Cinder-Liza
A Pride & Prejudice Vagary

By Shana Granderson, A Lady

CONTENTS

DEDICATION

This book, like all that I write, is dedicated to the love of life, the holder of my heart. You are my one and only and you complete me. You make it all worthwhile and my world revolves around you. Until we reconnected I had stopped believing in miracles, now I do, you are my miracle.

ACKNOWLEDGEMENT

First and foremost, thank you E.C.S. for standing by me while I dedicate many hours to my craft. You are my shining light and my one and only.

I want to thank my Alpha, Will Jamison and my Betas Caroline Piediscalzi Lippert and Kimbelle Pease. A special thanks to Kimbelle for her forthright and on point editing. To both Gayle Serrette and Carol M. for taking on the roles of proof-readers and additional editing, a huge thank you to both of you. All of you who have assisted me please know that your assistance is most appreciated.

My undying love and appreciation to Jane Austen for her incredible literary masterpieces is more than can be expressed adequately here. I also thank all of the JAFF readers who make writing these stories a pleasure.

INTRODUCTION

No fairy godmother or magic in the story although there is some imagery we would expect to see in a Cinderella adjacent story – my apologies to those who thought there would be magic based on the title. **

Mr. Thomas Bennet married the love of his life: Miss Fanny Gardiner. She gave him three children, Jane, Elizabeth and Tommy. 2 years after Tommy, Fanny was taken from her loving family birthing a second son, who was stillborn.

Another branch of the Bennet family, cousins to the Longbourn Bennets, are titled, the Earl and Countess of Holder, who live in Staffordshire with their 5 children. The two families are extremely close and after Fanny dies Bennet's cousins, at his request, keep and raise Tommy. In his grief Thomas Bennet doesn't think he can raise a 2-year-old at the same time as his two daughters. He also feels Tommy needs a mother figure in his life.

Martha Bingley is the widow of an honourable tradesman, Mr. Arthur Bingley, who had died of a heart attack. Bingley senior was a minor partner of Edward Gardiner in Gardiner and Associates. They had three children, Charles, Louisa, and Caroline. Unlike canon, the Bingleys are not very wealthy, and the girls have small dowries of £2,000 each.

Bennet is introduced to Martha at his brother-in-law's house. The Bingleys live in a leased house a few houses down from the Gardiners on Gracechurch street. Martha has always dreamed of climbing up the social ladder, raising her family above their roots in trade, so she compromises Bennet as he is a landed gentleman with an estate. Being an honourable man, and against advice of friends and family, he marries her.

Our *'prince'* in the story is of course none other than His Grace Fitzwilliam Darcy, Duke of Derbyshire, Earl of Lambton. Like canon his parents have already passed away. Dear old Lady Catherine de Bourgh will do anything to make her sickly daughter with a nasty disposition a Duchess. At some point the Duke purchases Netherfield to be closer to London so his sister, Lady Georgiana, will have her preferred music master close by.

Bennet never reveals the existence of his son or his relations, who are peers of the realm, to his new wife, who he dislikes intensely. The neighbours, none of whom like the new Mrs. Bennet or her children, keep the Bennet's secrets without question. Bennet allows his new wife to believe the entail on Longbourn is away from female line giving her the impression that on his death, she and her three spawn will be evicted from the estate by a distant unnamed cousin.

Sometime after sending Jane to live with his cousins, for reasons that will be revealed in the story, with Lizzy refusing to leave her father's side, Bennet has an accident which kills him. When no heir presents himself to throw her and her children, still at Longbourn, into the hedgerows, the stepmother feels more secure at the estate.

Several the usual suspects are present as well as some other characters. This is a story of hope and survival and the eventual triumph of good over evil.

PROLOGUE

T homas Bennet was devastated. His wife, Fanny, who he loved beyond all reason and had married in January 1786, had been taken from him trying to birth their second son. It was a risk all women faced in birthing a child, but Thomas was angry with God as he had placed Fanny's safety in His hands, and He had taken her!

He was now a widower and father of two daughters and a son. Jane, his oldest, had been born in June 1787. She was followed in March 1790 by Elizabeth, Lizzy. The heir to Longbourn, Tommy, was born in February 1792. By the beginning of the current year, his beloved Fanny had become with child again. Neither he nor his wife considered her state a risk, as there had been no unexpected issues with her previous three confinements.

In fact, Mrs. Maud Carlyle, the midwife, had opined that Mrs. Bennet was built to deliver children. That had been the belief until her last child, was breech and by the time he had been delivered never drew his first breath, and Fanny had bled to death.

Thomas and Fanny Bennet were vastly different in character, but that was what made them perfect for one another. Where Bennet was unsociable and somewhat of an introvert, Fanny was an extroverted social butterfly. He loved books and scholarly pursuits and she fashion and company.

They had fallen in love with one another in October 1785, and by the following January they were married. He taught her his love of books, and she taught him to be more sociable. He tempered her sometimes inappropriate outbursts, and she made him feel whole. Against all the odds, and the advice of his late mother, they had worked.

Fanny had been the best of mothers, showering her three children with unlimited and unrestricted love. As the time for her confinement had drawn near, Bennet had taken his children to visit his cousin, Lord James Bennet, the Earl of Holder. Unless his cousin was in Town at Holder House on Grosvenor Square, he, his wife, and their three sons could be found at their estate in Staffordshire, Holder Heights. Jane, Lizzy, and Tommy knew their Aunt, Lady Amelia Bennet, as Aunt Amy. It was Aunt Lia to Tommy as he could not pronounce Amy yet.

Lord James Bennet had two sons, James Junior and Phillip, as well as three daughters, Marie; Cassandra, called Cassie; and Alicia, called Allie. Phillip was around the same age as Tommy, just as Cassie and Allie were similar ages to Jane and Elizabeth, respectively. The children loved to spend time with their cousins, so their father sending them to Holder Heights did not concern the three Thomas Bennet children. Even though Tommy was only two, he was as enthusiastic as his older sisters to visit 'Unca Jamey,' 'Aunt Lia,' and his cousins, especially Phillip who would soon be three.

Thomas was thankful that his children were not at home when their beloved mother passed. He was not looking forward to explaining that they would never see their mama again, especially to Elizabeth who was wise beyond her years and had been extremely close to her mother.

Bennet wrote the most difficult letter of his life to his wife's younger brother, Edward Gardiner. There once were three Gardiner siblings, but Hattie, the oldest, had been taken some fifteen years earlier by influenza. After his father passed on, Gardiner sold his father's law practice and used the money to start his import and export business, Gardiner and Associates.

It was not widely known, but Bennet invested Longbourn's profits with his brother-in-law and was building a tidy sum. It was not a large fortune, but it was enough to provide his daughters with at least ten thousand pounds each, as well as a small legacy for Tommy.

Longbourn was entailed, but not away from the female line. Two generations earlier, the master had had a son who liked to gamble. Before anyone could make a claim against the estate, he entailed it so that all or part could not be sold off under any circumstances, and only a Bennet by blood could inherit, male or female.

A miserly and illiterate distant cousin, Ned Collins, who had married one of Thomas Bennet's cousins, believed Longbourn was entailed away from the female line. It mattered not how many times he was told it was secure with a child of either gender, he could not fathom that a female descendant could take precedence over his claim. What further eluded him was that with the stipulation of being a Bennet by blood, the Collins line could never inherit, regardless of the circumstance.

Thankfully, the man's wife had eventually managed to make him understand that he was placing his energy into something for which there was no reward. More importantly, her son William understood this fact quickly, as he surpassed his father in acumen and common sense. Bennet did not bother with sending them a notification of his Fanny's demise. From the time that Ned Collins finally grasped the facts of the entail, there had been no further contact between the Bennet and Collins families.

The same day that Bennet sent the express to Gracechurch Street, Gardiner left his young wife, Madeline, at home and made for Meryton with all haste. Had the children been at Longbourn, his wife, even in her delicate condition, would have accompanied him, as the Bennet children loved their Aunt Maddie.

Gardiner, himself feeling bereft of his only remaining sibling, gave his brother a hug of support before sitting in one of the armchairs in Longbourn's study. "It is hard to believe I am the only Gardiner remaining now. My one comforting thought is that I hope Fanny has re-joined Hattie and our parents."

"Thank you for coming, Gardiner. I must make some hard decisions, especially about Tommy. I think it will be better for him if James and Amy agree to keep him there. Tommy will be with Phillip, who will be like a brother as they grow up, and he will have a mother figure. The girls and I would be able to spend the summer with them each year so he will never forget his father and sisters. I have much work on the estate and I am not equipped to raise a boy of two. Fanny did all of that," Bennet's voice choked up at the mention of his beloved.

"I am sure your cousins will do anything to help that they are able to, Bennet. Have you informed Philips that Fanny is gone?" Gardiner asked.

Jacob Philips had purchased the law practice from Gardiner and lived in the old Gardiner house with his wife, two sons, and a daughter. All Longbourn's legal issues were dealt with efficiently by Mr. Philips.

"Yes, he was here earlier, and I updated my will. Heaven forbid, if something happens to me and Tommy, then my oldest living daughter will inherit at her majority. Before you ask, yes, my neighbours still think I clear two thousand a year. In a way, that is true in a sense as the rest goes to you to add to my port-folio," Bennet told his brother by marriage.

After the funeral, Gardiner returned to his wife and business, and Bennet journeyed to Holder Heights to break the devastating news to his children.

~~~~~~~/~~~~~~~

Martha Bingley had never been happy married to Arthur, who had died of a heart attack some six months previously. He left her with, in her opinion, a small widow's portion, a far too small, leased house on Gracechurch Street near Cheapside, and three young children. They lived a few doors down from number 23, where the Gardiners resided. Martha was envious of the Gardiners' much larger house and their ability to afford far more servants, and often commented on it, which taught her children to believe the same.

Her oldest, Charles was ten. Louisa was eight, and Caroline was five. Martha had never wasted an opportunity to tell her children how important it was for them to rise from their status as wife and children of a tradesman to the ranks of the gentry.

She also oft repeated and ingrained in her children that their lot in life was not their fault. She blamed an amorphous *them or they*, though, if asked, she was never able to define who *them or they* were, nor what *they* had done to affect her family's lives. It was always useful, however, to have a scapegoat excuse for her to use for not making such an effort herself.

Her husband had moved them from Scarborough some three years previously to become a minor partner in Gardiner and Associates. He had promised that as the business grew, so would their fortune. There had been no visible improvement in their wealth as of his death, and to her chagrin, her daughters had a pittance of a two-thousand-pound dowry each. On his passing, Gardiner had bought out the late Bingley's stake in the company for seven thousand pounds, which had been placed in a trust for Charles until his majority and was to be managed by Edward Gardiner. Martha's widow's portion was two thousand pounds, but their living expenses were paid out of the interest and dividends earned by the principal that would one day be her son's inheritance.

The roughly seven hundred pounds per annum that Gardiner generated from the invested principal was enough to pay the rent and their living expenses while leaving a few hundred pounds to be added to the principal. Martha wanted to get her hands on as much of her son's inheritance as she could, but Gardiner had been charged with the management of the funds, and Arthur Bingley had placed strict guidelines on said management, as he had known who and what his wife was. He did so to protect his son's money from his avaricious wife.

Even though she disliked and resented the Gardiners for their apparent wealth and success, Martha kept up the pretence of a friendship with Gardiner's young wife, as it usually led to an invitation to dine with them at least once or twice a week, and Martha was not willing to jeopardise those invitations, as she and her three resentful children enjoyed the quality of the repast they found at Madeline Gardiner's table.

Madeline Gardiner was nobody's fool. She knew full well

the truth of Martha Bingley and her grasping children, but she also felt sorry for them after they lost the patriarch of their family. This led her to keep inviting them, even against her personal preferences.

When Madeline Gardiner had a miscarriage, she did not tell Martha Bingley, as she knew the woman was incapable of concern for any beyond her own selfish desires. Luckily, Maddie had the support of a loving husband to get her through her sadness over losing their first babe.

It was at one of the dinners the Bingleys were invited to that they met the widower Thomas Bennet. Martha saw the man as the answer to her prayers. He was a gentleman whose family had been on their land for a good number of generations, and he seemed to be reasonably well off. She was determined to marry the man, and incorrectly believed that would raise her and her children's status to the gentry.

No matter how much she fawned over Thomas Bennet, batted her eyelids at him, behaved coquettishly, or tried to employ any of her vast array of feminine wiles, the man showed no interest in her.

When she perused her reflection in the mirror, she saw a woman of not yet thirty who still had her looks about her. She could not understand how it was that she had not been able to turn Mr. Bennet's head at all. She decided that as he seemed like an honourable man, there was only one thing for it, she needed to compromise him, and she intended to conscript her children to help her.

Once she explained how their lives would improve as the son and daughters of a gentleman, her older two agreed to assist her in any way they could. The opportunity came before Bennet was to return to Longbourn, when the Bingleys were invited to dinner the night before his departure.

Martha had not missed that her quarry sequestered himself in Mr. Gardiner's study after dinner, though she did not know, or care, it was his way of escaping her attentions. A half hour after her victim separated himself from the company, she gave Charles and Louisa a wink and then stated she needed to use the necessary.

On opening the study door slowly, she saw her victim had fallen asleep on the settee. She lay down next to him, freeing a breast from its constraints and placing his hand on it. Just then, as planned, Charles and Louisa opened the door and screamed.

"What are you doing in here, woman?" Bennet demanded as he pushed her off of him and she landed unceremoniously on the hard floor, her breast still hanging out of her dress.

"Oh, but Thomas, you were saying how much you wanted me before we were discovered," Martha stated with a straight face.

Maddy and Edward Gardiner shook their heads at the obvious compromise. Unfortunately, several servants had come running when the two Bingley children screeched, so it seemed there was no hushing up the event. Even if the Gardiners could hush their servants, they were sure that the despicable woman and her spawn would crow about it to one and all.

Bennet's honour would allow him to do naught but marry the woman. "I need to return to my home and inform my daughters of my impending marriage," Bennet spat out with distaste. "I will return in a sennight."

The look he gave the self-satisfied woman would have been enough to wilt a flower, but she cared not. She had achieved her aim; she was to be the wife of a gentleman!

CHAPTER 1

February 1795

T he first thing that Bennet did on his return to Meryton was to see his solicitor and friend, Jacob Philips. Just as Gardiner had, Philips advised his friend to not allow the woman to get away with her scheme.

"As much as I would like to walk away from the disgusting woman, my honour will not allow it. I want a settlement that will reflect my disdain for the woman. The two thousand pounds she has will be invested in the four percents, which will give her eighty pounds per annum. By my calculation, that is less than seven pounds per month. I will raise it to eight pounds, but no more.

"Then, there is the son's inheritance invested with Gardiner. It will be shifted to the four percents as well. After the behaviour of her children, Gardiner will do no more than the father's will charges him to do. Of the four hundred eighty pounds per annum the boy's money will earn, ninety pounds, thirty each a year, will be disbursed for the children's allowance. One hundred fifty pounds per annum will be paid to me for their board and lodging, as I refuse to spend one penny on that woman's children. The other half will be saved to send young Bingley to school as his father requested." Bennet was firm on the matter of the woman and her children receiving as little as possible from Longbourn's coffers.

"I see that you want the entail mentioned, but not defined. I like this," Philips pointed to his friend's notes. "The woman and her offspring may stay in the house until your heir claims it, should you pass before that time. It will be an incentive for the conniving woman to make sure you stay hale and healthy. What about Tommy and your cousins?" Philips asked.

"Never will that social climbing shrew or her devil's spawn know of Tommy or my cousins! She would try to engineer a compromise between one of her daughters and poor Jamey as soon as he was old enough. I would no sooner trust her and her offspring around my cousins than love her! When I travel to Holder Heights to inform my cousins and my daughters, I hope to convince them to stay with James and Amy. I will not attempt to force them, for you know how stubborn my daughters are wont to be," Bennet smiled warmly as he thought of his children. "As far as Tommy goes, the neighbours will not mention him; they are all disgusted with the woman for what she did to me!"

"I am to change your will to name Gardiner executor and the Holder Bennets' guardians if you die before all three reach their majority?" Philips read more of the notes.

"Yes, for even if I am no longer alive, that woman will *not* sink her claws into my children's future. Can you believe the temerity of the witch? She suggested I adopt her children and give them the Bennet name. That will *never* happen! Before I forget, I want all merchants informed neither the woman nor her children are allowed to charge anything to my accounts without my express, in-person permission. If a merchant does so against my wishes, then the unauthorised bill will *not* be paid by me! Also please make it known that the three children are Bingleys, *not* Bennets!" The men stood and shook hands, after which Bennet mounted his steed Orion and rode the one mile to Longbourn. Once in his study, Bennet composed a letter to his cousin James, informing him of what had occurred.

~~~~~~~/~~~~~~~

As promised, Bennet returned to Gracechurch Street a sennight later. Unlike his wife-to-be, he had honour and kept his word. As he sat with Gardiner in his study, Bennet derived much pleasure from seeing the pinched look on his *betrothed's* face as she read the settlement.

"I am only to have *eight* pounds a month pin money? And

my poor children will only have two pounds and a half-sovereign! You are a landed gentleman; how can it be that we will be no better off than we are now?" Mrs. Bingley screeched.

"*You* chose to compromise *me*, madam! I will not reward your behaviour in any way. Longbourn is a small, entailed estate, and I will not harm my budget to indulge you and your spoiled children. Before you ask, I will NEVER share your bed! There is only one woman that I will ever love, and I will not sully her memory with the likes of you—which is why you will *not* be occupying the mistress's chambers. If this is not to your liking, you are free to withdraw from the betrothal," Bennet offered hopefully.

Martha Bingley seriously considered taking the out she had been offered but decided being the wife of a gentleman would be worth it—after all, she could work on him to change his mind after they were wed as no man would be able to resist her charms when she had time and privacy to work her wiles. "Mr. Gardiner may sign on my behalf. Why do we wed in only a month?" she asked.

"I have things to see to, Mrs. Bingley—things that do not concern you. I will return in a month. You are free to find another man in that time if waiting is not agreeable to you," Bennet sneered at the despicable woman.

Martha Bingley would have done so had she access to the social circles where she would meet gentlemen or, better yet, a member of the first circles. It was her ultimate aim for her son and daughters to gain access to that lofty social circle. As it was not an option for her, she would have to cool her heels for one more month in the small, rented home.

~~~~~~~/~~~~~~~

"Thomas, are you out of your senses, giving in to this woman that you describe as being a fortune hunting social climber!" Not for the first time, Lord James Bennet, the Earl of Holder, berated his favourite cousin in an attempt to stop him from walking down a ruinous path.

"James, you know me; I felt I had no choice. Even if this

woman has no honour, I do! It is too late now; we have a signed settlement, and I will not bring dishonour to our family or to my children under any circumstances," Bennet responded forcefully.

"I know that is the kind of man you are, and I respect you for it. However, to be sentenced to be husband to such a woman as you have described! I feel for you, Cousin. Know that Amy and I will do *anything* we are able to, in order to help you," the Earl pledged.

"You are already raising Tommy for me; there is no amount of thanks sufficient for the service you are doing me in that quarter. If I am able to convince my stubborn daughters to remain at Holder Heights, I will do so. In that endeavour, I am not hopeful. You know Jane and Lizzy; they will not want to leave me," Bennet stated with resignation. "My only hope is that I am able to convince them that staying with you will be a way of helping Tommy."

"Knowing my young cousins, who I count as nieces, there is little chance of them not wanting to be with you, my friend," the Earl commiserated.

~~~~~~~/~~~~~~~

"*No*, Papa, we *will not* live without you!" Jane, who would be eight in June, insisted, while Elizabeth, who was about to turn five, nodded her head in emphatic agreement. They had already planned to celebrate Elizabeth's birthday with their family before returning to Longbourn.

"You have to teach me, Papa; I want to be with you," Elizabeth insisted, stamping her foot as an almost five-year-old child is wont to do.

"As I offered you girls the right to make the decision for yourselves, you will come home with me." Bennet was not surprised. He knew that he could have exerted his fatherly authority and ordered them to remain with their cousins, but he had given them a choice and he would honour that choice. "It shall be as you wish, and I promise you, we will visit Tommy every summer for at least three months, and we shall all be here for

Christmastide each year as well," Bennet promised his daughters.

Jane was blond, with deep blue eyes, and would be tall like her grandmother had been. Elizabeth looked just like her mother, Fanny. A slight olive complexion, chestnut curls, the greenest of eyes, but shorter than most girls of her age. Bennet supposed the likeness that his beloved Fanny had seen in their Lizzy had endeared the young girl to her mother. Fanny had never shown favouritism, but it had not been hard for Bennet to see she had an especially warm place in her heart for Lizzy.

"Now tell me what you have been doing since I was last here, my darling girls," Bennet asked, as he kissed each one on her forehead in turn.

"We met a mark-ess, Papa," Elizabeth said jubilantly. "And vi'count, and his younger brother, Richard. Richard was ever so much fun!"

"A mark-ess?" Bennet repeated in question.

"Lizzy means a Marquess, Papa. Lord Fitzwilliam Darcy, the Marquess of Pemberley, but he prefers we call him Lord William. His father is the Duke of Derbyshire, Earl of Lambton. He is sad because his mama went to heaven like our mama did after his little sister, Gigi, who is one, was born. Lord William is the same age as our cousin Jamey. The viscount is Andrew Fitzwilliam; he is the son of the Earl of Matlock, and a good friend of Uncle James. He is almost sixteen while his younger brother Richard is fourteen, a year more than Jamey and Lord William," Jane filled her father in.

"Gigi?" Bennet asked. "I have never heard such a name."

"Silly Papa, that is a nickname, her name is Lady Georgiana Darcy," Jane explained.

"She is too young to play with me!" Elizabeth pouted, her lower lip pushing out just as far as she was able.

"If you see her again in a few years then she will want to play with you, my Lizzy. She will be old enough then," Bennet assured his second daughter.

"Fine, Papa," Elizabeth recovered fully, as would be expected of one so young.

"We will depart for Longbourn on the morrow girls, so have fun with your brother and cousins today. We will be back for the summer," Bennet reminded them.

"The new mother…" Elizabeth started to say.

"She will not be your mother but your stepmother. She has three of her own children. They will be your stepbrother and stepsisters, but no more. They will *never* have the name Bennet as you do," Bennet corrected.

"Will they be our friends?" Jane asked innocently.

"I do not know, Jane dearest. You will have to see when you meet them," Bennet averred. He believed that there would be no friendship between his daughters and *her* children, but he would allow Jane and Elizabeth to come to their own conclusions without poisoning their minds beforehand.

The girls went to find their brother and cousins and Bennet remained in his chambers to think. He was not certain that he would find even the smallest measure of happiness with the soon-to-be Mrs. Bennet. It killed him how *that* woman would have the same title as his beloved Fanny, and he had no doubt the title was the only attribute his late wife would ever share with the woman, for good and ill.

~~~~~~~/~~~~~~~

"How was your time at Holder Heights with your Fitzwilliam cousins and the Bennets?" Lord Robert Darcy, Duke of Derbyshire, Earl of Lambton asked his son after the Matlock carriage had dropped his son at Pemberley before returning to Snowhaven.

"It was enjoyable, Father," Lord William answered his father with his normal formality. He was but thirteen and on his way to Eton in September, but ever since Lord Robert's beloved Duchess passed away, his son had become much more serious and introverted. "The Earl's cousin's children from Hertfordshire were visiting. They, too, lost their mother last year."

"I miss my Anne every day, Son," the Duke said softly. Unlike most of his station, Lord Robert Darcy, then Marquess

Pemberley, Viscount Kympton, had made a love match. His late wife's older sister had done everything to try to become the next Duchess of Derbyshire, including an unsuccessful compromise. It left relations between the sisters strained, and Lady Catherine had a tantrum of epic proportions when the betrothal between Lady Anne and Lord Robert had been announced.

The lady did not know when to give up. If she could not be the Duchess, then she was determined that her spoilt, sickly daughter with an extremely sour disposition and no accomplishments or education, would be the one to succeed where she failed.

While his Anne was alive, her sister attempted to browbeat his wife into agreeing to, as Lady Catherine put it, 'a cradle betrothal', which Lady Anne had steadfastly refused to allow. As soon as his beloved wife had succumbed after gifting him Gigi, the letters from his sister-in-law had begun, demanding the formalization of the phantom promise that Lady Catherine claimed.

The Duke had written back one time only, telling the termagant that she would be sued for slander if she mentioned one word of the made-up betrothal to *anyone* in society. He also informed her that he would *never* sanction a match between his heir and her insipid daughter. Although Lady Catherine was unaware of it, the Duke had a codicil written into his will refuting any claim the lady might try to make after his passing. He sent a copy of the codicil to his brother-in-law, Lord Reginald Fitzwilliam, the Earl of Matlock, and brother to his late wife.

"Is that a letter from Rosings, Father?" William asked as the butler placed the salver on the Duke's desk.

"It is, William. In the fire please, Son." The Duke ordered with a flick of his wrist. With a slight grin, the son complied. There was a knock on the study door. "No William, stay," the Duke commanded, as his son started to stand. "Enter!"

"You requested that I come see you and bring my son, your Grace," Pemberley's steward Maxwell Wickham bowed. His son George, twelve, bowed and smirked at Lord William, thinking his effort to cause the prig of a marquess trouble had succeeded.

"Mr. Wickham, do you remember how you requested that I stand as godfather for your son not long after your wife went to her eternal reward?" the Duke asked.

"I do, your Grace," the steward answered deferentially. Young George thought that he might become the godson of a duke.

"Based on your son's behaviour, I cannot and will not fill that role," the Duke stated matter-of-factly.

"Y-your G-grace," George Wickham spluttered. "W-why do you s-say t-that?" George had been most confident that he had hidden his behaviour from the Duke, surely the children he bullied had not told on him!

"Do not try and affect innocence with me, young Wickham. I know about your bullying, the way you order my servants around as if you are a member of the household. Worst of all, I *know* you left the gate to the stables open after my son left. What you thought you would achieve by painting my son in a bad light, I do not know. Whatever it was, you failed. You were seen in the stables and more than one person witnessed your leaving the gate open. It was closed right away after you left." The Duke did not look amused. George Wickham squirmed under the withering glares he received from the two men and the Marquess.

"I do not know why I did it; I think I was envious of Lord William as he has so much and I have nothing in comparison," George hung his head as he gave an honest answer.

"We all make mistakes, young George. So while I will not be your godfather, it does not mean that I will not assist you, but only if I see a significant and permanent change in your behaviour and attitude. Do you have any idea how much responsibility comes with my position, and William's? How many souls for whom we are responsible? To whom much is given, much is expected. Nothing will fall into your lap; you will have to work hard and then you will reap the rewards.

"The countryside is littered with estates that have been

gambled away by idle landlords who looked for a fast way out of their financial problems. What we receive without putting forth an effort, we do not value. I cannot choose for you; you need to choose the way forward for yourself. One way will be hard and satisfying, the other will lead to a life of dissipation, and quite possibly, debauchery leading to you becoming a profligate wastrel, or worse, a libertine." The Duke waited as the boy assimilated what he had been told.

"I will work to correct my behaviour, your Grace. Lord William, please accept my apology for attempting to cause trouble for you, for no true reason above pettiness," young Wickham stated sincerely.

After he was dismissed from the study, his father turned to his master. "I want to add my voice to that of my son's, your Grace. You could have demanded I punish him, or even dismiss me. Instead you helped point my George to the path of redemption. I promise you, your Grace, I will make sure my son remains on that path and will be worthy of your trust in the future, and Lord William's," the steward stated, contritely. He bowed and left the Duke's study.

CHAPTER 2

Two days after returning to Longbourn, Bennet sat with his daughters in the drawing room. "Do you understand why we cannot tell the new Mrs. Bennet and her children about Tommy, the actual state of the entail on Longbourn, or our cousins?" Bennet asked as his two girls sat on the settee next to him.

"Papa, is it not a lie if we do not tell the full truth?" Jane asked. "And have you not always told us to lie is unacceptable?"

"I do not want to lie, Papa!" Elizabeth exclaimed, looking concerned.

"In a manner of speaking, it is an untruth. There are times in life when we need to withhold some information from another person, and for good reason. This is one of those times. When you are older, I give you my solemn word I will explain this all to you when you are able to understand the circumstances. For now, I ask you to trust your Papa, and do as I say. You are both intelligent young girls, and you know I would never ask anything like this of you, unless I felt there was no choice, do you not?" Both girls nodded emphatically. "What I am asking you to do is for the good of our family, and especially Tommy. It is also for your own protection."

"What will happen to us if you go to join Mama in heaven, Papa?" Jane asked with concern.

"Do you both remember what a contingency is?" Bennet asked. Both of his daughters loved to read, and Elizabeth was starting to read more advanced books and had come across the word not too long ago.

"I remember, Papa; you told me it means making plans in case something occurs," Elizabeth remembered, proudly.

"Yes, Lizzy-bear," which was the endearment that Fanny had called her second daughter, as she gave the best hugs. "That is correct. Firstly, you will not get rid of your *old* papa so easily, but if, heaven forbid, something happens to me; I have made contingencies with both Uncle James and Uncle Edward. In a few years, I will be able to explain everything in detail to you, but please remember how important it is not to answer any questions about the entail, our connections, or your dowries if the new Mrs. Bennet or her children ask you."

"What is a dowree?" Elizabeth asked.

"A *dowry* is a lady's fortune that she brings with her when she marries. As neither of you know the amount of yours, you will not have to prevaricate and will be able to honestly answer that you do not know. My preference, if any of them should ask you questions about the subjects I have mentioned, is that you refer them to me." As Bennet completed his speech, there was a knock on the study door and Hill announced a lady that Bennet had been expecting.

"Miss Jones, welcome; please sit." Bennet looked at his manservant and butler all in one. "Hill, please request a tea service from your wife." Hill bowed and departed the study and Miss Jones sat in the seat that Bennet indicated.

After Mrs. Hill poured tea, weak for the two girls, she curtsied and exited the study, pulling the door closed. "Who is this lady?" Elizabeth asked directly.

"This lady, Jane and Lizzy, is your governess, Miss Anita Jones. She is sister to Mr. Jones, the new apothecary and doctor in Meryton. She will be working with you and making sure that you are busy. I will repeat what I already told you when we spoke previously, Miss Jones. The new Mrs. Bennet will be my wife, but she is *not* the mistress of this house. I, and I alone, am the only one who will be allowed to issue instructions regarding my children, and unless I specifically tell you otherwise, the Bingley children are *not* to be included in lessons with my children." He turned to his daughters, "I wanted you two to hear this from my own mouth in case anyone tries to gainsay me when I am not in the house." Both girls nodded. "Miss Jones will commence on the morrow, and she will stay to look after you when I go to Town to ..." Try as he might, Bennet could not force himself to say the word *marry*!

A few days earlier, Bennet was talking to Mr. Jones when he mentioned that he was looking for a good, dependable governess. Jones had told Bennet about his younger sister, Anita. They had grown up on a small estate in Bedfordshire; Jones was a third son. The family had saved money for the education of their three sons and daughter, but the younger two sons needed to find a profession and shift for themselves.

The middle son had chosen the church, while the third had chosen medicine. He had learnt both disciplines, doctor and apothecary, as he correctly believed most small market towns needed both but did not have the population to support two men. Bennet had met with Miss Jones, who did not want to be a burden to her parents or her older brother, so was seeking a position. It had not taken long for Bennet to realise she would be perfect for the position. His daughters took to Miss Jones almost immediately, which sealed the proposition, and so, she was hired.

One of the contingencies that Bennet put in place was that regardless of his being alive or not, the servants would all be paid through Gardiner, so the new Mrs. Bennet would have no say over the firing or hiring of servants. If she wanted personal servants for herself or her children, she would have to pay for them out of the fifteen pounds and half a sovereign they would have each month, if they combined their allowances.

That afternoon, Bennet had occasion to visit the general store where he met with the proprietor, and his friend, Mr. William Lucas. The Lucas family owned a nice sized house behind their store. His wife Sarah had been close to the late Fanny Bennet. His oldest was Charlotte, who was almost fourteen. His sons Frank and John were eleven and seven, respectively. They all helped in the store whenever they could. Their unanticipated baby, Maria, was not yet one year of age, and demanded much of her mother's time.

Besides being the owner of the local store, William Lucas was also the mayor of Meryton. It was a largely ceremonial position, but Lucas enjoyed it, as he was a jovial and sociable fellow. While Bennet was ordering some of his favourite port, Lucas was regaling his friends of how in about a sennight, the King and Queen would pass through Meryton and, he, though only a lowly merchant, would make an address to his Royal Majesty because he was the mayor.

Lucas was a rather loquacious chap, but that did not bother Bennet. The only thing that counted was the Lucas family were loyal friends of long standing and how either would do anything in their power to help the other. Even though Charlotte was almost five years older than Jane, she often enjoyed spending time with the Bennet sisters, declaring each of them as friends well before either of his two daughters had learned to say the word.

Unexpectedly for Lucas, Bennet asked if they could speak in the store's office. With his wife there to assist the customers, Lucas led the way. Bennet filled his friend in on *all* of the happenings, and Lucas pledged himself to help and support as required. He would make sure his wife and children knew never to disclose any information about the Bennets to the new Mrs. Bennet and her offspring.

After Lucas, Bennet spoke to his friends Spencer Goulding and Johnathan Long; both pledged to assist as and when needed. Before his departure to London, Bennet met with Philips several more times to make sure his will and all other relevant documents were as they should be and that there were more than three copies to disperse throughout the land.

As Bennet travelled to London during the latter half of March 1795, he cheered himself by thinking of Lizzy's fifth birthday and how much fun they all had. He was also diverted with how the King, for a reason known only to himself, had been enamoured with William Lucas's drawn-out speech, and would knight him as a reward for it, at St. James Palace in early April. His friends were now, or would be after the investiture, Sir William and Lady Lucas.

~~~~~~~/~~~~~~~

Lady Catherine de Bourgh was seriously displeased, though for those who were her servants it seemed to be her permanent state. No matter how many letters she wrote about a claimed agreement with her sister, who she often declared stole the man and rank that was her due as the older sister, there had not been a single answer—other than the one with a warning even she would not test.

If that were not enough, it seemed Anne was getting more sullen. The stories that she would one day be a duchess were the only things that interested her. At ten, Anne was not like others her age. Until she was six, she had been a normal, vivacious girl, but then she had contracted scarlet fever. Although her mother did not want to acknowledge it, Anne's heart had been weakened, and there was a true possibility that she would never see her thirtieth year, or perhaps only her twentieth.

Anne de Bourgh knew everyone thought her spoilt and a sour person, yet they would feel the same if her mother was theirs. Anne was fully aware that she was uneducated and had no accomplishments, for her mother always spouted her, 'if my Anne had been healthy enough to learn...' nonsense.

The truth was, Anne would have loved to have learnt to play, to draw, and to do many other things, but had always been denied the opportunity by her officious and overbearing mother. Her mother thought Anne was not aware that once she attained the age of five and twenty, fifteen years in the future, she would become the owner of Rosings, the de Bourgh House in town, and the de Bourgh fortune. As the estate was unentailed, she would be able to will it to whomever she chose.

To Anne, the possibility of marrying her cousin represented a way to escape the stifling confines of living with a mother who wanted to control every aspect of her daughter's life. Hence, the desire to marry her cousin became her wish as well, for vastly different reasons than her mother believed.

Lady Catherine was ranting about her brother-in-law refusing to do his duty to her by betrothing his son to Anne, thereby combining the fortunes of Pemberley and Rosings Park. It was the only way Lady Catherine could see where she would retain control of the fiefdom she had created for herself since her husband had drowned some five years previously.

Anne shook her head out of her mother's line of sight. The Darcys owned eight estates, and outside of the main Pemberley estate, three of them were as large, if not larger than, Rosings Park. Why ever would they need an estate in Kent? Even at her tender years, Anne was sure her mother's push was about herself gaining access to the Darcy coffers after failing to entrap her Uncle Robert some years ago, and, in truth had nothing to do with her daughter's happiness, for it was long established that anything which would give her pleasure was not to be borne.

~~~~~~~/~~~~~~~

The deed was done. Bennet was married to the last woman he would ever choose to marry. "You could have looked a little happy," Martha Bennet whined as her husband handed her into the carriage after her children.

"I have no reason to be happy. You fully know this is not what I desire. Let us depart; I want to return to my daughters as soon as may be." Bennet said, as he closed the door.

"How is it that you are only telling me you have children now?" Martha asked carefully.

"If you had not deigned to compromise me, and had I been even a little interested in you, I would have shared everything about my family with you." The woman had the decency to turn red at that statement.

"Well, at least now your unfortunate daughters will have a mother," Martha drawled.

"Let me be rightly understood," Bennet wheeled his head around toward her with a thunderous look, "I give you *no* authority over *my* children. You may not question them, discipline them, or anything else. They are not now, nor will they ever be, under your care! Do I make myself clear?"

For the first time, Martha was afraid of Bennet and decided

that, for now anyway, she would obey her husband. She was still confident she would be able to use her feminine wiles to bring him to heel as it had never failed to work before. Her former husband was compliant and had never questioned that none of his children looked even a little bit like him.

Charles was tallish with sandy blond hair and grey eyes; Louisa had mousy brown hair, brown eyes and was plump, to put it nicely, for she never saw any food that did not call to her. Even Martha had to own the fact that her older daughter was homely. Caroline had orange hair, almost yellow eyes, and was a bony young girl, quite the opposite of Louisa. Unfortunately, she was homely as well, if one were being generous in their description of Caroline Bingley. Martha had hoped that her daughters' appearances were not obvious, as the disparity between her daughters' looks and her husband's was great.

Martha did not know how yet, but she had to convince her husband to adopt her progeny so they would have the name of a gentleman and not a tradesman. She would just have to seduce him. It was as simple as that.

~~~~~~~/~~~~~~~

Four hours later, with Bennet riding ahead, they arrived under the portico at Longbourn. Martha was not happy, for there was no one to receive her, no servants lined up, and her husband's daughters were also nowhere to be seen. "You would think my new daughters…" She got no further as Bennet interjected.

"Madam, I will tell you one last time. *My* daughters are *not now,* nor will they *ever be* your daughters! If you make me say it again, *Mrs. Bennet*, you will have a choice before you: annulment or divorce!"

"You would not do that; either would cause you scandal!" For the first time Martha began to realise she may have underestimated her husband.

"If you break a single rule of my house, I most certainly will. No matter the cost or the scandal, I will be rid of you. Before our wedding, I explained that you are not mistress of this house;

in truth, you have say over *nothing*, most particularly, my children. Under no circumstances will you or your children claim they are Bennets to anyone! Do I make myself clear, or do I need to summon my solicitor and begin proceedings to rid myself of you and your spawn?" Bennet demanded. His anger was palpable, and Martha knew now was not the time to test his will. She may have to bide her time, but at some point, she *would* prevail.

As she was standing in shock, two of the prettiest girls she had ever beheld burst out of the front door and jumped into their father's arms. As homely as her daughters were, her husband's daughters were at the very opposite end of the scale. She immediately resented the two girls who were receiving love from their father in a most unreserved way.

Louisa and Caroline stared wordlessly at the visions before them. No matter how much they told themselves otherwise, when they saw their stepsisters, they saw what beauty truly was, and it was not what they found when they looked in the mirror. Caroline especially hated the two beauties, for all they had, from the quality of their dress to their looks, things she apparently would never have, as her new father had said he would buy them nothing!

Charles was almost twelve and had a habit of spying on his sisters when they changed or bathed. When he saw the two Bennet sisters for the first time, his eyes opened wide, especially when he saw the older of the two—a blond angel. He, however, soon learned he would have no opportunity to ply his trade with his stepsisters. His mother, his sister, and he were shown to chambers on a different floor from the family. Between them, they had three small chambers and they were told, in no uncertain terms, that there would always be a footman on duty in the hall below that led to the family chambers.

As a safety measure, Bennet moved his daughters into a bedchamber next to his and out of the nursery, which was on the floor where his wife and her children had been placed. Miss Jones was then ensconced in the bedchamber next to Jane and Elizabeth.

There was an uneasy truce among the inhabitants of Long-bourn, which lasted for a little more than six years.

CHAPTER 3

June 1801

Nothing had gone as Martha Bennet, formerly Bingley, had imagined. When she had attempted to go to her husband, a footman would not allow her to pass, and when her shouting woke him, Bennet had exited his bedchamber and told her, in no uncertain terms what he thought of her charms. That was three years ago, and she never made a second attempt.

She and her daughters had food and a place to live, but no more. If they wanted new dresses, they had to use some of their pittance of an allowance. At least Charles was in his second year at Eton, his expenses paid from the trust the officious Mr. Gardiner controlled. No matter how she ranted at him, the man looked at her as if she were offensive and adamantly refused to release a penny more than her and her children's allowances.

Martha was pleased Charles would be home from Eton in a few days. He would be able to report on his success at ingratiating himself with sons in the first circles. Martha could not understand how, with her perfect instructions, her son had not succeeded in making any high-born friends as of his last term break.

One of her greatest vexations was her husband and his daughters, who at fourteen and eleven, had grown even more beautiful, especially as the older had begun to show womanly curves, and would travel at Easter, Christmastide, and for the whole of the summer, never telling her where they were going and never inviting her or any of her children to join them.

While the Bennet daughters had been educated by their

governess and masters from Town, her daughters had received no training, as she could not afford to spend her meagre resources on educating her daughters on anything except the art of the compromise.

When her daughters pointed out that their mother's compromise had not garnered much success, or as much as she had expected, Martha Bennet could not argue the point. Nothing had been as she had wished it to be.

She had tried to charge items to her husband's accounts in Meryton and had been roundly refused, and the only time she had gained a little extra was one time when the owner of the haberdashery gave into his lust and exchanged her, *services,* for some ribbons. It was the first and last time anyone in Meryton had been interested in trading services.

The servants were polite but accepted no orders from her or her children. If Martha could go back six years, she would not compromise her miserly husband. On the other side of the house, the Bennets were as happy as could be expected.

The only time they would see the interloping Bingleys was when they shared dinner. The Bennets were up with the sunrise, while Martha and her children usually ambled down at noon after taking a tray in their chambers. For the first few months they had expected warm, fresh food waiting for them when they deigned to rise from their beds. Bennet had disabused them of the notion with alacrity—hence the trays.

As their father promised, each Christmastide and summer had been spent with their cousins and Tommy. After the first year of *them* being at Longbourn, Easter became a time to hie to Holder Heights as well.

Since Charles Bingley had begun at Eton, their summer trip north would normally commence a few days before his expected arrival, as neither Bennet sister felt comfortable with the way that he stared at them, especially Jane. This year, they were delayed a few days as their father had to take care of an issue on the estate that would not wait for three months.

Charles Bingley arrived home, and, as was his wont, leered

at Jane Bennet. No amount of spying on his sisters could come close to the lust he felt when viewing Jane, and that was when she was fully clothed. In his imagination, he had undressed her so many times from so many different dresses there was a veritable mountain of cast-off dresses in the room his mind had created for them.

The day before their scheduled departure from Longbourn, Jane escaped the house to walk in the little wilderness on one side of the park. Charles Bingley saw her leave but did not follow her right away. Luckily, when he followed Jane, Elizabeth noticed, and asked one of the footmen to follow her outside.

Before Jane saw him, she felt a presence behind her and whirled around just as Charles Bingley attempted to grab her with one hand and place his other hand over her mouth. Thanks to her sudden movement, his hand went into her mouth instead of over it and she bit down onto the offending limb with all her might.

Charles Bingley let out a scream like a stuck pig, and soon he saw blood running from his injured right hand. Like the coward he was, he lifted his left arm to strike a blow to the chit who injured him. Had his mother not told them to always take what they wanted? Did she not say it was their right? Then why did this girl bite him? He would make her rue the day.

As his hand began its arc down towards Jane, and she, being close to him thanks to his attempt to detain her, remembered what her father had told her about sensitive areas on a man. Before his hand reached her, her knee, with as much force as she could muster, connected with his most sensitive area.

His previous scream was nothing to his caterwauling after he got his breath back. "Jane, are you well?" Elizabeth and the footman ran up to her. They had witnessed the whole of the attack but had been too far away to stop it.

"Oh, Lizzy," Jane fell into her younger sister's arms as the fight went out of her and she realised how close she had come to something distasteful in the extreme. Jane burst into tears as the tension was released from her body.

Bennet arrived with his wife in tow, the two of them followed by her two daughters. "What have you done to my brother?" Caroline, who was twelve, screeched.

"Your lecherous brother tried to attack my sister, and she defended herself," Elizabeth bristled.

"You lie," Caroline retorted, and would have said more if not for the footman, who stepped towards her threateningly. By now, Jane had ceased crying and was sniffling into her father's chest.

"Jane, my dear, can you tell us what happened?" Bennet asked softly as he rubbed his daughter's back.

"He," Jane pointed at the still writhing Charles Bingley, "tried to grab me and cover my mouth at the same time. I bit him, then he was going to strike me, so I put my knee into the spot you showed me, Papa."

"I am sure Charles was just trying to play a prank on his step-sister," said Martha, trying to defend her son.

"Does he play a prank when he spies on his sisters as they change and bathe?" Bennet thundered. Young Bingley blanched as he was trying to stand up.

Louisa and Caroline turned to their brother and yelled in unison, "CHARLES!", while Martha did not dispute what was said. She had caught him in the act a few years back, and he swore to her it was the only time and he would never do it again.

"He is to leave my home on the morrow and never return," Bennet stated, brooking no dissent.

"Where will he go?" Martha pleaded.

"I care not. He can apply to Gardiner for some of the interest for rent, or he can go to his uncle in Scarborough. Where he goes is his problem. If he approaches any member of my family again, I will see him in gaol, and you will find yourself and your daughters thrown out of my house. Do I make myself clear?" Bennet demanded.

Charles Bingley held his peace, but as he stared at Bennet sullenly, he swore to himself that he would avenge himself on the man he hated. He would also have to find a way to pay back the chit who injured and humiliated him.

~~~~~~~/~~~~~~~

That night, when their packing was complete, Bennet called his two daughters into his study. A footman was posted outside because either Martha, or her youngest daughter, had been caught trying to eavesdrop at the study door on more than one occasion. Although the door was of heavy oak construction, Bennet preferred to be careful, nonetheless.

"Jane and Lizzy, I want you to remain with my cousins when I return to Longbourn. The less you are around these interlopers, the happier I will be," Bennet informed his daughters.

Unlike the last time he had talked about living with their cousins, Jane did not object. Of course, Elizabeth was another story. "I will remain with Jane and Tommy until after Twelfth Night, but I will return home with you in January, Papa. I will *not* allow these people to chase me from our house!" Elizabeth insisted.

"We will talk again when I return for Christmastide, Lizzy," Bennet told his second daughter, who sat with her arms akimbo and a determined look on her face. "Time for bed, you two. In case you are worried about that disgusting young man, there will be a footman outside his door all night and two in the hall outside our chambers. I promise you, he will never be in this house with us again." Bennet kissed both his daughters on their cheeks and then walked them back to their chambers, acknowledging the two footmen on duty.

~~~~~~~/~~~~~~~

The next morning, a sullen Charles Bingley was escorted to the post and placed on the stage to London. The men watched until the coach was out of view. Charles Bingley would get funds from Mr. Gardiner and then take the post to Scarborough to be with his father's younger brother until school began again.

Bennet had sent an express to Gardiner the previous afternoon apprising him of why the young man was never allowed to return to Longbourn. Unbeknownst to Martha, Bennet also changed his will to state that even should he die, that Charles

Bingley being allowed back into Longbourn would be grounds for himself, his mother, and his sisters to be permanently removed from Bennet lands.

"How could you attempt such a thing with my niece?" an angry Gardiner demanded, as he supported his weight on his fists, leaning forward towards the cowering young man. "If your father were alive, he would have disowned you!"

"It was just a silly prank," the younger man tried to prevaricate.

"And is that why my niece bit your hand and put her knee in your ballocks? Is part of a prank trying to strike the object of the prank when it is a young lady?" He raised his hand to stay the next lie before it was uttered. "If you ever go near *any* of my family again, I will make you disappear. I know many men of varied backgrounds, so believe me when I tell you that no one will find your miserable body. Take your money and get out but remember my warning well. It is not a jest!" Gardiner stated dispassionately.

Charles Bingley felt a cold shiver traverse his spine. He could read in Mr. Gardiner's eyes that this was no idle threat. He would have to rethink his desire for revenge, because it was not worth losing his life over. Thus, for the first time in his life, he began to question his mother's way of doing things.

An hour later, he was on the stage headed north.

~~~~~~~/~~~~~~~

George Wickham stood in the Duke's study, much as he had some six years previously, and, like before, his father and Lord William were present. Lord Robert Darcy was impressed at the way that the young man had turned his life around. Since the last time they had met in the study, there had not been a harder worker than George Wickham when he was presented with a task. At times he would even take the initiative to perform tasks he saw in need of completion rather than attempt to pawn it off on another!

The best part was that it was not for show. The younger Wickham had been observed in candid moments when he was unaware he was being watched and his behaviour was never found wanting. Even though their stations were enormously far apart, a true friendship developed between the heir to Pemberley and the steward's son. George had also been accepted into Darcy's circle of friends, which included Andrew and Richard Fitzwilliam, as well as a few others.

"I have been most pleased by the way you have changed direction since the last time we met in my study some years ago. What have you learnt from your endeavours, George?" the Duke asked kindly.

"I thank you for your encouraging words, your Grace," young Wickham gave a half bow. "There are two main things that I have seen, your Grace. Firstly the only way to make true friends is to be honest to a fault and be willing to give as much, sometimes even more, than one is apt to take or receive. Secondly, when I work for something, apply myself, and especially when I help others, there is a fulfilment I would never experience when I tried to gain what I did not deserve by trickery and prevarication," young Wickham stated evenly.

It had been hard, extremely hard, for the younger Wickham in the beginning. He had railed against the unfairness of his situation, telling himself he would get *his due*! His late mother had always told him that he should aspire to attain more and with all the Darcys possessed, they would not feel it to give him a small fortune to set him up in life. But Mrs. Henrietta Wickham had been an envious and avaricious woman who was never happy with her lot.

Then young George had started to observe those around him—his father, the tenants, and even the servants—each seemingly had a contentment in them which he could only dream of attaining. He had started to talk to his father, and the more they spoke, the more he realised his mother was wrong and she had started to direct him down a path that would only lead to his ruination, or worse.

George Wickham started to address faults in his own character and make the changes his father suggested, starting with a few smaller steps. Not a few times did he reflect on the fact that, had he stayed on his previous path, he would have ended up a libertine living a life of debauchery and dissipation. The Duke had been right, as much as he had doubted such in the beginning now George had no cause to believe otherwise. He was never more grateful for the Duke's calling him on the carpet to disabuse him of his notions six years previous. It had been the shock he had needed to seek his father's help and become the young man he was today.

"You are the one who has made the effort to change, and we," the Duke indicated his son and the steward, "are all impressed with who you are now." Lord Robert paused. "Have you thought about what you would like to do for a profession?"

"As you know, your Grace, my esteemed father made sure I was educated; that was another thing I learned—the value of education. Without a university education, however, I find my choices limited to a trade, for I will not allow my father to use his hard-earned savings to send me to university," young Wickham responded firmly.

"Your feelings do you credit, young man, but indulge me for a moment! If you had a university education, what would you do with your life?" Lord Robert probed.

"I know myself well enough to know I am not suited to be a clergyman, so I could read the law and then follow my father into his profession of stewardship. But if I am honest, my first love is the army. I have been speaking to your nephew, Richard, who has just completed university. Lord Matlock has purchased for him a lieutenant's commission in the Royal Dragoons. That would be my first choice, your Grace." George Wickham had a glint in his eye when he spoke about the army, the sight of it proving that his words were not idle talk.

"You would go into the regulars where you can be sent into battle and risk the chance of not surviving? Why not the militia?" the Duke pushed.

"As much as I respect militia officers, I find I would prefer to serve King and country in a more active way," young Wickham insisted.

"It is my intention to gift you a university education at Oxford," the Duke held up his hand to stay the protest he saw forming on the young man's lips. "It is exactly the reason you deserve this; you did not change for gain or reward. This is my choice because I feel you deserve it. Apply yourself, keep your nose to the grindstone, do well in your studies, and keep away from gambling and cavorting with women. When you graduate, you will receive a lieutenant's commission in the Dragoons, just like Richard has."

"Just thank my father," Lord William grinned, "for you well know how obstinate we Darcys are when we make a decision."

"I thank you from the bottom of my heart, your Grace," George bowed to his benefactor.

"Papa, I missed you," little Gigi, just seven, in a blur of blond ringlets and light blue skirts, launched herself into her father's arms.

"My apologies, your Grace." The governess, Miss Karen Younge, curtsied, looking chagrined at having lost control of her charge. "Lady Georgiana took off before I could catch up to her," the out-of-breath and harried woman explained.

"It is fine, Miss Younge. I know my daughter's propensity to run at times. I will send her back to you after she has had some time with her old Papa." After he dismissed the governess, he looked to the Wickhams. "Unless there is something else from either of you?" Both bowed and left the family in the study.

A half hour later, Lord William took his little sister by the hand and led her back to her waiting governess.

~~~~~~~/~~~~~~~

Lady Catherine de Bourgh was at her wit's end. She had been writing to her brother-in-law, who, by all rights, should have been her husband, for years with no response. Not only was there never an answer, but all invitations to Pemberley, Darcy House, Derbyshire House, or any of his other properties had ceased more than five years previously.

Worse, no invitations to Rosings Park were answered. Her

sickly daughter was sixteen; in but nine years Rosings would become hers, and Lady Catherine could not allow that! She refused to be relegated to the dower house.

Being denied and worse, ignored, was not something that sat well with Lady Catherine, who believed she could shape events with just the force of her will. She did not know how yet, but, with her *brilliant* mind, she was sure she would come up with a solution soon enough. She just had to get Anne into her cousin's company so she could engineer a compromise that would be more successful than the one she attempted on Lord Robert Darcy.

For Anne's part, she too despaired. It seemed the betrothal her mother kept going on about might not be a fact, and if it were not how would she escape the bonds of her mother's strictures?

~~~~~~~/~~~~~~~

After a most enjoyable summer at Holder Heights, Bennet was not happy to return to *that woman* and her daughters. At least the insipid, lecherous son would no longer darken his property.

He had hardly crossed the threshold when his termagant of a wife started pleading her son's case, begging for Bennet to relent and give her 'dear Charles' another chance. After about five minutes of her whining, Bennet had had enough.

"Do you remember what I told you would happen to you and your daughters if your son sets foot on my lands again?" he asked with asperity.

"You meant that? Surely you jested," Martha hoped.

"*NO* madam! It was no jest. You should know my will was changed. If I should die and if your son arrives on my property before my heir takes possession of the estate, you and your daughters will be evicted. It will be my heir's decision what happens after taking over the estate." Seeing she was about to protest, he held up his hand. "I tire of this subject; not another word, madam!"

Mrs. Bennet got a pinched look, one that her younger

daughter had perfected as well, and left the master's study in a huff. She had made a serious misjudgement, for this had not been the gentleman to compromise!

CHAPTER 4

"Mama, why are we never included when our stepfather and his daughters travel?" Caroline Bingley whined. At twelve, she was even more homely than she had been as a younger girl. If one were to own the truth, she was simply ugly!

"He does not care about you, my child; he only cares about his own children. Have you not seen all they have, while we receive nothing?" Martha repeated her oft-told refrain, shifting the blame away from her own actions and onto someone else.

"As they are away, why can we not take some clothing and jewellery from their chambers?" Caroline asked.

"The doors are locked when they are away, Caro; there is no way to enter their bedchambers. Besides, Jane and Eliza usually take most of their possessions with them."

"They have been away since June, Mama. Will they return?" Louisa asked between mouthfuls of biscuits. "And when they do, do we have to hate them, Mama?" the fifteen-year-old asked.

"You most certainly do," Martha replied indignantly. "It is because they are jealous of you that their father treats you so ill!" Before Louisa could challenge the logic of her statement, Martha changed the subject. "I heard from your brother. He is with Uncle Jack in Scarborough for Christmastide. After Twelfth Night he returns to Eton for his final term."

"It is most cruel of our stepfather to never allow Charles back at Longbourn, for all he wanted to do was prank that high and mighty Jane!" Caroline complained.

"Sister, do you forget what he was doing to us?" Louisa asked, aghast.

"I am sure it was a misunderstanding," Caroline waved her sister's concerns away. "Have some more biscuits, sister dearest," Caroline added spitefully.

"Mama!" Louisa appealed.

"Now girls, you need to get along. Remember, we are the ones who are being ill-used. One day we will get our due, I promise you that!" Martha insisted.

~~~~~~~/~~~~~~~

"Welcome, Papa," Tommy threw his arms around his father. The nine-year-old boy missed his father greatly but understood why he lived with Uncle James. He was vastly pleased his two older sisters had been with him at Holder Heights, and for a stint at Holder House in Town, for the last six months. Even better, Jane told him she would be remaining with him and not returning to Longbourn.

"My, my, Tommy. You are getting quite big, Son. Have you been attentive to all of your lessons?" Bennet asked after he hugged his son.

"I have, Papa. Phillip and I learn together. It is less fun when Jamey is at Cambridge, and I do not mind my girl cousins too much. Marie and Cassie are often with Jane while Allie and Lizzy are always together," Tommy reported.

"What else have you been up to?" Bennet asked.

"The Fitzwilliams were here a few days before your arrival, Papa. Ewww, you should see the way the Viscount looks at Marie and she at him!" For his part, Tommy was certain that girls were very strange creatures indeed.

"Marie came out in October as she is eighteen already, and they are courting," Bennet explained. "One day you will understand."

"I will *never* court a *girl!*" Tommy exclaimed emphatically. "I forgot; Richard Fitzwilliam is a Lieutenant in the Dragoons! I want to be an officer when I am big!"

"He has a profession because he is a second son. You will

inherit Longbourn one day, so you will not need a profession," Bennet clarified.

"I would rather be in the army!" Tommy stuck his bottom lip out in an exaggerated pout.

"Where are Lizzy and Jane?" Bennet asked after he stopped laughing at his son's antics.

"They are with our cousins in Marie's sitting room, Papa," Tommy informed his father. "May I go play with Phillip now?"

"You may, Tommy, after you collect your sisters and ask them to join me in my sitting room." Bennet sent his son on his way with a playful tap on the posterior.

Not more than fifteen minutes later, Bennet was accosted by his daughters, who seemed most pleased to see him. "Papa, you always like to surprise us!" Jane chastised. "If we had known when you were to arrive, we would have waited for you in the entrance hall."

"Did I not achieve my goal? Are you not surprised?" Bennet grinned.

"You had Tommy send for us, Papa?" Elizabeth asked after she received a warm hug from her father.

"Lizzy, you remember when I brought you girls here in June? I told you that you and I needed have a discussion. Jane has accepted that her place will be here until I find a way to rid us of that woman and her daughters. The son is forbidden to return, but given his obsession with Jane, I feel it is safer for her to be here," Bennet told his daughter.

"Papa, are you ordering me to remain here with Jane and Tommy?" Elizabeth asked, her eyes downcast.

"No Lizzy, I am not ordering you. However, I would feel better should you remain with Aunt Amy and Uncle James. You are a highly intelligent young lady, and I am sure that you understand the reasoning behind my request." Bennet sat back and allowed his daughter to cogitate.

"I do understand, Papa," Elizabeth said carefully after a minute or two. "Unless you order me to stay here, I would like to return home. You cannot do everything yourself, Papa. That woman has not a clue how to be the mistress of an estate or how to help the tenants when needed. I know I will only be twelve in March, but I also know that I am willing and able to help you. Those interlopers will not chase me from Longbourn!"

"As I promised, I will not order you to stay with my cousins, Lizzy. Your willingness to help me warms my heart. You may return to your cousin's daughters, and I will see you at dinner," Bennet released the girls.

Not long after, Bennet was sitting with his cousin in the latter's study. "Port, Cousin?" the Earl offered.

"You know I will never refuse good port, James, thank you," Bennet responded.

"So Lizzy responded as you believed she would?"

"She did. Truth is, she made some valid points. I *will* need a certain amount of help, and she is a most capable girl." Bennet raised his glass in toast to his younger daughter.

"We are both blessed with a surfeit of intelligent children. In that, we are fortunate." The Earl took long swallow of his port. "I know we cannot change the past, Thomas, but you know my opinion. You should never have married the woman; even had she been found naked and riding you astride in your bed! It was the greatest mistake you ever made! You never consummated the marriage, did you?" Bennet shook his head. "Why not an annulment, for goodness sake?"

"She is a widow, so not a maid. It would be my word against hers. My honour will not allow me to do that. I have drawn certain lines in the sand, and should she cross one of them, I will divorce the woman," Bennet related, with some anger. Allowing his honour to rule in this case had in fact been the worst mistake of his life.

Bennet's cousin changed the subject to one more palatable. "I received a notice some days ago that we have inherited a rather extensive estate, a plantation I believe they call it, near Kingstown in Jamaica. Who would have thought I would have property in the British West Indies?"

"I was not aware we had a relative in that part of the

world," Bennet stated.

"We do not. It was a branch of Amy's family, and we are the only remaining cousins, so it fell to us by default. I understand from the information given to us there is an effective overseer who has held the post for going on ten years."

"Does the plantation keep slaves?"

"I do not know, but I am writing to the man in charge to tell him, if there are slaves, they are to be freed immediately and I will pay them as servants going forward. In addition, I am authorising five and twenty pounds a year in back pay for all former slaves if they are being used at the plantation. I abhor the practice and will not have it attached to my name," the Earl stated emphatically.

"You are to be lauded for your principled stance. If only all members of the empire practiced the same! Even though the practice is outlawed in England, I am disgusted at those who bring in *indentured servants,* which is merely slavery with an-other name. How sad when making money trumps humanity," Bennet opined.

"I suppose I will have to go see the place at some point," the Earl stated, as he refilled both glasses.

"Do you have an idea when?" Bennet asked.

"Jamey has two more years to complete Cambridge and then his Grand Tour. After the terror in France, I am not sure the son of a peer should visit that country, so I suppose I will have to negotiate with Jamey. In short, it will be about three years. It will be before Phillip and Tommy are to attend university, so it will be the ideal time," the Earl laid out.

"I assume that, by then, Marie will be Viscountess Hilldale? While relaying his aversion to girls, Tommy shared that Marie and the Fitzwilliam heir are courting," Bennet cleared up for his cousin.

"Tommy's information is correct. As much as we like the Fitzwilliams, we did not push the two together; they came to it on their own," the Earl explained. "Cassie will be too young to be courting yet, so one of my daughters will be with Jane. If we go at that point, we will time it to return in time for your eldest's coming out."

"The Darcys, the Duke of Derbyshire and his family, are to join us in two days. Have you met Lord Robert yet?" the Earl asked.

"I have not, but I remember Lizzy telling me about them some years ago," Bennet replied. The two talked for a while longer until retiring to change for dinner.

~~~~~~~/~~~~~~~

The Duke of Derbyshire was about to follow his children into his travelling coach when a most unwelcome visitor pulled into the internal courtyard. There was no missing his sister-in-law's carriage and four.

"Why are you here, *Lady* Catherine?" Lord Robert demanded, when the uninvited woman descended from her conveyance.

"Is that the way to greet your nearest relation, Robert?" Lady Catherine smiled sweetly.

"First, you are not even *close* to being my nearest relation, and I am *your Grace* to you, Lady Catherine!" the Duke stated icily. "I ask again, what are you doing here?"

"It is time for Fitzwilliam to do his duty..." The indignant lady got no further.

"Did you not get the message? Did you not know I have been consigning your lying drivel to the fire all these years? I must thank you for helping to warm my house. Do you remember what I threatened if you spewed your lies about William being betrothed to my niece in public?" the Duke demanded.

Lady Catherine was taken back by his visceral reaction and emphatic response. Mayhap it was time to change tactics. "Why Ro—your Grace, I thought you were jesting."

"You know very well, I was not. Mention this phantom engagement one more time, and I will make good on that threat!" The Duke stepped toward Lady Catherine, and, towering over her, used his size to intimidate her, hopefully for the last time. "Now climb in your coach and return to Rosings, or if not, to the lower hell you truly belong in!"

"How can you be so cruel, your Grace? My Anne is in no shape to travel once again so soon; you can see for yourself," Lady Catherine indicated her daughter wrapped with many thick blankets against the freezing temperatures.

The Duke knew his sister-in-law would not hesitate to use Anne as a pawn in her schemes, but he could not punish his beloved late wife's namesake for the sins of her mother. "You have a *maximum* of two days for my niece to recover. At that point, I care not if you go to the inn in Lambton, and Lady Catherine," the red-faced lady turned to look at him with hate-filled eyes. "If you dare arrive at my estate or one of my homes without an invitation written by me, you will be turned away regardless of who is in the carriage with you."

"The lady spluttered but did not dare gainsay her high-ranking brother-in-law. "If that is your decree, your Grace!"

"It is," he turned to his son. "William, I think you should take Gigi and go visit your aunt and Uncle at Snowhaven until our *guests* have departed. I will send a note when you may return," the Duke instructed. Lady Catherine started to protest, but one quelling look from the Duke silenced her.

"What about the Holders, Father?" Lord William asked.

"I will send a note forthwith," the Duke assured his son.

~~~~~~~/~~~~~~~

Within an hour, one of the Derbyshire carriages departed for Snowhaven, a mere fifteen miles distant. Lady Catherine and her none-too-happy daughter were shown to their suite on a guest floor.

"Mother," Anne screeched as they gained the shared sitting room. "You promised I would soon be a Marchioness and a duchess! Why did my uncle deny I am betrothed to my cousin when you continually tell me I am?" Anne had long suspected it was a fantasy of her mother's, but she had long held onto the hope that she would leave her mother's company.

"It is a misunderstanding, Anne, and one I will clear up tonight!" Lady Catherine promised her daughter.

After midnight, Lady Catherine slipped out of her chambers and made for the family floor, more importantly to the master suite. She had failed to compromise Robert Darcy before, but she would not fail again!

As she opened the door to her brother-in-law's chambers, she failed to notice the Duke was standing in an alcove in the dark, with his valet at his side. With the aid of the moonlight she stole into the master's chambers, and after blowing out the candle she had used to get there, she climbed into the bed with the male form she could just make out.

"Robert, we were meant for one another, do not fight it," Lady Catherine snaked her hands around the man's chest. "It is time to make me your duchess."

"Sorry, missus, but if ya marry me, ya will no' be any duchess, but a footman's wife," a smiling man still in his livery looked back at the dismayed woman.

"Why are you in my brother's bed!" Lady Catherine blustered.

Suddenly, the chamber was bathed in light as candles were lit. "That is my question for *you*, Catherine! Had your misguided scheme succeeded in compromising me all those years ago, the result would have been the same as it would have been this night. I would not marry you, even if you were the *only* woman on this earth! Thompson, Hampstead," the Duke looked to two burley footmen, "escort this *lady* to her chambers. Post a guard there, more than one, in fact. She is to be in her coach and departing Pemberley by ten this morning. The gatehouse is to be informed that she is not allowed back onto my lands, *no matter what* she tells them!" The two men nodded, and before she could protest, each took an arm, lifted her off her feet, and marched her to her chambers.

As the Duke had instructed, the de Bourgh carriage departed Pemberley on time.

~~~~~~~/~~~~~~~

"It is good to see Longbourn again, Lizzy," Bennet told his daughter as they rolled down the drive. It was Saturday, the eighth day of January 1802. Bennet and his second daughter had departed Holder Heights the day after Twelfth Night with his cousins, who turned off towards Town some hours earlier.

"It is, Papa. I understand why Jane and Tommy are not here, but I do miss them so," Elizabeth stated wistfully.

"I miss them all the time as well, Lizzy, but we will see them in three short months at Easter. As happy as I am you are with me, I wonder if I did the right thing by not ordering you to stay with Jane and Tommy," Bennet questioned himself.

"Well, I for one think you made the correct decision!" Elizabeth insisted.

"I hope so, my Lizzy," Bennet kissed her forehead as the carriage halted under the portico. Neither missed the sour looks on Mrs. Bennet's and her daughters' faces.

CHAPTER 5

August 1805

"Papa, did you receive a letter from Jane? Have they arrived?" Elizabeth bounced on the balls of her feet. She was fifteen, more beautiful than ever, and had grown taller and womanlier. As ladylike as she normally was, the prospect of news from her sister and brother about their long voyage made her natural exuberance come to the fore. "Mr. Hill told me the post was delivered and there was an especially thick letter delivered!"

"I was about to call for you, my Lizzy. Yes, I received a letter from Uncle James and Tommy, and this one," Bennet put the missive in his daughter's eager hands, "is for you."

Elizabeth squealed with excitement when she saw Jane's handwriting. "I apologise, Papa; that was childish of me." Elizabeth blushed.

"Think nothing of it, Lizzy. They travelled for over two months, so I understand your desire for news; I felt the same way," Bennet assured his daughter.

Father and daughter had spent as much time away from Longbourn as possible during the last three years to keep away from the constant complaints of ill use from Mrs. Bennet and her youngest daughter.

Louisa remained homely and overweight, but when she was away from her mother and younger sister, she could be pleasant, and Elizabeth had warmed to her stepsister. The more time Louisa spent with Elizabeth, the more she came to realise how much inaccurate information her mother fed them.

Through Elizabeth, Louisa apologised for her part in the

compromise ten years earlier. She was ashamed it had taken her so long to wake up to the fact and beg Mr. Bennet's pardon. After Elizabeth conveyed the sincerity of her new friend's contrition, Bennet had accepted it without reservation, and through Elizabeth told Louisa he understood she had been only ten and had done what her mother told her to do. The forgiveness lifted a great weight off Louisa's shoulders.

Louisa had also become friendly with Charlotte Lucas, who was Elizabeth's best friend in the neighbourhood. The three would meet without the mother or the youngest Bingley being aware, and they enjoyed their time together immensely. The three friends spent as much time with one another as possible, often at Lucas Lodge where Caroline Bingley was not welcome.

While Bennet was aware of the burgeoning friendship, his wife and her youngest daughter were not. The younger one had moved from homely to plain ugliness as she grew. At sixteen, her body had developed few womanly curves; she was tall for a lady, with long, spindly, skinny limbs that were not in proportion to her smaller body. Her burnt orange hair colour and almost translucent skin did not help, as they highlighted her stark features.

When Caroline Bingley spoke, it was more of a screech than a voice, and it was grating to any who heard it other than perhaps her mother. Her mother kept telling her how well she looked and how all other women would be jealous of her, especially her stepsisters. Now that her eyes were wide open, when Louisa heard her mother spout this nonsense, she had to do everything she could to not burst out laughing.

After three years of constantly denying her requests, Martha Bennet still importuned her husband from time to time about allowing her son to visit. The answer was always the same, a resounding '*no*' with a reminder of what would happen should he cross his property line!

Charles had graduated, albeit just barely, from Oxford, as he had been more interested in gambling, cavorting with women, and running up debts than in his studies. No matter what hogwash he wrote to his mother, Bennet knew the truth, as he had a man keeping an eye on the Bingley heir. Bingley had just come into his inheritance. Gardiner had been only too pleased to rid himself of the money and complete the charge laid on him by the wastrel's late father.

Bennet was sure the money would be gone inside of a year. As it was, there had been two to three hundred pounds in debt that Bingley had to discharge as soon as he had received his inheritance. It was that or debtor's prison. Bennet could only smile as his wife waited day after day for her son to send them some money to help her purchase new gowns and fripperies for her daughters. It was no surprise to him that the expected money never arrived.

Elizabeth sat and eagerly broke the seal on her missive from Jane.

June 4, 1805
Sugar Hill, Kingstown, Jamaica

"Papa, it took almost two months for the letter to arrive!" Elizabeth exclaimed.

"The packet ships must have had good winds, Lizzy; it can take weeks longer than that at times," Bennet replied.

I cannot tell you how happy I am to be on dry land again, Lizzy! Thank goodness we will be here two months before we must return on an interminable voyage again! It has been four days since we arrived, and only today am I steady on my legs while walking on land. As the captain warned us we would, it felt like we were still on-board ship until today. I expected the ground to rise and meet my foot, or to dip below it as I walked!

Enough complaints. What an interesting place this is. On the one hand, there is so much beauty here, but on the other hand there is slavery. How can such beauty co-exist with such cruelty and evil?

Many of the landowners are unhappy with Uncle James because he freed those who were slaves on his estate, a plantation as it is called it here, and on top of that, he paid them back wages. Some chose to return to the countries from which they were stolen by the vile men who perpetrate this most disgusting of acts, but most elected to stay and work at Sugar Hill of their own volition.

The other landowners think it will give their slaves hope. I, for one, hope it does! How can these supposed good and upstanding Christian men justify treating a human being as a possession? It is so sad, Lizzy; men, women, and children <u>owned</u>! Uncle is trying to influence his fellow landowners to follow his lead and prove to them they will still make healthy profits. I pray he is successful in this endeavour.

The beauty I spoke of is wonderous. The flowers and animals! Lizzy, you would not believe your eyes. You remember we saw a few parrots at the menagerie? Here they fly about, wild and as common as a robin back home. The colours, variety, and sizes! And Lizzy, you would never guess; some of them talk! I was most shocked when I heard one using extremely off-colour language!

All the houses are painted white here, as I am told it helps with the heat. It is so humid here, Lizzy; your hair in particular would be impossible to style! I am told that, even in the winter, it never gets really cold. And I heard there are sometimes massive storms they call hurricanes. I am hopeful we will not experience one of those, as I am told they can be devastating.

Next week Uncle and Aunt are taking us to a Town, Saint Anne on the northern coast of the island, to a group of eight rivers they call Ocho Rios. You know what that means from your Spanish lessons! There is jungle that ends at the most inviting and beautiful white sand beaches that we saw already. I am told it is more the norm than the exception here.

I am hopeful that Aunt will take Cassie, Allie, and I sea bathing. We will have to find a private place as, unlike us, the natives are not modest. They, especially the children, think nothing of swimming naked! I know it will shock your sensibilities, but who are we to tell them they are wrong? Are we not the visitors, and they the owners of the land and its traditions? I would not dare do such a thing in the company of any but my aunt and female cousins!

"Papa," Elizabeth laughed freely, "could you imagine our modest Jane swimming naked as when she was born in front of anyone? Even our aunt and cousins?" Bennet just shook his head, chuckling at the surprise he imagined his Jane having expressed.

Do not be angry with me if I do not write too much while I am here, Lizzy, for there is so much to do! Instead I will keep a journal, sister dearest, and you will have it to read it when I return to you.

Your loving sister,

Jane

"I wish now I had taken Uncle's invitation and gone with them!" Elizabeth lamented.

"It is easy to look into the past and say I should have, would have, or could have. It does not help, my daughter. What have I told you?" Bennet asked.

"Only remember the past as that remembrance that gives you pleasure?" Elizabeth parroted, grinning at the words for now she knew exactly what that implied, Jane having told her about parrots literally parroting what it had heard.

"Yes, Lizzy, that is the one. If Uncle must return to Jamaica and you are yet unmarried, then you will travel with him next time," Bennet assured his daughter. "Mayhap you will be lucky enough to marry a man who will show you the world."

"Like you did when you married Mama, Jane and I have pledged that we will only marry for the deepest love," Elizabeth insisted.

"That is my wish for both of my girls," Bennet said gruffly as he became emotional every time he thought about his beloved Fanny.

~~~~~~~/~~~~~~~

"Did you forget to salute me, Lieutenant?" Captain Richard Fitzwilliam demanded.

"Hello to you too, Richard," Wickham gave his friend a jaunty salute.

"Welcome to the Dragoons, Wickham; I am impressed. When you told me this is what you wanted, I thought you were just paying lip service. You have the gift of the gab, you could have been a good barrister," the Captain told his friend.

"I think I felt a calling like you did, my friend. I have no doubt I would have done well in the law, but then I would not have been able to help give Boney a bloody nose." Wickham stated with purpose.

"How was William when you saw him last?" Captain Fitzwilliam asked.

"He was well, Richard, working hard to learn everything from his father. He has deferred his grand tour until he is able to go to the continent again," Lieutenant Wickham informed the Captain.

"At least we have not been sent to fight the French yet; however, I believe it is but a matter of time," the Captain opined.

As the two were talking, a private ran up and saluted the two officers. He handed each a black-edged letter. At first Richard feared it was his father, mother, or brother, but it was none of them. Uncle Robert was dead. He looked at his friend and saw true despair.

"Wickham, what is it?" the Captain asked with concern.

"My father is dead!" the Lieutenant stated looking lost.

"Good Lord, your father as well as Uncle Robert! Come Wickham, we must see Colonel Atherton; he will authorise as much leave as we need. Let us be away. My parents, brother and sister are yet at Matlock House; we will travel together." Richard shook his friend out of his stupor, and they made their way to the Colonel's office.

~~~~~~~/~~~~~~~

When the lead carriage passed the gate house at Pemberley, the black cloth hanging on the posts and gates was impossible to miss. An hour later, the Matlock carriages pulled into the enclosed courtyard. There were black wreaths hanging on the large oak doors leading into the manor house.

Wickham wanted to go directly to his father's house, but the Earl advised that they all find William and find out what occurred to leave both men dead on the same day. The butler, Douglas, showed the Fitzwilliams and Wickham to the study.

Lady Marie asked where Lady Georgiana was, and she and the Countess left the group to go see the grieving girl.

Lord William Darcy, now his Grace the Duke of Derbyshire, Earl of Lambton, was sitting behind the desk looking at nothing in particular. He looked haggard, with dark rings under his eyes; he had obviously had little or no sleep.

"William, WILLIAM!" Richard called twice, before his cousin noted their presence. As soon as he saw Wickham, he walked around the desk and threw his arms around his friend.

"They are both gone, George!" the new Duke stated, with a hitch in his voice.

"How William—your Grace, how did they both die on the same day?" Wickham asked with obvious anguish in his voice.

Lord William sat with his friend on a settee, as the three Fitzwilliam men found seats around them. "Still William, my friend. It is almost five days ago now; our fathers went to inspect a problem at the Cox's. You remember they are in the northwest corner of the estate." Wickham nodded. "They took my father's curricle, just the two of them as was their wont," Lord William choked up as he relayed the story, pausing for a drink of water to be able to carry on. "They were approaching the bend, the one with the forest on the left a mile from Cox's house, and we do not know what, but something spooked the horses. Later, we found a fox on the side of the drive; he was bloody and there were hoof prints. We believe that he darted under the horses' feet, and they panicked. There is a ten-foot drop to the side, and when the curricle broke loose, it turned over and fell over the edge. Our fathers were trapped inside under the wreckage. It is not much of a consolation, but the doctor opined that death was instantaneous."

"They died doing what they loved, taking care of the estate," Wickham stated philosophically.

"George, if you want to withdraw from the Dragoons after this, no one will think anything less of you," Richard informed his grieving friend.

"I will be back, Richard. I will mourn here, and then I will return. I need an occupation to keep my mind busy, and nothing has changed with my desire to serve the King and the country," Wickham said with purpose.

"In that case, I will make sure you join my unit when you return, George," Richard clapped his brother-in-arms on the back.

"You will need to hire a new steward, William; I will pack up the house as soon as may be," Wickham offered.

"No need. Your father reported the under steward he trained, Mr. Edwin Chalmers, was ready a few months back; he has been searching for employment. I have appointed him on a trial basis, and by all accounts he is happy to remain in his house, so take as much time as you need, George," the Duke assured his friend. "Now that we are here, and if George agrees, we will have the interment tomorrow. Our fathers are in the icehouse, given the temperature. Your father will be buried in the family plot, my friend." It was the first time since receiving the news that George Wickham cried.

As they were preparing to leave the study, a well-known and unwelcome voice was heard. "Where is my daughter's betrothed! He will do his duty to her!" Lady Catherine pushed the study door open without knocking. When she saw five pairs of eyes looking at her with disdain, she was momentarily silenced.

"Why are you here, Lady Catherine? Did my father not warn you what would happen if you spouted your lies again?" the new Duke demanded.

"But your mother…" she started to say.

"Give it up, Cathy! There is no one in this room who does not know it is a lie. Do you think Robert did not tell us what you attempted when you were here last? Only you would try and take advantage of a house of mourning to further your own desires! Now unless *his Grace* objects, you will leave and return to Rosings Park, and you will not leave there until I say so!" the Earl thundered.

"But Anne is weak…" This time, Lord William cut her off.

"Have you no decency, madam? Do you think I will fall for

the same ploy you attempted last time you were here, where you ended up climbing in bed with a footman, while trying to compromise my father? If Anne needs to rest, there are perfectly good rooms at the Cock and Bull in Lambton, or at other coaching inns on the Great North Road on your way back to Kent. Leave, now! I am in no mind to see you, or to listen to your lies!" Like his father had the last time she was at Pemberley, Lord William towered over and glowered at the now-quaking lady.

Seeing there was no option, Lady Catherine withdrew. She could not understand what went wrong with another of her well-thought-out plans. The boy was supposed to be weak with grief, not surrounded by men, and certainly should not have the same backbone of steel as his father before him!

She would return to Rosings Park and lick her wounds, and then come up with a plan which could not end but with her daughter wed to her nephew. She could not become a duchess now, but her daughter would be! Of that, she was certain!

~~~~~~~~/~~~~~~~~

Father and daughter were ensconced in the study on the first Sunday in August; and they would have invited Louisa to join them if it would not have caused trouble with her mother and harpy of a sister.

"Do you think they have left Jamaica yet, Papa?" Elizabeth asked enthusiastically.

"We cannot be sure, Lizzy, but I believe so, both by Jane's estimation and that of my cousin's, in his letter to me," Bennet opined.

"I cannot wait to see Jane again, Papa, and to read her journal. She will have so very much to tell!" Elizabeth gushed.

Half a world away, *The West Indies Trader* had departed Jamaica, starting its two-month plus voyage to England with the Bennets on board. They were sailing between Cuba and Haiti toward the Bahamian Islands. The passengers were asleep when a storm of epic proportions hit them, one which Jane had called a hurricane in her letter to her younger sister.

CHAPTER 6

December 1805

Both Bennet and his second daughter were beside themselves with worry. It had been confirmed from Jamaica that the cousins, Jane and Tommy, had boarded *The West Indies Trader,* and she had sailed as scheduled. Two days after their departure, a massive storm, one called a hurricane, had descended on the area without warning.

No wreckage had been found, meaning there could be no official determination, and the Earl, Countess, and their family could not be declared dead for seven years. Bennet took Elizabeth with him to visit the last remaining family member they were aware of, Lady Marie Fitzwilliam, at Hilldale House in London. She had married Andrew Fitzwilliam, Viscount Hilldale, a year previously.

"Uncle Thomas," Marie's cheeks were stained with tears. She saw Elizabeth and enfolded her younger cousin in her arms. "Lizzy, I am so very sorry, Jane and Tommy, all of my family!" Lady Marie descended into a fresh round of tears, and her husband extracted her and took her into his arms tenderly.

"It is my choice to hope, Marie!" Elizabeth stated, her back stiff as a board. "Until the wreckage is found, and we are told all hope is lost, I *choose* to believe all of our family are alive and waiting to be rescued! My hope always rises when things look bleakest."

"I will pray you are right, Lizzy," Marie said with a tremulous voice.

"Are you managing my cousin's assets?" Bennet asked the Viscount.

"I am, Bennet," the Viscount replied. The two had met soon after Marie accepted the Fitzwilliam heir's offer of marriage. "Everything will be held in trust until, as we hope and pray, they are found and returned to us hale and healthy, or seven years pass. Marie and I leave for Holder Heights in a few days, and we intend to remain there and manage the Holder holdings as best we can."

"If you want to communicate with us, please send any letters to the care of my solicitor, Mr. Jacob Philips of Meryton. I am sure you know the reason," Bennet stated dryly.

Two days later, the same day the Viscount and Viscountess departed London for Staffordshire, Bennet and Elizabeth returned to Longbourn.

~~~~~~~/~~~~~~~

Shortly after their arrival, they were accosted by Martha Bennet. "Did you learn any news about your precious Jane?" Martha asked spitefully.

"Madam!" Bennet growled a warning and turned on his heel. The slamming of the study door reverberated throughout the house. The truth was Thomas Bennet was wracked with guilt. If he had kept Jane and Tommy at home, they would have been with him now and not, as he suspected, at the bottom of the sea somewhere.

The only glimmer of joy in his life was his Lizzy, who spent many hours talking and reading to him in his study. As he withdrew into himself more and more, he began to spend almost all his waking hours in the study with a book and his port.

When Elizabeth wanted to have a meal in the company of her father, or spend time with him, she would go into his study. He was always pleased to see her, but she did not miss the looks mingled with anguish and guilt on her father's face, and he would not talk about the subject with her, so he continued to stew in his misery.

It was during this time Elizabeth slowly, but surely, took over the running of the estate. A month after his new habit of closeting himself in his study, Elizabeth invited Mr. Philips to

Longbourn and cared not if her father wanted to be left to his own devices. At her request, she had Philips set up a trust he would administer and to which she had access.

Before her father had begun to sink into the doldrums of despair, he had taken an active role in running the estate—now all he cared for was his port and books. Bennet knew Lizzy needed him, but he could not motivate himself to do any more. Feelings of guilt paralysed him, and he was doing as much as he was capable of.

Without Bennet being as present as he was before, Martha and her nasty daughter started to take advantage of the situation after having seen no change in his behaviour in the following months. Louisa tried to blunt their verbal attacks through diversion, but they simply ignored her.

Not long after her sixteenth birthday on the fifth day of March 1806, the loneliest one Elizabeth ever celebrated, Caroline Bingley slapped Elizabeth when she refused to give her a bracelet her father had aside for her birthday before the tragedy. It was gold with some delicate scroll work, and had diamonds spaced four to five inches apart.

In her younger days, Elizabeth had been taught to punch by her male Bennet cousins. She drew her hand back and allowed her fist to fly. Caroline Bingley landed flat on her back after Elizabeth delivered her blow to the shrew's upper left shoulder, a little above where a breast would have been had Miss Caroline developed any of note.

Mrs. Bingley had been proud of her daughter when she slapped a high and mighty Bennet girl but was incensed when the chit retaliated. "How dare you?" Martha Bennet screeched as she stalked toward Elizabeth with her arm cocked, ready to put the chit in her place.

"I would think twice about striking me if I were you *Mrs. Bennet!*" Elizabeth hissed. Martha Bennet stopped her advance, not nearly as confident as she had been before. "I know all about my father's rules for you. While I may not be willing to disturb him, I am quite capable of communicating with Mr. Philips and,"

Elizabeth indicated the servants, including the Hills watching, "they would take pleasure in restraining you, should I ask it!"

"You hit my dear daughter," Martha tried to bluster.

"After she slapped me, as I would not give her something that belongs to me!" Elizabeth retorted.

By now Caroline was sitting up and wailing. "Punish her, mother!" she whined.

Elizabeth looked at her stepmother in a challenging way. The woman had a modicum of good sense, so, after helping her shaking daughter to stand, she withdrew to her chambers, taking her caterwauling daughter with her.

No matter how Elizabeth tried, she found nothing that would alleviate her father's dark moods. She knew that many nights he now fell asleep on his sofa in his cups. He was unshaven and unkempt many days and was losing weight as he hardly ate solid foods. As the summer of 1806 wore on, Elizabeth had no idea how to coax her father out of his study and to entice him to start living once again.

~~~~~~~/~~~~~~~

What nobody in England knew was that the hurricane which had caught the ship unawares in August of 1805 had killed most of the officers and crew who had been above decks as they battled to sail the ship during the raging storm. The ship, mostly intact, had been blown onto and over a reef that almost entirely surrounded a small, uninhabited island that was part of the chain of islands comprising the Bahamas. There were a few hundred known islands in the chain, and hundreds more unknown.

James, Amelia, Jamey, Cassandra, and Phillip Bennet, along with their cousins Jane and Tommy Bennet, were among the handful of survivors who walked away, uninjured for the most part, from the wreck that finally broke apart and sank in the lagoon between the reef and island. It seemed only those few who were below decks had survived.

Once the section of the ship they had been in came to rest in the lagoon, the Earl led his family out of the hulk. His family and three crew members were able to reach the beach in the dark of the night, made even blacker by the still raging storm. The survivors huddled under trees they found within a few hundred yards of beach. At some point a few hours later, there was an eerie calm followed once more by the intense fury of the storm.

The Bennets and the remaining crew rode the storm out until it finally abated as the dawn broke. Once the clouds cleared and light was able to reach them, they all walked out from under the trees onto the beach. *The West Indies Trader* had been turned into matchwood! There were timber and trunks floating in the lagoon. They could not find a single longboat which had survived the ordeal.

The Earl took charge and organised the survivors into groups of two or three to explore and return to the beach in a few hours. Luckily for them, the storm had provided a bounty of downed fruits as well as some birds and some small animals which had not survived the storm.

Jane, Cassie and Tommy walked up a hill a mile from the beach. The summit was flat and gave them a vantage point from which to see that the island, although not huge, was not tiny either. As they walked around the summit to see all sides of the island, they saw there was a stream that ran into a natural pool to their west. That was when they learned they would have plenty of fresh water. The reef seemed to circle the island except to the south, close to where they had come ashore, where there was a gap of mayhap a hundred yards where the angry sea had free access to the lagoon.

On their return to the beach, it was determined they would have more than enough food and water for a lengthy stay, but they had no knowledge of whether or not the island was on any of the shipping routes. They did not know when or if they would ever see another ship sail close to them.

Their first task was to collect as much useable material as they could, including timber, canvas from the sails, and trunks. As the three surviving crew members were all seamen, they naturally deferred to the Earl, and he to them for their areas of expertise. One had been the cook/surgeon, the second a carpenter, and the third a seaman who used to help set the sails.

A fortnight later, a utilitarian structure had been built and made waterproof with canvas from the mainsail. The men had hauled a good supply of wood up to the summit of the hill, where a rotating watch was set to keep an eye out for a ship. It did not take long for the social distinctions that would have separated them in England to be all but forgotten.

~~~~~~~/~~~~~~~

Lord William Darcy, Duke of Derbyshire and Earl of Lambton, walked his friend to the carriage that would bear him back to his unit as his three months of deep mourning were at an end. A month into their shared mourning period, Darcy had given Wickham a cottage for his own use, where the contents from his father's house had been placed. The commanding Colonel of Dragoons had approved his extended leave without a thought.

Richard Fitzwilliam had recently been promoted to major and made company commander. George Wickham was keen to return, as he would be a platoon officer in his friend's company. The fact they would be shipped to the Iberian Peninsula in January of 1806 was not lost on the Duke.

Even though there had been no major battles with the French Imperial Army since the declaration of war in 1803, the young Duke was sure it would only be a matter of time. He respected his cousin and friend for their commitment to their duty, but he could not help but worry for their safety.

At the reading of his father's will, there were no big surprises for him. Neither Wickham nor Richard had anticipated the legacies that were left to them--fifteen thousand to the former and fifty thousand to the latter. Both elected to invest their money, and there had not been a moment's thought about selling out or resigning from the army.

Richard had been made co-guardian of Lord William's young sister. Georgiana missed her beloved father terribly, as he was the only parent she ever knew. Miss Younge had been a godsend in helping Gigi though the grief her young mind could hardly comprehend. At four and twenty, the new Duke was not ready to think about a wife yet, but he was now brother, father, and mother to a sister more than twelve years his junior.

"Godspeed, George," Lord William clapped his friend on the back as they stood in the enclosed courtyard.

"Must you depart?" Lady Georgiana asked plaintively. Wickham had been almost like another brother to her since her father's tragic end.

"I must, Gigi, I have my duty, and it is especially important to me to fulfil it. Just like your duty is to look after William now," Wickham winked at the young girl.

"Well, in that case, I will take care of William for you," she answered, seriously. The adults around her did their best to keep straight faces.

With a last shake of his friend's hand and a light kiss on the top of the girl's head, Wickham mounted the conveyance and was soon off. Brother and sister watched until the vehicle made a turn out of the courtyard onto the main drive and was gone from view.

~~~~~~~/~~~~~~~

By the time 1805 drew to a close, Bingley had managed to gamble and whore away more than half of his legacy. Luckily for him, he realised at that pace he would burn through his money before the end of the approaching year.

His mother was not an option as her allowance and his sisters' allowances were a pittance thanks to his tight-fisted stepfather. As much as he had a selfish disdain for the feelings of others, he well knew the penalty of showing up at Longbourn to see his mother and sisters, and worse, still—he could hear Gardiner's threats in his ear of what would happen to him if he had any contact with Bennet's family again.

He left London in the direction of Kent and Surrey. He had briefly considered asking Mr. Gardiner for work, but he knew there was no chance the man would hire him, even were he capable of any work which would be tasked to him.

When he considered what occupation would have a

reasonable return for the minimum of work, he realised that he would need to take orders. He had completed his degree with no distinction, passing only by the kindness of his professors, as he had been too interested in extra-curricular activities at Oxford. He found a small seminary not far from Hunsford in Kent where, for fifty pounds, the head of the school was willing to cut the time needed to take orders from twelve months to six months.

So it was that in mid-1806, when Lady Catherine de Bourgh was seeking a man for the living Rosings Park had within its gift, for another fifty pounds the head of the school sent the *great* lady one name: Mr. Charles Bingley.

~~~~~~~/~~~~~~~

As they approached the one-year mark of the date the family should have returned from their long voyage, there had been no improvement in Thomas Bennet. As he no longer countermanded his wife's orders, she slowly but surely began to fulfil parts of the role of mistress, as best she knew how.

Worried more about her father than what the woman was up to in the house, Elizabeth did not challenge her. Martha was not able to hire or fire staff, but she had started to redirect some of the maids from their normal duties to be personal servants to her and her daughters.

The maid who was lucky enough to serve Louisa could breathe easier as the older Bingley daughter was infinitely more pleasant and respectful than the other two harpies. The friendship between Elizabeth, Charlotte, and Louisa had continued to flourish, even if Elizabeth had less time to be a carefree young lady as she had to keep Longbourn running.

Luckily for Elizabeth, her stepmother did nothing overtly against her. As mean of understanding as Martha Bennet was, she knew the reason the estate was running efficiently was because of her stepdaughter. While she and her youngest daughter often made comments about how unladylike all her activities were, they did nothing to interfere with her tasks.

As long as her husband, who she hated with a passion,

stayed alive, and his daughter ran the estate, she and her daughters would not be turned out into the hedgerows by the heir, whoever the mysterious man was. Over the years she had asked about the heir, but she received no answers to her enquiries.

Elizabeth could have put a stop to Mrs. Bennet's encroachment regarding the duties of mistress, but she had so much to worry about with her father and keeping the estate running, it was a fight that she decided to defer. Her father's equanimity, such as it was, was more important to her than reining in her stepmother and her youngest spawn.

Her father used to gift Elizabeth books they would read together. The last one before he had withdrawn had been *Utopia* by Sir Thomas Moore, which she reread many times over. It became a treasure that represented how her father used to be.

~~~~~~~/~~~~~~~

Thomas Bennet was aware of his monumental failure to protect his family. One day he sat cataloguing his failures as he saw them: He had allowed his damned honour to rule and marry a woman he should never have married. That had led to him leaving Tommy permanently with his cousins. Bringing that woman into his house had brought her lecherous son into his household as well, which had led to Jane staying with his cousins.

He still had one child left; he knew that, but he could not overcome his feelings of guilt as his mistakes had cost the lives of two of his beloved Fanny's children. As much as he had always loved spending time with Lizzy—reading with her, debating what they had read—each time he saw his beloved daughter, it was a stark reminder of his perceived failures.

A few days after the one-year anniversary of the date the ship should have returned to England, the day he had again listed all his perceived failures, and after having been drinking all day, in the afternoon, Bennet ordered Orion saddled. The groom had hesitated before saddling the stallion as his master was clearly foxed, but in the end, he had done as he had been bade, for the master was in no mood to listen to anything the groom said.

Bennet rode out of the area around the stables much faster than normal and tore across a field. Being in his cups, he was not seated as he should have been and was not holding the reins as tightly as needed. Orion jumped a small culvert, something horse and rider had done many times before. This time, however, with his state of inebriation, Bennet slid off the speeding horse and hit the ground with a tremendous force that snapped his neck. In an instant, Thomas Bennet was no more.

When Orion returned riderless to the stables, the grooms mounted an immediate search, and an hour later one of them found the cold and lifeless of the late master.

CHAPTER 7

Elizabeth did not want to believe what the groom was telling her when he returned from the spot where the master's body had been discovered. She hoped beyond hope that there had been some sort of mistake and that her Papa was just injured, was not dead, as she had been told. How could it be that her father, who had been the rock that anchored Longbourn until he allowed grief and guilt to consume him, was no more?

When they brought her father's body home for the final time, Elizabeth had sobbed great wracking sobs of grief as the reality hit home. She was alone at Longbourn, except for her loyal servants. Louisa was her friend, but she had to be circumspect around her mother and younger sister. It hurt Louisa that she could not go to her friend and offer her succour.

Elizabeth knew she could write to Marie and Andrew with a request for their help, but she was cognisant of how much they were having to manage, what with Holder Heights and the Holder holdings in addition to their own estate and concerns. They also had a babe to contend with. Elizabeth chose not to add to their burden. Uncle Gardiner would take care of the money aspects, but she would not impose on him more than that. He and Aunt Maddie had two-year-old Lilly at home and another babe on the way.

Mr. Philips would take care of all the legal issues and make sure her father's wishes were honoured. Elizabeth knew full well that if both Jane and Tommy were declared dead in six years, then she would become the owner of Longbourn. Her only problem was the way her father's will had been written—the evil woman and her younger devil's spawn were allowed to live at the estate until it was claimed by the heir. She could not be angry with her papa, as there was no world in which he could have imagined the scenario which had taken place.

After he was stricken with grief and guilt, he had become an indolent man who was in no way comparable to the man she had known most of her life. Elizabeth reckoned if he had been more his old self, he would have changed his will to reflect the new reality. As he had not done so, she was left to live with the reality and not what might have been, which would have been far more preferable.

While she wanted nothing more than to curl up in a ball and mourn her father, Elizabeth did not have that luxury. She had been effectively running the estate for a year, and now there was no choice. So much loss, but she firmly reminded herself that Jane, Tommy, and the rest of the Bennets were alive! They had to be! Her Jane and Tommy could not have left her so alone in the world.

As Elizabeth did at least once a week, she sat down and wrote a letter to Jane that would never be posted. She knew writing to Jane helped her relieve her stress, and helped her feel connected to her sister. How she would have loved to have Jane's calming influence with her! *'Jane and Tommy, I* know *you are alive,'* Elizabeth told herself, a mantra she reiterated more than once each day. *'You* have *to be!'*

~~~~~~~/~~~~~~~

When Martha was told her husband had lost his life in a riding accident, she cared not a whit that the man himself was dead. In fact, she thought he deserved such a fate after the way he treated her! She was, however, very much afraid of what it would mean for her and her daughters. How soon would the heir arrive to throw her out of the house?

She knew Charles had just been awarded a living at Hunsford in Kent, but she had so far received no invitations from her son. She was not content with how Charles seemed uninterested in assisting his mother and sisters. He had let them know he would ingratiate himself with his patroness, Lady

Catherine de Bourgh, but it would take time, so he would be too busy to see them in the near future.

Things were not ideal for her at Longbourn; it was nothing like she imagined her life would be after she engineered the compromise. Martha had imagined seasons in London coupled with her power of persuasion would have been enough to have her husband adopt her children and give them his name. None of that happened! When the children had used the name Bennet in Meryton after their arrival in the neighbourhood, one and all had derided them, as her husband had made it known how he had *not* adopted his stepchildren and their name was *not* Bennet.

She remembered the humiliation she had experienced when she and her children had attempted to charge their purchases to the estate's accounts, only to find out her miserly husband had expressly forbidden the merchants to allow her to use his accounts unless they did not want remuneration. How was she to know her husband was serious when he informed her about the accounts at the time of their reading of the settlement?

At least they were in a comfortable house with a roof over their heads. Martha had attacks of nerves as she worried she would soon be in the hedgerows and homeless with two dependent daughters. Where would she go?

She had alienated her first husband's brother in Scarborough when she had attempted to seduce him. Who knew he took his vows to his wife seriously? Now the uncle refused to allow Charles or any of them back into his home, all because of a little thing when Charles was discovered trying to watch the daughters of the house bathing.

The day her late husband's solicitor was due to arrive to read his will—the copy that would be disclosed to her—Martha had flutterings and palpitations of her heart as she was convinced she would have days to vacate the property with only the two thousand she brought into the marriage. Her daughters had two thousand pounds each, but their money was secured and could not be touched until they either married or turned five and twenty.

Mr. Philips turned over her widow's portion of two thousand pounds to her and reiterated that *all* rules Mr. Bennet had instituted during his life regarding the treatment of his remaining daughter and of Charles Bingley not being allowed on the property were codified in the will. He also explained the profits from the estate would be placed into a trust account and would be turned over to the heir when said heir claimed the property, effectively cutting off the avaricious woman's hope she would have access to estate money.

Philips was clear if Mrs. Bennet wasted her portion, she would not receive a farthing from the estate for her pin money or any of her personal needs. He opined she should invest the money in order to continue to receive a monthly allowance.

"Am I not to know who this mysterious heir is that holds my fate in his hands?" Martha demanded.

"When it is time, you will be notified. You are aware you may not discharge any of the servants, unless they are ones you hired and pay out of your own funds, do you not?" Philips asked.

"I am well aware of that fact!" Martha replied, acerbically. "Is my stepdaughter, a young woman, going to continue the unladylike practice of managing the estate?"

"If I do not do so, *Mrs.* Bennet, then it would not be long before you had no food on the table or servants to take care of your demands!" Elizabeth challenged. Martha had no answer and looked away, petulantly.

"In that case, we are done here," Philips stated as he gave the twice-widowed woman a withering look. "You, madam, *will* observe a year of deep mourning, and do not let me hear of any additional inept attempts at seducing men in the town to help you with your needs and disrespecting the memory of your late husband!" Seeing the outraged look the woman affected, he added, "You are reputed to be a strumpet, which is why none of your seductions have succeeded!"

There was a loud, wounded gasp by the woman, but neither Philips nor Elizabeth paid her mind. Philips stood, bowed, and left. "Do not look so smug, *Miss* Bennet! Your father and sister both died rather than be with you!" Martha stated spitefully and then flounced out of the drawing room. Until that moment, Elizabeth had not believed her stepmother so very evil and unfeeling. *'Papa, if only you had amended your will to remove the woman if you were no longer with us!'* Elizabeth remonstrated.

The reality was what it was, so she would have to make the best of a bad situation.

~~~~~~~/~~~~~~~

According to the notches on the tree, they had been on their island for a year. With the tools and other items recovered from the doomed ship, they had built two wooden cabins raised off the floor of the jungle. There was a large one where the Bennets slept, and a smaller one for the three surviving crew members.

The Bennet males and the crew members divided the daylight into four-hour shifts where one of them manned the top of the hill on the lookout for a ship. After the first major rain—and it rained often—they learnt to cover the dry wood with some of the canvas from the doomed ship's sails. Flints had been recovered from the wreckage, so lighting the kindling that would fire the wood would be as simple as striking two flints together.

No ship had been sighted, except for one, two months previously. The Earl was taking his turn at watch when he spied a ship. He was about to light the fire when he decided to use the spyglass that they kept on the summit to view the vessel. He thanked God he did, as it was flying the standard of a privateer. As much as it depressed him not to light the fire, he stepped back and placed the flints in their place.

When his watch was complete, he shared what he had seen with his wife, Cassie, Jane, Jamey, and the two crew members not on watch. There was universal agreement that he had made the correct decision. There was no reason to leap from the frying pan into the fire.

The jungle provided more than enough fruit and wild vegetables. There was no shortage of water, and the secluded pool seen on the first inspection of their island was ideal for bathing. The mornings were reserved for the males while the afternoons were for the females.

Phillip and Tommy had found a young parrot shortly after arriving on the island that had an injured wing, they surmised it was from the storm. He or she was simply named Parrot, and after a year, Parrot became very vocal. During their waking hours, the vibrantly coloured bird could be found perched on one of the boys' shoulders. James and Amy Bennet thought that, even if Parrot were able to fly, it would not leave the boys who always made sure there was an ample supply of fruit on hand for it to feast on.

'How I hope Papa and Lizzy are well and not suffering too much not knowing our fate,' Jane thought one day shortly after the one-year anniversary of their being stranded on the island, which the children had dubbed New England. It was a name accepted by all. 'Please do not give up hope for us to be discovered; I have to believe we will be found. If there are privateers in the area, then our Royal Navy cannot be far away either. Please God, send us a ship to rescue us.' Jane lifted her eyes to the heavens to repeat her daily prayer for deliverance.

She smiled as her thoughts turned to how close she and Jamey had become. Jane wondered if she would feel like this about her cousin had they not been stranded and thrown together as they were on New England. After all, if they were home, Jamey would have been busy on his estate, Glenmeade in Leicestershire, making their time in company together limited. After a lot of thought, she decided that the chances were a resounding yes, it may have taken longer, but she had a sneaking suspicion she and Jamey had been formed for one another.

As the group entered their second year stranded on New England, they all kept hope alive that one day they would be rescued and reunited with their families at home.

~~~~~~~/~~~~~~~

The first few months after her second husband's death, Martha Bennet had been on edge waiting for the heir to arrive and claim his inheritance. As her confidence grew with each passing day the heir did not arrive to claim his property, Martha once again asserted herself as mistress of the estate.

It would have been easy for Elizabeth to disabuse the woman of her pretentions, but she decided with the limited power available to her stepmother, it took some of her duties off her plate. As long as the interloper had no control over the purse strings and no power to engage or fire servants, Elizabeth would allow her to believe she was the mistress of the manor. She was perfectly happy that Miss Jones, their former governess, was now her companion. Miss Jones was a link to her sister and brother, just as her precious book was a link to her father.

About three months after her father's death, when Elizabeth changed from full to half mourning, Mr. Philips was visiting the estate to make sure all was running as it should be and Mrs. Bennet had not crossed any lines stipulated in her late father's will.

"No, Mr. Philips, she has refrained from anything that would contravene any of Papa's rules," Elizabeth reported as they sat in the study, now effectively *her* study. She unconsciously patted her pocket to reassure herself that the copy of *Utopia* her father had gifted her was on her person, as it always was when she was awake.

"What of her usurping your authority as mistress?" Mr. Philips enquired.

"I have decided to allow her to believe she is mistress..." Elizabeth explained her reasoning to Mr. Philips.

"Be wary of that one, Lizzy, you give her an inch and she will want a mile," Philips warned.

"Yet she will only receive an inch," Elizabeth stated with determination.

Just then the subject of their discussion barged into the study without so much as a knock on the door. "Why should you meet with my stepdaughter when I am mistress here?" Martha demanded.

Philips was about to disabuse the brash woman of her pretentions when Elizabeth gave a slight shake of her head. "Mr. Philips meets with me about estate business, as I manage it," Elizabeth stated evenly.

Martha sniffed with disdain and looked to Philips. "Where is this heir who was supposed to inherit? If he does not want his inheritance, then my Charles should be made the master here!" she stated primly.

"There are a few issues with that statement, Madam," Philips replied slowly, so his words would not be misunderstood. "Firstly, you know what will happen should your son set foot onto Bennet lands, do you not?" Martha barely nodded, her pinched expression proving her irritation with the rule still being in affect. "Next, only a Bennet *by blood* may inherit, so there are no circumstances under which any of your progeny might inherit the estate and Bennet holdings." He paused to allow his words to sink into the woman's thick skull. "The reason the heir has not been made known is a matter of law. Until seven years from the loss of the ship passes and all on board are declared dead," Philips reached over and squeezed Elizabeth's hand as she grimaced when he said the last, "then the heir will claim the inheritance."

"So, I have six years left to live here with my daughters?" The woman lit up with pleasure as she realised there were years ahead of her before she would have to consider finding a new home. She already had a plan for Caroline to compromise the heir when he finally showed himself, and then they would finally get full control of the estate and its funds.

"Technically correct, as long as you do not commit any of the infractions that will have you removed from the estate without warning," Philips reminded the woman, whose face became contorted with a pinched look of deeper irritation at the reminder that they were always monitored and still unwelcome.

"Well, I never!" the woman spat out as she sailed out of the study without closing the door.

~~~~~~~/~~~~~~~

"Please, brother," Lady Georgiana Darcy beseeched her

brother. "I would love to study under music master *Signore* da Funti! As you are aware, he does not travel more than forty miles from London.

"Without making a promise, Gigi, I will see if there is aught I can do. Before you suggest it, you know how much I eschew society in Town, so our townhouses are out. Your staying with our aunt and uncle at Matlock House would be a possibility," Lord William said soothingly.

He knew that, at twelve, his sister was far more advanced than many twice her age on the pianoforte, and to study with the music maestro was one of her dreams. It had been a few years since Miss Younge had been able to teach his sister anything on the instrument. The Duke had hired masters from Derby, but they were not *Signore* da Funti and could only take his sister so far.

"I would hate to be away from you for months at a time, Wills; we are all that is left of the Darcy family," Georgiana said sadly.

"As I said, I will look into options and attempt to find a solution. In the meanwhile, as much as I hate Town, we will spend a month there every now and again so you may start some lessons with the *Signore*. I know you want more time with him. As soon as I find an acceptable solution, I will let you know, Gigi," Lord William compromised.

He had been hunted enough by debutantes and their families, as had Marquess Pemberley. Now that he was a Duke at four and twenty, the huntresses would be relentless. After his sister skipped out of his study, the Duke picked his quill and penned a note to his man of business to seek properties for sale fifteen to forty miles from London.

CHAPTER 8

In the last two plus years since her father's death, life had not been pleasant for Elizabeth all the time. Mrs. Bennet had moved herself into Jane's chambers. She would not have chanced using the master suite, as she suspected it was one of the infractions that would have her removed from the estate.

Mrs. Bennet had ordered Elizabeth to switch bedchambers with her Caroline. Elizabeth could have stopped it, but with the woman in the adjoining bedchamber, Elizabeth accepted the edict with no argument. As Louisa, who was treated with almost as much disdain as Elizabeth by her mother and younger sister, would remain in her bedchamber, the move was easy for Elizabeth to make.

The friendship between the two stepsisters blossomed out of view of the vicious mother and daughter. They spent as much time with Charlotte and Maria Lucas as they were able so as not to have to be in the company of either the mother or younger daughter any more than was absolutely necessary. Part of the reason Louisa was looking so much slimmer was that she had begun to join Elizabeth on her morning rambles before the other two were awake.

"Here comes Cinder-Liza!" Caroline Bingley said meanly. "How ill you look with cinder soot on your face, always reading that useless book next to the fire," Caroline cackled.

About six months after the swap of bedchambers, Caroline had begun to call Elizabeth, who she used to call Eliza, Cinder-Liza due to the fact Elizabeth would often fall asleep close to her fireplace in her room reading her beloved *Utopia* by the light of the flames and would rub her face with her hands that sometimes had cinders or soot on them, occasionally leaving black smudges along her cheeks and forehead.

It riled both mother and younger daughter that Elizabeth never reacted to the moniker Caroline had gifted her. They were not allowed to physically harm her, so they intentionally attempted to insult her verbally, but more often than not they two came away frustrated that they had not elicited the desired reaction from Elizabeth in either tears, or anger.

"How ill you look, Stepdaughter. If you did not spend so much time with your head in your books, you would look somewhat more ladylike, although with those masculine features, one never knows," Martha evaluated her stepdaughter meanly.

"If I did not spend so much time with *my* books, *Mrs. Bennet*, then we would not eat. You forget I keep this estate running!" Elizabeth returned, hotly. It was an oft repeated conversation as it seemed the woman refused to acknowledge what Elizabeth did to run the estate.

"What is that to me if you will not give me any pin money?" the woman demanded.

"Whose fault is it you wasted over half of your principal on dresses for *that*," Elizabeth pointed at her skinny, ugly stepsister, Caroline, "and on useless baubles for yourself?"

"Do not dare talk about my beautiful daughter in that way, or I will whip you!" Martha screeched ineptly. There was no denying the fact that her youngest had become uglier as she grew older. She had no womanly assets of which to speak, and her face was long and angular with a thin line for lips. On the other hand, Louisa was looking much better. She no longer ate as much and was not nearly as portly as she had once been. She could not be called comely, but neither could she any longer be called homely, a word when applied to her younger daughter was a kindness.

"Please do so, Stepmother dearest, as that will remove you from Longbourn without waiting another four years! You know full well what will happen to you should you lift a hand to me!" Elizabeth challenged, watching with satisfaction as the woman visibly deflated at having her threats declared impotent.

To Martha Bennet, the worst crime her stepdaughter continually committed was her beauty. Her daughters in comparison were ugly—or at least, her favourite Caroline certainly was. Elizabeth had a penchant for taking long rambles out of doors and would get darker in the summer, but even then, she had the temerity to always look pretty, even healthier! Regardless of what Martha said to her stepdaughter, she was thankful the girl was a homebody and outside of some close friends, she did not socialise.

Martha could not understand why her stepdaughter bothered with those so decidedly below her; they *were* there to serve the estate after all. One day when Elizabeth was out of the house visiting tenants, she noticed the chest at the end of Elizabeth's bed was unlocked. She opened it and found the most beautiful dress she had ever seen within.

It was obviously part of the girl's trousseau, more than likely her late mother's wedding gown. It was a shimmering light blue silk with a gossamer overlay that shimmered in the light with tiny blue trinkets sown into it. As much as she would have wanted the dress to fit her youngest, she knew that no amount of making the dress over would make it fit her daughter, as Elizabeth was petite in stature.

Underneath it she found the shoes. They were glass with the same blue colour of the dress infused into the glass. When she held one up, the refracted light made a display that looked like stars on the opposite wall.

"Why are you touching that which is not yours?" Elizabeth demanded as she entered her chambers. "You do know stealing from me is a reason to be removed from this house, do you not?"

"I was not *stealing* anything!" Martha spat back as she dropped the glass slipper onto the bed. "I was just looking! Such a pity your masculine build will not fit into this dress," she stated with a sniff, as she flounced out of the room.

Although she dismissed almost anything the woman said, her words did bother Elizabeth on some level when her stepmother said such things to her, but she knew the woman was wrong about the dress as she tried it on every now and again to feel close to her beloved, late mother to keep her memory alive.

After catching her stepmother digging in her mother's chest, Elizabeth had Mr. Hill take it to the house of a tenant she trusted, as she did not trust Mrs. Bennet at all, and so would not take any chances with something as important to her as this. Except for the amber cross she wore, which her late father had told her belonged to her late Grandmother Beth, his mother and Elizabeth's namesake, the rest of her jewellery was locked in a safe in Mr. Philips's office. After the incident when Caroline tried, and failed, to take her bracelet one year, Elizabeth moved the few pieces of her jewellery still at Longbourn to the safety of a strong box.

On the fifth day of March, Elizabeth turned nineteen. There was no celebration at Longbourn, but Elizabeth and Louisa, leaving separately and at different times, joined the Lucas family at Lucas Lodge where her birthday was celebrated. Lady Lucas had a cake baked to help Elizabeth celebrate the day with them.

Charlotte was six and twenty and had as yet not found a man to value and marry her. Louisa was three and twenty, and if anyone had thought about approaching her, they were scared off by the antics, pretentions, and machinations of her mother and younger sister. Maria Lucas was the baby of the group of friends at fifteen.

It was at her birthday party that Sir William Lucas informed everyone that he had heard from his friend Paul Morris that he had sold Netherfield Park at last. The estate had been unoccupied for some years after Mr. Morris inherited a much larger estate in Dorset. He had initially leased it, and one or two tenants had rented it for short periods of time since he had moved, but in the end, it was too much trouble, so he placed the estate on the market.

Sir William had no information about the new owners of

Netherfield Park. Elizabeth hoped they were pleasant people, as the estate was but three miles from Longbourn.

~~~~~~~/~~~~~~~

Jane was betrothed to Jamey Bennet, Viscount Glenmeade. They had been betrothed some eighteen months previously. Their official betrothal, however, was pending her father's approval after they finally were rescued. Her Uncle James was allowed to act in her father's stead, but she wanted her father's blessing and consent. For propriety's sake, Jamey slept in a third wood cabin that had been constructed on the other side of the one where the remaining crew members slept.

There was no question they were in love—deeply in love—but they both refused to consider marrying before Jane's father could bestow his blessing, though at two and twenty Jane no longer needed his consent. Additionally, they wanted to marry in front of all their family with a Church of England clergyman officiating.

Given the situation in which they found themselves, they were able to meet away from their dwellings quite often sans chaperone. Both being honourable, they had not anticipated their vows, but had come close. As happy as Jane was with her betrothed and thankful for the fact that they were alive and healthy thus far into their stay, she missed both her father and Lizzy terribly.

Once they were rescued—and for her sanity she had to believe they would be one day—she never wanted to eat another fish in her lifetime. It was their main source of meat and there are only so many fish one person could willingly consume. Thankfully, the carpenter had fashioned some bows and arrows, so occasionally they would have some small animals like rabbit, birds, and other creatures for which they knew not the names. Whenever they ate the birds, however, Phillip and Tommy apologised to Parrot before they consumed their meal.

The men wore breeches that ended at their knees and nothing more below that, the supply of stockings being long exhausted. They all became adept at remaking old clothing into garments they could use—clothing that would have been thrown into the ragbag at home.

Phillip, already sixteen, and Tommy who was fifteen, were almost as tall as Jamey. Given how much manual labour there was, combined with the fact that if they wanted to go anywhere on *New England* it was with their own legs, they looked very fit and well built, as did the rest of the men. When Jane looked at her younger brother, she saw a younger version of her beloved father.

There had been some sad happenings, however, besides being stranded for about three years. About a year earlier, one of the massive storms such as the one which caused them to be stranded on *New England,* hit the island without warning. The sky had blackened, but that was not unusual when it was about to rain.

Rather than rain, it had been a massive storm. One of the three crewmembers, the seaman, had been returning from his watch on the hill when the storm struck. Part of a tree had cracked off the of trunk and had fallen on the unfortunate soul. They had buried poor, unfortunate Jack Sparrow a few hundred yards from the dwellings, and the carpenter had fashioned a cross as a marker for the man's grave.

Then there was the monotony. Each day was almost the same as the one that came before it, so it sometimes seemed they were living the same day over and over and over again. Thankfully, Jane had the company of her cousins—Cassie, who was one and twenty, and Allie now nineteen. Jane was always close to her cousins but was even more so now. Jane and her female cousins would assist Aunt Amy in making over old clothing for all of them to wear, sometimes combining two old items to make one.

Some months before, Phillip was on watch with Tommy keeping him company. The two had always been close, but now they were much more like brothers than cousins. Tommy spied a sail, and when Phillip looked in the spyglass, he saw the unmistakable skull and crossbones flying proudly. The boys were extremely frustrated.

They heard a boom in the distance and saw a Royal Navy ship; the pirate ship was obviously running from them. The boys debated whether or not to light the fire and decided against it. They were sure the navy ship would not break pursuit to investigate, and if the pirates evaded their fate and returned after seeing the smoke, it could spell disaster for them. More importantly, the ships were sailing away from them and making the chances of the smoke being seen almost naught.

The two friends watched until the ships were out of sight, after having noted the navy ship was gaining on her quarry. They were relieved by the Earl, who agreed they had made the prudent decision not to light the fire with a privateer in view and the direction the ships were sailing.

Jane had been working on clothing repairs with her aunt and cousins when the two lads returned from their watch and relayed what had happened. It was now four months later, and not another ship had been sighted.

'Papa, Lizzy, we are here, alive and well! Please do not give up hope,' Jane beseeched the expanse of sea before her.

~~~~~~~/~~~~~~~

Charles Bingley hated his life as a parson, especially as he had to bow and scrape to Lady Catherine de Bourgh. More than two years previously, he had quickly learnt that his patroness required a sycophant in the position, so that is how he presented himself, which earned him the living.

With his glebe lands and the money he received from his parishioners' tithing, he had an income of over five hundred pounds per annum. It was a Godsend, as he had managed to lose the rest of his legacy at the tables, and at the time owed more than five hundred pounds to men one pays back—if he values his life. It had taken two years to pay back a little more than six hundred pounds, but he was finally debt free. In this at least, Bingley had learnt his lesson; other than playing for small amounts, and never more than her had on his person, he kept away from the tables.

He dined at Rosings twice a week, and from what he could

tell he was the only guest that ever visited the ladies who resided at the grand house. When he either dined or joined her ladyship for tea, he very seldom had to talk, as Lady Catherine did not require answers, just someone to listen to her thoughts on many subjects—for most of which she had no idea of what she spoke.

The subject the lady pontificated on most often was the failure of her nephew, some duke or the other, to do his duty and marry her daughter. Personally, Bingley could understand why this duke, or any other man who did not need her fortune, would not be interested in marrying Miss de Bourgh.

Said sickly daughter, the heiress of Rosings Park, was present when she was well enough to attend. Bingley thought about how he could compromise the insipid woman to gain all he surveyed. Yes, the decoration was gaudy, the furniture overly ostentatious and uncomfortable, but he thought it was the way of upper society. If he were able, it would not stop him getting his hands on all of this. From what he knew, the estate's profits were more than five thousand pounds per annum.

An income of five thousand a year was more than he could imagine earning and it would allow him to do so much. He might even help his mother—a little. He had not come up with any workable plan as of yet.

It did not take long to realise that Miss de Bourgh's companion, who was more of a nurse, never left her mistress' side. The only time Miss de Bourgh was not securely ensconced in the manor house was when she drove her pony-drawn small phaeton. The problem was, she was never alone.

He tried to charm her, but his charms had no effect on her and only earned him a glare from the companion, Mrs. Jenkinson. His effort earned him a severe tongue-lashing from his patroness as Mrs. Jenkinson reported all to her, and he had endured a lecture about breeding and the distinction of rank.

When he was allowed to get a word in after half an hour, he had prevaricated, saying the companion misread his intention as he only wanted to be friendly, as he was to all. His patroness had accepted his explanation to a certain degree but warned him

—she would not tolerate another instance of familiarity with her daughter, no matter the reason.

After leaving his patroness in high dudgeon, Bingley had slithered back to the parsonage to consider other plans that would net him an easy fortune. He knew although the appointment was for life, Lady Catherine could make that life very unpleasant and could also apply to his bishop, allege wrongdoing, and have him removed or even defrocked. Given this, he knew he would have to be much more circumspect.

~~~~~~~/~~~~~~~

For the last few years, they had been spending more time in Town than the Duke had wanted to, in order for his sister to be able to study with *Signore* da Funti. As much as he hated it, the Duke would accept the occasional invitation, but only to dinners or a musical evening, never a ball, where he would be obliged to dance.

Thus, it was a great relief when his man of business informed him of Netherfield Park, an estate just over twenty miles from London in Hertfordshire near the market town of Meryton, that was for sale. Lord William had his man find all the information possible.

His man returned after viewing the estate with Mr. Philips, who was the agent and a local solicitor. He reported how it was in all ways perfect for what the Duke was seeking. The manor house had been rebuilt within the last thirty years as there had been a fire and was thus in excellent condition. Most importantly, there was a large music room where Lady Georgiana would be able to practice and study with *Signore* da Funti.

The Duke trusted his man, as he did his stewards at his various estates, but he had learnt from his father that, when making an important decision, he should have all the facts and that meant viewing the property for himself. The day after he met with his man, Lord William set off just after daybreak on his stallion, Zeus, accompanied by his two enormous personal bodyguards, Biggs and Johns.

Just over three hours later, the Duke and his bodyguards

rode up the drive leading to the manor house at Netherfield Park. So far, his man of business had been correct. Everything he saw told him this would be the ideal place for his needs. Mr. Philips met him on the front steps after their horses were led away by grooms.

"Your Grace," Philips bowed low, as was befitting courtesy to one of the Duke's rank.

"Thank you for meeting me on short notice, Mr. Philips," Lord William returned.

Philips introduced the Duke to the butler and housekeeper, Mr. and Mrs. Nichols. Mrs. Nichols led the tour of the house and, when they were done, the Duke of Derbyshire, Earl of Lambton saw nothing that would inhibit him from purchasing the estate. His final task was to ride the estate. After refreshments were served in a wonderfully comfortable drawing room, furnished as the Duke preferred with understated elegance, the steward was introduced, and he led the Duke and his men on a ride to view some of the fields and tenant farms.

They started with the home farm, where no fault was found, and then visited a selection of tenant farms. At the last one they visited; the lady of the house was out of sorts. When the Duke asked if there was anything he could do to assist, the lady pointed to the retreating form of a lady with long chestnut curls and said, "Miss Elizabeth visited me, sir, an' gave me some elixir from Mr. Jones."

When they reached their horses, the Duke looked at the steward questioningly. "Miss Elizabeth Bennet is from Longbourn, your Grace. If you look to where the young lady just crossed the stile in the fence, that is Longbourn. As there has been no master here for some time, Miss Elizabeth looks in on the tenants from time to time," the steward related.

"That is quite singular," Lord William said in wonder. He could not imagine any other gentlewoman walking all over her estate to take care of not only the tenants of her estate, but those of the neighbouring estate as well. Just then a memory stirred. "Mr. Hampstead, do you know if these Bennets are related to the

Earl of Holder, Lord James Bennet, by any chance?"

"Sorry your Grace, I have been here but two years and have never heard mention of any other Bennets. All I know is that Miss Elizabeth's father died in a riding accident some three years past. I heard there was another sister, but I do not know what happened to her, or what her name was," Hampstead related.

"Bennet is not an uncommon name, so I am sure it must be another family about which I am thinking. Thank you, Hampstead; I am extremely impressed by what I have seen." The men mounted their steeds and rode back toward the manor house along the border fence between the two estates. The young lady turned and looked at them for a moment, and the Duke could have sworn he saw a pair of the greenest eyes looking at him. Then she turned and continued her walk.

Lord William decided his eyes must have played tricks on him, as they were too far distant to be able to see her features. By the time they returned to the manor house, the Duke had pushed thoughts of the intriguing young lady to the recesses of his mind. During negotiations to purchase the estate, he never asked the one man who would have been able to give him the correct answers, Mr. Philips.

Before the Duke departed, a price was agreed upon, and papers signed. As soon as the funds were transferred to Mr. Morris's bank account, which would be within a fortnight, the sale would be final.

~~~~~~~/~~~~~~~

Richard Fitzwilliam and George Wickham had both earned field promotions. The two had fought side by side at the Battle of Roliça, the Battle of Vimeiro, and the Battle of Sahagún. The first two had been in August of '08, while the last in December of the same year.

Richard was promoted to Lieutenant-Colonel, replacing the man who was promoted to command the battalion when Colonel Atherton had been promoted to Brigadier General. After Wickham had saved the lives of a group of men, including Richard Fitzwilliam's, he was promoted to Major and assumed command of the company his friend formerly commanded.

So far, by the Grace of God, both had escaped any serious injury. There had been some cuts and bruises, but nothing that would keep a good officer down. The two men had grown as close as brothers and watched one another's back on the battle-fields. When they were able to sleep, they shared a tent.

In January of '09, they went into battle again; this time it was The Battle of Corunna, also known as Battle of Elviña. The newly promoted colonel was struck down on the first day, and Richard Fitzwilliam found himself a full colonel before the next day of fighting.

There was particularly bloody fighting at Corunna, and both Major Wickham and Colonel Fitzwilliam were injured. Wickham had a bullet wound in his right arm, the one that wielded his sabre, and Richard was shot in the muscle of his left thigh, making riding a horse impossible. Neither one felt easy about leaving his men behind when they were ordered back to England. Thankfully the generals decided that the dragoons deserved a break from being the tip of the spear, so the entire battalion was ordered back to England to rest and recuperate.

By mid-March, the friends went to the railing on the ship that they were on to see the welcome sight of white cliffs rising out of the sea ahead, signalling that they were close to England once more. After being gone for more than two years, it was a most welcome sight to the brothers-in-arms.

~~~~~~~/~~~~~~~

"Mama, I heard that the new owner of Netherfield is a *duke*! And he is unmarried," Caroline Bingley screeched in excitement.

"A duke! A single man with such a fortune must be in want of a wife; how good this will be for you, Caroline! My daughter, a duchess," Martha Bennet imagined.

Elizabeth and Louisa looked at one another and had to employ all the self-control they processed not to burst out into raucous laughter.

CHAPTER 9

February/March 1809

"We must go introduce ourselves, Mama," Caroline Bingley demanded. The four residents of Longbourn were seated at the dinner table.

"Oh yes, my girl, that is what we will do," Martha Bennet gushed.

"Far be it from me to stop you, Mrs. Bennet, but you may find yourself tossed out of Netherfield Park for that impertinence," Elizabeth smiled.

"Shut up, Cinder-Liza! What do you know?" Caroline spat out at her stepsister.

"Of the two of us, stepsister *dearest*, which one of us grew up a gentleman's daughter? Which of us do you think would know the protocol for visiting a new neighbour?" Elizabeth asked, amused at the pinched look mother and daughter sported.

"As you seem to know all the rules of it, Cinder-Liza, elucidate for us," Martha ordered.

"Use my correct name, and I will consider it," Elizabeth returned.

"Tell me, Eliza," Martha tried again. Not being able to strike the chit was most annoying as her stepdaughter had no fear of her at all.

"That is not my name, and well you know it," Elizabeth pushed.

"*Elizabeth*! Are you happy? Now tell me what I want to know," Martha almost whined, and Caroline, pouting that her stepsister had managed to humiliate them once again, turning the conversation to her advantage.

"Under normal circumstances, when the new arrival is of equal or lesser rank, the *man* of the house would call on his new neighbour. *However*, as a duke is far above any in this area, it is his prerogative to initiate contact and request introductions. If I were to have my guess, then his Grace may make an appearance at the upcoming assembly in Meryton so he can meet a good number of the residents in one controlled area," Elizabeth explained. "However, if you do not believe me, then please go right ahead and show up at the Duke's estate uninvited and introduce yourselves. I would wager you never get close to the front door."

For all her bluster, Martha was aware she knew not the ways of the gentry in general and the *Ton* specifically. She hated to do so, but she decided that, in this case she had to assume that her stepdaughter was correct. She and Caroline stood, without a word to Elizabeth or Louisa, and exited the dining parlour with their noses in the air.

"Is everything you told my mother true?" Louisa asked. She did not doubt her friend, she simply did not know.

"It is, Lulu, every word," Elizabeth assured her friend.

"I know how much you dislike my mother and Caroline, especially for that derisive moniker she gifted you—Cinder-Liza indeed! So why did you stop her from being thrown out of Netherfield Park?" Louisa was confused; she thought her mother and sister's humiliation would have amused her friend and all of those in the neighbourhood.

"Firstly, no matter how much I dislike them, I would not want to see them be humiliated in such a fashion, and second, as your mother's last name is Bennet and connected to Long-bourn, I have a selfish reason for not wanting my family name and estate to be the subject of neighbourhood gossip. Heaven forbid if word reaches so called *polite* society in London!" Elizabeth explained.

"What do you mean *your* estate?" Louisa asked.

"The one I live on silly, that my family has had for generations," Elizabeth hedged.

"Do you really believe the Duke and his party will attend the assembly?" Louisa wondered.

"I do think there is a good chance, but I may be wrong," Elizabeth owned.

"Mama had purchased new gowns for Caroline out of her widow's portion, but she told me she has no money to spare for me," Louisa lamented.

"Meet me at the dressmakers at eleven Louisa, and we will make sure you have something to wear; we have a few days yet," Elizabeth assured her friend.

"Elizabeth, I did not tell you so that you would acquire a dress for me," Louisa protested.

"I know you did not, Lulu, which is the exact reason why I am doing it! I will not be gainsaid, so you had better grin and bear it!" Elizabeth smiled, as she saw acceptance on her friend's face.

"And when Mama asks me where a new dress came from?" Louisa asked with concern.

"Your mother only worries what her other daughter wears, and that sister of yours is far too self-centred to notice what you are wearing, so I believe all will be well," Elizabeth soothed.

The sad thing was, what Elizabeth said, was true.

~~~~~~~~/~~~~~~~~

Tommy was on watch at the top of the hill when he spied a sail. "Another pirate, I am sure," Tommy said in exasperation to Parrot, who was eating a banana. Tommy opened the spyglass and pointed it at the vessel. It took him some seconds to see the ensign of the Royal Navy flapping in the wind from the quarter-deck of an English man-of-war.

Tommy pulled the canvass off the enormous pile of wood, splashed some water onto the top pieces as Uncle James had instructed to make more smoke, and struck the flints to the kindling. He was so excited the first two tries failed to produce a spark, but the third one did.

As gently as he could, he blew on the small embers that

settled into the dried grasses and twigs. Within thirty seconds, he had flame, and he gently pushed the burning kindling to the base of the tower of wood that they had collected, with the kindling there quickly catching fire.

Within five minutes, the flames took hold and a thick plume of black and white smoke rose towards the clear blue sky. On the beach, the family and the two remaining crew members saw the smoke, and they all dared to hope as they had not allowed themselves for some years.

~~~~~~~/~~~~~~~

HMS *Charger* was a six and thirty gun frigate of the Royal Navy. She was charged with a patrol area among some of the unknown and believed to be uninhabited islands of the Bahamas chain. She had been sent to this particular location as a pirate ship had been found, chased, and ultimately sunk in the area.

Captain Nevin Sandiford had commanded HMS *Charger* for over five years and he, his crew, and his vessel had been stationed in Nassau for just over a year. They had been on this patrol for over three weeks and had a few days left on the patrol before returning to port. They had stopped at a few uninhabited islands to take on fresh water and the crew had foraged for fruits and wild vegetables. Fishing was a daily occurrence. It seemed like a normal day of seeing no quarry when the man in the crow's nest yelled, "Smoke ahoy!"

The Captain pointed his spyglass, as did his executive officer, a Lieutenant-Commander, and a sub-Lieutenant who was on watch. Sandiford looked at the hill from which the smoke was emanating and saw a boy or young man waving a Union Jack! He dropped his sight line to the beach, and there he saw a group of people, men, and women all waving furiously.

"Make for that island with all speed, Mr. Chandler," the Captain ordered his executive officer. "I see a reef line, steer southwest. There is a break in it where we will anchor and launch the long boats." The Captain turned to the junior officer, "Have a contingent of Marines at the ready, Mr. Barlow," he commanded.

~~~~~~~/~~~~~~~

As soon as Tommy saw the ship change course towards them, he took off down the hill as fast as he safely could. By the time he reached the beach, the warship could be seen plainly with the naked eye, and he joined the group rejoicing on the beach. After more than three years, their odyssey was about to come to an end.

Some were kneeling and offering thanks to God, others were hugging each other, and not a few of their number, men included, were crying tears of joy. His sister and her betrothed were hugging one another tightly, unashamedly crying tears full of so many emotions one could not fathom separating them one from the other. Soon, they would be able to marry. Poor Parrot was squawking, not at all sure what all the noise and excitement was about.

"What is she?" Phillip asked the carpenter, who was standing next to him on the beach.

"She be a frigate, six and thirty guns, I believe," the ecstatic man responded.

It took about two hours until the ship's sails were lowered, and she anchored outside of the reef line near the gap. The group on the beach watched in wonder as four longboats were lowered, and then men, some sailors and some in the uniform of the Royal Marines, scrambled down the netting that had been lowered down the side of the hull and smartly took up positions in the longboats.

Eight oars were raised in each boat, four on each side, and then as one they were lowered into the water, and again as one as the men started rowing. It took about twenty minutes for the four boats to reach land. An officer approached those on the beach.

"Lieutenant-Commander Chandler at your service, executive officer of *HMS Charger*. Who is in charge here?" he asked. The marines standing behind him had their weapons shouldered but were ready for anything.

"I am Lord James Bennet; Earl of Holder, and I am in charge of this group of survivors of *The West Indies Trader*. We have been here since August 1805. We have the ship's log that we were able to save." The Earl did not miss the looks of shock and surprise on the faces of the officer and the men.

"Your Lordship, everyone believed *The West Indies Trader* was lost with all hands," Mr. Chandler shared.

"I think I still remember some of the protocols from England," the Earl jested. "My wife Lady Amelia Bennet, Countess of Holder, my oldest son James Bennet Junior, Viscount Glenmeade, my daughters Ladies Casandra and Alicia and my youngest son, the Honourable Phillip Bennet." Each made a curtsy or bow when their name was mentioned. "This young lady is Miss Jane Bennet of Longbourn in Hertfordshire, and her brother Thomas Bennet Junior; they are my cousins. Lastly, Smith and Jones, the last two remaining crewmembers of the ship."

"I will wager after three years stranded here you wish to be away?" the Lieutenant-Commander noted dryly. "Is there anything you wish to bring with you?"

"Only Parrot," Tommy spoke up.

"A parrot?" the officer asked.

"Yes, he, we think it is a male bird, but his name is Parrot," the Countess explained.

"To the boats," the Lieutenant-Commander ordered.

Soon, all were seated in the boats, and some of the seamen pushed them into the lagoon and then jumped on board themselves. The men rowed efficiently, and soon they were alongside the hull of the frigate. Bosun's chairs were lowered for the ladies, and once they were all safely standing on the deck above, the men climbed up the netting.

At the Earl's request, the executive officer introduced his Captain and fellow officers. When the Captain heard who they had just rescued, he was speechless. "My Lord, I think you are familiar with my father. I grew up on Falconwood and being a third son I chose the navy," Captain Sandiford stated.

"Yes, of course, your father is Mr. Cedric Sandiford. Falconwood is but twenty miles south of Holder Heights!" the Earl confirmed.

"We have a few more days of patrol left and then we will return to Nassau. Unless it is a dire emergency, I do not have the authority to leave my patrol, my Lord," the Captain explained.

"You will hear no argument from any of us, Captain, after more than three years on *New England*, we are overjoyed to be leaving our island home behind us." Seeing the Captain's quizzical look, the Earl explained they had dubbed the island with a name that tied them to the home country for which they longed.

"Captain," Jamey called the commander's attention to himself. "Do you carry a clergyman on board?" he asked hopefully as Jane blushed becomingly.

"We do happen to have one with us on this patrol; may I ask why?" The Captain inquired, though he had a fairly good idea the reason the Viscount was asking.

The couple explained how they had been betrothed for over eighteen months, and as much as Miss Bennet wanted her father and sister present, they did not want to wait any longer. They decided that they would have a celebration after their return home, and if her father desired, Jane stated they would renew their vows, to which Jamey had no objections.

The parson was called to meet the 'castaways.' He confirmed that, as the bride was of age, he would issue a common license. So, the wedding was set for the morrow, the seven and twentieth day of February 1809. Parrot loudly told everyone he wanted some fruit as if he also wanted to celebrate the upcoming nuptials, which led to much laughter.

~~~~~~~/~~~~~~~

"I need money for Caroline's new dress; she must impress the Duke at the upcoming assembly!" Martha demanded, as she stood across the desk from her stepdaughter in the master's study.

"Are you telling me, madam, you have frittered away your widow's portion, have no more of your monthly allowance, and due to your inability to manage your money you now expect the estate to pay for your profligate ways?" Elizabeth asked, amazed at the hubris of the woman.

"Listen to me, Cinder-Liza, I am the mistress of this estate, and you will provide me the funds I need!" Trying to intimidate Elizabeth, the woman leaned over the desk with her arm raised as if she were about to strike her.

"Go ahead, stepmother *dear*!" Elizabeth challenged. "Strike me, and you and your daughter will be gone before the sun sets in the west this very day!"

Martha shrank back. How she hated the chit, but there was no option. If she did something to be removed from Longbourn now, they would be destitute. She again missed that her stepdaughter had used the singular connotation rather than the plural when she referred to her daughters.

"Did you again forget what Mr. Philips told you the day he read my father's will? All the funds are kept in trust for the heir and *Mr. Philips* disburses funds, not I! Even if I wanted to, and I do not, he would not give you a penny to reward you for wasting your money on nothing of value," Elizabeth stated firmly. She had no doubt the woman hated her, but the woman's fear of being cast out with nothing was stronger even than the hatred.

The woman straightened up and flounced out of the study, leaving the door open as was her wont. After Elizabeth closed the door, she sat back in her father's comfortable armchair. Next to *Utopia* it was the thing that made her feel closest to her late father; she could almost feel his presence in the chair.

'*Oh Papa, why did you ride when you were so deep in your cups? Even though you locked yourself in this study, you were still here and now you are gone!*' Elizabeth dashed away the tears that had collected in the corners of her eyes as her memory drifted back to the fateful day. '*I have hoped for so long that Jane and Tommy will return, but after three years, is it not time for me to accept it is a dream that will never be? Jane and Tommy, how I ache for you; I will try and keep hope alive, but it becomes harder with each passing month! I am sorry Janey, I only write to you once a month, I pray you will forgive me.*'

~~~~~~~/~~~~~~~

"Will you attend the assembly, your Grace?" Mr. Harold

Hurst, the Duke's private secretary asked. Hurst had joined the current duke some two years ago. He was the fourth son of a gentleman who owned a small estate, Winsglade, in Yorkshire.

"I think I must. Miss Younge will remain here with Lady Georgiana as she is not out yet. I know sometimes in the country girls are out locally earlier than in Town but given my sister's shyness and the amount of fawning I will have to endure, it is not a situation to which I would expose her," the Duke replied.

"At least it seems the residents are aware of protocol, as none have called on you at Netherfield, your Grace," Hurst informed his employer.

"So it seems, Hurst, so it seems. Where is Lady Georgiana currently?" the Duke inquired.

"Your sister is in a lesson with *Signore* da Funti. As you requested, Miss Younge and a maid attend her at all times," Hurst reported.

"Did we receive the report on the populace of the neighbourhood that I commissioned?" the Duke wanted to know.

"We did, your Grace. There is nothing exceptional, rather like the population of Lambton. That is, except for the Bennets," Hurst related.

"What about the Bennets? Did you find a connection between them and the Holder Bennets, who were lost at sea?" Lord William asked with interest. In the recesses of his memory, he remembered the impertinent slip of a girl with green eyes, the likes of which he had never seen before or since.

"It is easiest to answer the second part of your question first, your Grace. If there is a connection between these Bennets and the unfortunate family from Staffordshire, for some reason it has been well hidden, as the investigator found no trace of such a connection." Hurst then proceeded to relate that there were three Bennet children, only one remained at home, and there was no clue as to the location of the other two.

He related the story of the compromise, the marriage in name only, how Mr. Bennet refused to allow his stepchildren to use his name, and how the town's folk disdained the new Mrs.

Bennet and her three children, named Bingley.

"Bingley you say? I remember in my final year at Eton, there was a Charles Bingley who attempted to ingratiate himself with those of high birth. As far as I know he never succeeded and there was talk about him lacking character. I wonder if it is the same family?" the Duke mused.

"I believe so, your Grace, for the former Mrs. Bingley's children are Charles, Louisa, and Caroline. The son is not allowed to return to Longbourn. From what I am reading here, the son was not seen again after the compromise and before the Bingleys arrived at the estate. The older Bennet girl left at the same time the Bingley boy was banned from ever setting foot on Bennet lands again. In my estimation, the only ones you need to be wary of are Mrs. Bennet and her youngest, Caroline Bingley." Hurst placed the report on the Duke's desk as he concluded his report.

"I will have Biggs and Johns near at all times. Have we stationed some men around Meryton to keep their eyes and ears open?"

"Per your wishes, your Grace." Hurst was dismissed soon after.

Lord William sat in his study cogitating. If the Bennets were related to his uncle's and aunt's daughter-in-law and Lady Marie's family, why would they hide the connection? The obvious answer must be that there was no connection.

~~~~~~~/~~~~~~~

"Well, that is not very friendly of William not to be home to receive us!" the hobbling Colonel jested as he leaned on his crutch in the entrance hall at Darcy House in London.

"To be fair, Richard, we did not inform William of our coming. You did want to surprise your cousins after all!" Wickham grinned at his brother-in-arms.

"You used to allow me to have more fun, George," Richard gave a chuckle. "How was I to know that my parents would depart London before the end of the season to assist Marie and Andrew with the running of the Holder estates?" Richard got an idea. "Killion, where is my cousin?"

This was information the butler would give only to a select few, the Colonel being one of them, the Major another. "His Grace and Lady Georgiana are at his estate, Netherfield Park, near the town of Meryton in Hertfordshire," Killion shared.

"What does my cousin need with another estate? Never you mind! What say you, George? I feel like a travelling to this Meryton; it is early, and we will arrive this afternoon," Richard said, with a mischievous glint in his eye. "We will still be able to shock my staid cousin."

A half hour later, the two officers and their batmen were in a Darcy coach headed for the estate in Hertfordshire, where they arrived in just over four hours. When Mr. Nichols answered the door, he saw two officers he did not know and looked to Biggs, who nodded his head. The officers asked not to be announced and were pointed to the music room where they could hear sweet sounds from the pianoforte.

Lord William looked up when the door opened, as he wondered if he was needed. Through the door, supporting himself on a crutch, hobbled his cousin, and behind him, his friend George, his arm in a sling. Both were grinning from ear to ear.

Before he could say a word, the playing stopped. "*RICHARD!* Mr. Wickham!" Lady Georgiana shouted with glee. In an unladylike but understandable display, Lady Georgiana Darcy launched herself at her cousin but pulled up short when she noticed his crutch.

"Do not worry, Gigi; I am on the mend, as is my friend George here. In a few more months we should be back to full strength." By the time Richard had finished speaking his cousin was before him and both brother and sister hugged Richard. Lady Georgiana curtsied to Wickham, and he, too, received a bear hug from Darcy, who was careful not to go near his injured shoulder.

Mrs. Nichols was summoned and asked to prepare rooms in the family wing and have hot baths readied for both men.

CHAPTER 10

Charles Bingley was more scared than he had ever been before. One of Lady Catherine's goons had caught him attempting to watch some young ladies bathe through the window of their cottage. The man had frog-marched the errant clergyman to his mistress, where he now stood, sweating, before her *throne* in the drawing room.

"I knew you were not to be trusted when you looked at my Anne the way you did! Spying on young maidens! What kind of libertine are you, Mr. Bingley?" the great lady spat out. "Do not try to answer; there is no excuse for the way that Dryden discovered you!"

"W-what w-will you d-do to me, y-your Ladyship?" Bingley managed to get out. If only he could control his urges, he told himself, for it was the same overwhelming impulse as when he tried to drag the delectable Jane Bennet away. He had to believe a base need controlled him rather than the other way around. It was easier not to look at his behaviour as a cause of his problems.

"As I see it, there are two choices here. One is that I contact the Bishop and you will be defrocked and never be allowed to be even a curate, never mind a vicar." Lady Catherine paused allowing her words to sink into the disgusting pastor's consciousness.

"I will do anything you require, your Ladyship, just please do not summon the Bishop. Bingley was well aware he was already treading on thin ice with the Bishop, so there would be no returning from this.

"Your mother just wrote to tell you that the Duke of Derbyshire has recently taken up residence in an estate neighbouring the one where she is mistress, did she not?" Lady Catherine asked, seemingly changing the subject.

"She did, in fact, relate that news. I do not understand…" Bingley started to say when the lady held up her hand.

"You will soon enough. She told you his sister, Lady Georgiana, is also reputed to be with him, did she not?" Bingley nodded. "I have a task for you. Succeed, and I will give you a character so you may seek a new parish along with ten thousand pounds. Fail me and your Bishop will hear all!" Lady Catherine stated.

"What is it you would have me do?" Bingley asked with trepidation. Especially where her nephew was concerned, he knew the lady bordered on the insane.

"You will visit your family on the estate that neighbours my nephew's," she stated flatly. Bingley's stomach roiled as he had never shared how he was not allowed to set foot on the estate. "You will find a way to compromise my niece! Despoil her, or Dryden here," she pointed a bony finger at the man, "will end your miserable life for me! I want enough done that I will be able to force my nephew to finally do his duty to his betrothed, my daughter! You have your choice. What is your decision?"

Bingley was not sure what he would do once he reached the Meryton area, but he had to make her think he would do as she desired to buy himself some time. "I will do as you ask. You realise it may take me a little while to get close to her, do you not?"

"Do you take me for a fool?" Lady Catherine slammed her cane down. "I am not a simpleton; I know you will not be able to walk through the doors of their Netherton estate, or whatever its name is, and simply have access to her! I expect updates at least once a week. If not, Dryden will come and visit you! Do I make myself clear?"

"It is Netherfield, your Ladyship." Bingley then convinced the lady that he would need funds for travel and to purchase some clothing that would make him look the part of a man who would be noticed by the sister of a duke. Lady Catherine gave him a hundred fifty pounds and told him it would be deducted from his final payment. Charles Bingley was on a carriage from Bromley headed towards Meryton by stage early the next day.

~~~~~~~/~~~~~~~

"It will be the finest gown I have ever owned!" Louisa gushed as Elizabeth and Charlotte watched her while she was being fitted for the gown Elizabeth was gifting her at the seamstress in Meryton.

"You look very well in it, Lulu," Charlotte assured her friend.

"Charlotte has the right of it, Lulu; it is perfect for you. Louisa blushed with pleasure not being used to compliments about the way she looked. She quickly changed, and the three friends departed.

As they walked down Meryton's main street, Elizabeth spied her stepmother and Caroline exiting the jewellery store, which was also Meryton's pawnbroker. "Charlotte, I will meet you and Lulu at the tearoom; there is some Longbourn business I must take care of." She crossed the road to Smithers Emporium and rang the bell for Mr. Smithers, who looked decidedly guilty when he saw her.

"What did that woman sell you Mr. Smithers?" Elizabeth asked sharply, her arms akimbo.

"J-just some old pieces of hers, Miss Bennet," the man hedged.

"Mr. Smithers, you may tell me now, or I will return before you know it with Mr. Philips, the magistrate, and the constable! Now, I ask again, what did she sell you?" Elizabeth demanded.

The man crumpled, knowing if he were convicted of buying and selling stolen goods, he would lose his business and be transported. "Some of your father's first editions," the man owned.

"Is this the first time she has sold Longbourn's property to you?" Elizabeth asked.

"Just one other time. She sold me a pair of silver candlesticks. They are in the back." the defeated man acknowledged.

"If you do not want the law involved, you will have all of my property sent to the Halverson's farm. I will not reimburse you one penny, as you were warned along with every other merchant in Meryton. She is not to be trusted. At the very least, you should have told her you needed time to appraise the goods and called me or Mr. Philips. Which you will do *if* she attempts to sell you anything else, will you not?" Elizabeth stated, leaving no room for argument. The man nodded, summoned his man and had him load whatever the woman sold him with instructions to deliver the items to the Halverson's farm.

Elizabeth stopped at the tearoom and told her friends she needed to return home urgently and was gone before they could protest.

After the two friends completed their tea and pastries, they paid and left the tearoom. Louisa was turned, looking at Charlotte as she whispered her concern for Elizabeth, so she did not see the gentleman barrelling towards her as he too was distracted. The two collided, and Louisa would have fallen had the man not quickly reached out and caught her arms, saving her from harm.

"I am so sorry, sir," the embarrassed young lady stated with her head down.

"No madam, it was all my fault; I was preoccupied and did not see you," Mr. Hurst averred.

"Rather than argue who was more at fault, may we know who almost bowled my friend over, sir?" Charlotte asked, offering an amused, teasing tone when she saw how uncomfortable both were. She wondered when one of them would wake up to the fact the gentleman was still holding onto Louisa's arms. Charlotte said nothing, as she did not want to add to their embarrassment, but both of them seemed to find the contact comfortable enough to maintain it—that always boded well.

Just then both separated a step or two, blushing furiously. "Harold Hurst at your service, ladies. Private secretary to the Duke of Derbyshire, Earl of Lambton."

"Miss Charlotte Lucas, and the lady you accosted is Miss Louisa Bingley," Miss Lucas made the introductions from their side.

Hurst almost recoiled when he heard the chit's name, but

he schooled his features. As he remembered the report, it had stated that the younger Bingley, Caroline, was the objectionable one. He had the good fortune to bump into the one who was reported to be nothing like her mother or sister. She was standing demurely, waiting for his reaction and had not in any way tried to call compromise.

"Well met, Miss Lucas, Miss Bingley. I must be away, but may I be so bold as to solicit a dance from each of you at the upcoming assembly?" Hurst bowed to the friends. Both nodded, so he requested the second from Miss Lucas and the third from Miss Bingley.

~~~~~~~/~~~~~~~

The afternoon *The Charger* left *New England* behind, the Captain and his Executive Officer introduced the arriving Bennets to their wives. For the first night, the Countess and Jane joined Mrs. Sandiford in the captain's cabin while Ladies Cassandra and Alicia were billeted with Mrs. Chandler in the second-in-command's cabin. The two senior officers shared the Captain's day cabin with the Earl, while the Viscount, Phillip, and Tommy joined the officers in the wardroom. Parrot was not allowed in the wardroom but seemed mollified when he was given a perch near the crew's messdeck.

The night before the wedding, her Aunt Amy had given Jane *the talk*. It was, at the best of times, not the easiest talk to give, and when the Countess had talked to Marie it was easier than in this case, when the bride was marrying Jamey—notwithstanding the intimacy of their lives on the island. Both had made it through the awkwardness with a minimum of embarrassment.

Before she went to bed that night, Jane had found Uncle James. "I feel guilty that I am being selfish for not waiting until Papa walks me down the aisle," Jane admitted to her uncle.

"There are things you need to know, Jane. Your father's love for you is such that when he sees you again, all he will care about is that you and Tommy are alive and well. He would think it most selfish of himself to want you and Jamey to wait even a single day more than necessary. The second part is that, although you do not need it, being of age, you do have your father's consent and blessing, through me. Do you not think we both did not see you and Jamey were headed in this direction? Before we left for Jamaica, your father gave me full authority to consent to and bless your marriage in his stead if it were to happen before we returned." The Earl lifted his soon-to-be daughter's chin to see Jane was gently crying tears of relief.

Knowing she had her father's consent and blessing, even if not in person, lifted a great weight from her shoulders. The night before her wedding, Jane Bennet had the most restful sleep she had had in a long, long time.

The morning of the seven and twentieth of February dawned with a brilliant sunrise. Jane was assisted in dressing by her two cousins and soon-to-be sisters. The truth was over the last three years of their ordeal they had become as close as any sisters could ever be, and today would be the official ceremony that would match what they already claimed in their hearts.

At two bells—nine in the morning to the Bennets—all crew who were not integral to the sailing of the ship stood in two smart lines on either side of the deck in their best uniforms. The Chaplain stood in front of the mainmast with Jamey to his side, just in front of the capstan, with Phillip as best man standing to his brother's right. The Earl, Countess, their two younger daughter, two officers' wives, and the officers sat on chairs near the mast. Cassie walked toward her brother as she was standing up with Jane. Once she reached her place, the clergyman gave a signal, and those seated stood as the bosun piped the welcome for a senior officer on his whistle.

All Jane saw was Jamey standing waiting for her. They had waited for so long, and it was finally the day she had dreamed of from the time she fell in love with Jamey. Other than Jamey, she noted nothing of the beautiful view as the ship navigated between some of the hundreds of islands in the chain.

Jamey knew his betrothed was beautiful, but she never looked more so than she did as she walked towards him on

Tommy's arm. She wore a new gown, one that was on loan from the Captain's wife, and although it was a simple gown, it was perfect. Jane did not need adornments for her angelic beauty to shine through.

Tommy kissed his sister's cheek. Jane looked up at Tommy, who was no longer shorter than her, and had not been for almost a year. Tommy placed Jane's hand onto Jamey's arm and the couple took two steps to stand in front of the Chaplain as Tommy joined the rest of his family. The clergyman nodded his head and those with chairs were seated.

The clergyman opened the Book of Common Prayer and commenced the service. Before they knew it, they had said their vows and were pronounced man and wife. When Jane signed the register, she had to smile. Most brides signed their maiden name for the final time at this point in the proceedings, but it was not the case for Jane Bennet. The new Viscountess Glenmeade had married her cousin, James Bennet Junior.

The crew cheered and whooped loudly and were all released to receive a double ration of grog. The two crewmen, who had spent the years on *New England* with the Bennets, wished the newlyweds joy. They had been assimilated into the frigate's crew until they reached Nassau, but after three years together, they were honorary members of the family, and would always be. The Earl had spoken privately to his wife and pledged to help them and their families as much as he could, including the family of Jack Sparrow, the unfortunate soul in eternal slumber on *New England*.

For their wedding night, the newlyweds would have the Captain's cabin; the other ladies would make alternate plans for one night. Thankfully, in three days or less, *The Charger* would sail into Nassau.

~~~~~~~/~~~~~~~

As soon as Elizabeth arrived at Longbourn, she had the Hills and the other servants check the contents of the house against the inventory. Thankfully, the items Mr. Smithers claimed to have been sold to him were the only items missing.

Elizabeth had her servants pack anything of value into crates.

When Mrs. Bennet and Caroline flounced into the house looking well pleased with themselves, their looks changed to ones of horror when they noted all the valuables gone from their places.

"Cinder-Liza! What are you doing with *our* possessions?" Caroline screeched.

"Contrary to what your mother may have told you, nothing in this house, other than what you brought with you or purchased with your *own* money, is yours! Why would you care what I do with the heir of Longbourn's possessions? It is not like you would have stolen anything to sell in Meryton, would you?" Elizabeth asked innocently.

Mother and daughter blanched, and their pallor became decidedly whiter. It was then Louisa returned and saw the looks on her mother and sister's faces. "What has happened?" She asked.

"Never mind; go eat something, Louisa," Martha Bennet spat out spitefully as she turned on her heel and she and her harridan daughter beat a hasty retreat. Elizabeth then told Louisa privately what had precipitated her action.

"Why did you not report them to Mr. Philips?" Louisa asked.

"Everything is safe. These crates will join the recovered items and be out of their reach until it is time to restore them to their rightful owner," Elizabeth stated, cryptically.

Louisa knew there was something her friend was not telling her, but she did not push her.

That night after talking to her friend for an hour or two, where Elizabeth noted but did not point out the name Hurst was mentioned by Louisa three of four times, Elizabeth decided she would have to pay attention and help her friend find happiness, to free her of her mother and sister. Elizabeth had always known she would be free of them eventually, but Louisa deserved the same relief, and if it included the personal secretary to the Duke, it was a twist of fate she would gladly aid.

~~~~~~~/~~~~~~~

The next morning the Duke, as was his wont, had Zeus saddled and was off across the fields as the sun rose above the horizon, with only Biggs as an escort. At some point he crossed the boundary between his estate and Longbourn without noticing it. He slowed down as he approached an apple orchard, as he seemed to remember one on the estate, mayhap not as large as the one he rode into.

Lord William slid off his mount, picked an apple, and offered it to Zeus. He then repeated the action for himself and was about to take a second bite when an apple flew and struck him on the shoulder.

"Who do you think you are stealing my apples?" The angry launcher of the missile hissed. Elizabeth had an apple in each hand, just in case she needed it. It was then the Duke saw the green eyes flashing at him in anger.

"Do ya know w'o ya thowed your apple at?" Biggs asked as he advanced to take hold of the petite young lady. "Ya cannot 'urt 'is Grace like that!" The big man stopped as his master shook his head.

"I care not a whit if he is the King himself. That does not give him the right to trespass on my land and eat my apples without permission!" Elizabeth looked at the Duke, daring him to say anything. "Please leave my estate and respect the boundary unless you have permission."

Before the stunned Duke could retort, the woman turned, her loose chestnut curls flying behind her, and took off walking at a furious pace towards what Lord William guessed was the manor house. As her form retreated he heard: "Insufferable man!"

She obviously knew who he was and did not care a whit. Those eyes. He had only ever witnessed eyes that green and impertinent, such as she had just displayed, by one four-year-old girl. He could not remember the girl's first name, but those eyes were the same!

It took Biggs to remind the master they needed to return to

their own land to break the Duke out of his stupor. She had not fawned, had not simpered. She had treated him just like what he was—a trespasser. Any other lady, knowing who he was, would have told him to take anything he desired, including themselves, but not this lady. She must be the last remaining Bennet daughter at home, the one the report called Elizabeth.

~~~~~~~/~~~~~~~

As Elizabeth trudged back towards the manor house, much of her anger bled from her body. *'Did I just throw an apple at a duke? And then chastised him? Good heavens, he must think me an uncouth harridan! You have to learn to control your temper, Lizzy!'* she berated herself and then sadness overwhelmed her, as she knew those were words Jane had spoken to her on more than one occasion.

Elizabeth sat down on a log and considered all she had lost in her less than twenty years. First her beloved mother, then Tommy and Jane had disappeared along with her uncle, aunt, and her cousins except for Marie. Shortly after those tragedies, she lost her father. She was the only Bennet left, for Marie was a Fitzwilliam now.

Andrew and Marie wrote to Elizabeth in care of Mr. Philips. When they asked how she was, she would always say all was well. Her cousins had more than enough to worry about without her adding to their burdens. They had invited her to visit them from time to time, but she had always demurred. She just did not feel she could afford to be away from her beloved Longbourn; it was all she had left of her family.

What she did not know was the man she had just berated was, in fact, her cousin by marriage.

~~~~~~~/~~~~~~~

"You were attacked by a slip of a woman?" Richard guffawed as his cousin related the happenings of the morning.

"She did not fire grape shot at William, Richard, she fired apple shot!" Wickham ribbed his friend.

"Have your fun, you two. I would like to see you stand up against the force of nature I met this morning. Though I actually never met her; she was too busy berating me to worry about mentioning her name." Lord William took another sip of his coffee.

"Richard, do you remember, I think it was in '94, I was with you at Holder Heights, and we met this little impertinent miss, about four, green eyes, chestnut curls, little slip of a thing and as inquisitive as all heck?" Lord William asked.

"I remember her, Miss Elizabeth Bennet!" Richard stated his eyes wide with surprise at the intimation.

"Richard, are you sure that is her name? If it is, I believe the one I met today was the nineteen- or twenty-year-old version of that mite," Lord William whistled. His suspicion it was the same girl had turned ever more into certainty the longer he pondered it; now Richard had confirmed it. "If that is true, then she lost a big part of her family in '05."

"She lost a lot more than cousins, William. Her older sister and younger brother were with the Holders when they were lost. A year later, her father fell off his galloping horse and died instantly. She is our cousin, William! Her cousin Marie, the only surviving Holder Bennet, is Andrew's wife!" Richard explained. His mother had kept up a steady correspondence with him while he was in the peninsula. The letters he received were filled with news, and he had received the one where his mother had enumerated the tragedies of the Bennet families.

"She is our cousin, William, and she is all alone in the world?" Lady Georgiana asked, softly.

"So it seems, Gigi," Lord William replied thoughtfully. "Richard, why does no one here know of the connection to her Holder Bennet cousins?"

"From what I remember of what my mother told me at the time, when a despicable woman compromised Miss Bennet's father, he led her to believe the entail on the estate is away from females. It is not, but given the social climbing and fortune hunting tendencies of his new wife, he kept as much of the truth from her as possible," Richard recalled.

"At the moment, she thinks me an insufferable man who

thinks his rank allows him to take what he wants. I think, before we inform her of our connection, we should change her opinion of us," Lord William grimaced as he saw three sets of raised eyebrows pointed in his direction. "I know—me—not us!"

~~~~~~~/~~~~~~~

Charles Bingley had taken a bedchamber at the Golden Bull Inn in Steveton, a little town ten miles to the west of Meryton. He did not want to be seen yet, not until he knew how to approach the problem. Bingley had spent the journey toward Meryton contemplating why, of all the people Lady Catherine might know with disreputable characters, she chose her own parson to commit such a misdeed against her own family.

He was finally willing to admit that anything bad in his life had been at his own direction. He had spied on young women because it gave him a feeling of control and pleasure. He finally admitted he controlled it, not the other way around, as he had tried to tell himself to excuse his deviant behaviour. He began to admit the biggest lies he told were the ones he told himself.

His mother had taught him to take what he wanted, as it was his due. However, as he looked back with fresh eyes, fully open for mayhap the first time, he could see there was little his mother told him that had been correct. She had involved her eleven-year-old and nine-year-old children in a despicable scheme to entrap a man so honourable he married his mother. What mother uses her children in such a fashion?

He had gambled, drank, and whored away his legacy. It had not been a vast sum, but if he had invested it with Mr. Gardiner as he should have, he would have had a healthy dividend each year as well as being able to grow the principal. What an addlepated fool he had been!

He did not know how yet, but he must find a way to contact the Duke and tell him what Lady Catherine had charged him to do, and he would seek no reward. For the first time in his life, Charles Bingley intended to do something because it was the right thing to do.

CHAPTER 11

When the Duke was walking in Meryton a few days later, he bumped into none other than Miss Elizabeth Bennet, literally. He was surprised, and Elizabeth, already thinking he was an arrogant man who thought he could do what he wanted when he wanted, misread the look she saw as one of hauteur and disdain rather than surprise.

Before the Duke could say a word, she was off with a "Well, I never! Who does that man think he is? The King!"

Richard, whose leg was bothering him, had remained at Netherfield with Lady Georgiana. "Miss Bennet, I assume?" Major Wickham snickered at the surprise still evident on his friend's face.

"The one and only," Lord William drawled as he shook his head. Would he ever get to greet her without causing offense?

Mrs. Bennet and her grasping daughter had seen the interaction from across the street. "Mama, we must apologise to the Duke for Cinder-Liza's rudeness. It will bring me to his notice!" Caroline bleated.

"Yes, my dear, you are correct; let us cross the road." Martha took her daughters thin fingers and crossed the road. They stopped in front of the Duke and his party, and before Biggs or Johns moved, they genuflected as they would for the Queen.

"Your Grace," Caroline said, in her nasally, grating voice, "we must apologise for Cinder-Liza, she knows not how to behave around one as highborn as yourself," she simpered.

"Who are you to address me without my requesting an introduction? It is *you* and this other woman who know not how to behave in my presence, not *Miss Bennet*," the Duke replied angrily. Both women were taken back at the rebuke. They were certain all they would need to do was to introduce themselves and he would be under their influence.

"I am Mrs. Bennet, mistress of Longbourn, and this is my daughter, Miss Caroline Bennet," Martha fawned.

Mr. Hurst stepped forward. "Firstly, *madam*, how dare you lie to a duke?" Both women gasped. "It is well known that this," he speared Caroline with a look of pure disdain, "is Miss Caroline *Bingley*, the daughter of a tradesman." Caroline almost swooned with the humiliation. "And you are as much the mistress of Longbourn as I am!" With that, the Duke, Major Wickham, and Mr. Hurst turned away, cutting the women. Two huge bodyguards followed them, daring the gasping women to try to approach their master again.

"This is all Cinder-Liza's fault!" Caroline Bingley hissed.

"You are correct, my daughter. We will get even with that uppity chit!" Martha promised.

~~~~~~~~/~~~~~~~~

The day the *HMS Charger* docked in Nassau was the day the reality of their rescue hit the Bennets and the two former crew of *The West Indies Trader* fully. They stepped onto the quay and were met by no less than the governor, Lord Wesley St. George. A pigeon had been released a day out of Nassau, and from their reception as the frigate docked, it was obvious the bird's message had been received.

"Lord and Lady Holder and family, you are most welcome. This is a glorious day; it has been years since there has been any hope of your being alive and well. We feared it was to be naught but an impossible dream! Before we go any further, and you have a chance to relax at the governor's mansion, there is a packet ship departing in two hours. The post and goods she carries will reach England, God willing, in about two months. I expect there are those at home who would want to know you are alive and well," Lord St. George suggested.

It was decided with alacrity. The Earl wrote to his daughter, his cousin Thomas, Mr. Philips, and Mr. Gardiner, and Jane wrote to her father and Elizabeth, care of Mr. Philips. She would not take a chance the awful stepmother would intercept this most important of missives. The letters were sealed and delivered into the hands of the Captain of the packet ship.

The Earl stated the two men who had survived with them on the island were to be included in the party hosted at the governor's house, and Lord St. George did not object. Before the Bennets left the dock, they could not thank Captain Sandiford and his crew enough for rescuing them from *New England*. The Captain quipped that, instead, the Earl should thank the pirates, who tried to hide in the waters around the islands.

Parrot was happy sitting on Tommy's shoulder as the party was shown to their chambers; he squawked his approval. Oh, what a luxury, to sleep in a feather bed once again! Jane and Jamey were especially pleased to have a suite to themselves with thick walls rather than the thin boards that separated the cabins on board the frigate. The newly married couple found their enjoyment of the marriage bed increased exponentially when they could not be heard by others and were themselves unable to hear others.

Jane told her father and Lizzy of her marriage in her letters to them. She could not wait to hug them both again, which she was sure was true for Tommy as well. '*Wait until Papa sees Tommy is taller than him! Oh, I cannot wait to see his face,*' Jane giggled at the thought.

"Why are you giggling, Janey?" her husband asked, as he bestowed a long languid kiss.

"I was thinking about Papa's reaction when he sees how big Tommy is, and Phillip as well. Lizzy was always petite so Tommy will tower over her now." Jane smiled, as her husband captured her lips, and all thoughts of England and family were forgotten for a time.

The next day, with a letter of unlimited credit from the governor, the Bennet family went about the business of visiting seamstress and tailors. They had a few days before the ship that would carry them home to England departed. As much as they wanted to return home, they were not unhappy they would have some time in a thriving port town before going to sea again.

By the time the Bennets boarded the Dennington Lines ship for the voyage home, they once again looked like English gentry and not castaways. Before departing, the Earl issued an invitation to any of the officers of the frigate to visit him when they were in England once again.

~~~~~~~/~~~~~~~

"How dare you show us up like that, Cinder-Liza!" Caroline Bingley fairly screeched as she and her mother arrived back at Longbourn after their demeaning performance in front of so many denizens of the town.

"Of what do you speak, stepsister?" Elizabeth asked, not having a clue what the shrew was on about this time.

"You were rude to him, the Duke, and we had to apologise to him on your behalf!" Martha spat out, literally, with spittle flying in all directions.

"**He was so angry at you he cut us**!" Caroline screamed, at the top her lungs.

"Let me see if I have this right. The Duke bumped into *me*, he said nothing to me, and somehow it is my fault *you* decided to approach him even after I explained protocol to you. When he did exactly what I said he would, you chose to lay at my feet responsibility for your own actions. Let me guess, you introduced yourself and you introduced this doxy," Elizabeth pointed at the Caroline, placidly ignoring that she was shaking with rage, "as Miss Caroline Bennet when every single resident of the area knows that is a lie! Please explain to me how I have anything to do with ridiculous choices you made with no reference to me? You thought this was a chance to come to the arrogant man's notice. All this after I clearly explained he would ask for an introduction should he *wish* it!" Elizabeth challenged.

Both changed colours as Elizabeth hit the nail squarely on the head, and they hated her even more for being correct. Caroline advanced and tried to slap Elizabeth, but the intended victim was more than ready for the paltry attack and easily caught her arm.

"Would you like a reminder what happened to you the last time you hit me, Caroline *Bingley*? If you do not remember, the next time you raise your hand to me I will make sure you never again forget!" Elizabeth stated, with steel in her voice.

Caroline shrank back. The one and only time she had struck Elizabeth would not be forgotten, and she looked to her mother, pleadingly, for her intervention.

"You strike my daughter again and you will rue the day you were born, *Cinder-Liza*! If you had been more like a lady and less like a man, you would not have been in the Duke's way, and we would not have had to apologise for you!" the nasty woman unloaded her vitriol.

"And how did that apology work out for you, stepmother *dearest*!" Elizabeth knew she was goading the woman, but she cared not. Louisa sat quietly, ashamed again at being related to her mother and younger sister.

"Your family all went away and died to get away from you…" spewed forth from Martha's mouth when an unexpected voice rose in opposition and halted her tirade midway through.

"That is enough, mother! A halfwit can see that you and Caroline alone are the authors of your own problems. How can you be so evil as to say something like that to Lizzy? If it were not for her running this estate you and *that*," Louisa pointed at Caroline, "would be in the hedgerows you are always going on about! I am ashamed to be your daughter," she looked at her mother, "and Lizzy has been a friend and sister to me these many years, when you have allowed your selfish needs be your only guide, Caroline!"

"So, you stand against your own blood with Cinder-Liza!" Martha spat. "So be it, you are no daughter of mine!" Mother and younger daughter marched out of the drawing room with their noses in the air.

"Lulu, I thank you for your support, but you did not have to destroy what little relationship you had left with your mother and sister for me. You know I pay them no heed, no matter what they say," Elizabeth told her friend, as she hugged her.

"I did it as much for myself as for you, Lizzy, and you well know it was a long time coming. It has been some years now since she has been a mother to me; she is only interested in her own and Caroline's machinations. It is good I will not have to hide how I feel about you any longer. We are stepsisters, but you and Charlotte are sisters of my heart." Louisa hugged Elizabeth tightly.

The two soon retired to their chambers, where Elizabeth wrote a letter to Jane and then read her book in front of the fire. She finally crawled into bed a little after midnight.

~~~~~~~/~~~~~~~~

"We should have a masque!" Richard suggested, a few afternoons after the Bingley women's performance in Meryton—yes, he knew one was a Bennet.

"Are you in your right mind, Richard, suggesting that William host a ball, masque or not? You would have better luck having him walk over hot coals!" Wickham guffawed, as the three sat in the study with snifters of brandy.

"Actually, George, I think for once Richard may have a decent idea. It had to happen sooner or later!" the Duke ribbed his cousin.

"William, are you well? You understand as host you will be expected to dance, and you will not be able to stalk around the perimeter in that stupid manner you are wont to do," Wickham confirmed.

"Yes, George, I am well aware of what my duties would be. It would be a way of showing the neighbourhood I do not think myself so above them as to not socialise with them by choice," the Duke explained.

"Do you not mean you want to show such to one particular young lady, William?" Richard prodded.

"Yes, mayhap, I do not know. Be quiet, Richard!" Lord William was flustered, and he was never flustered.

"When will we have it?" Wickham asked.

"The local assembly is on the morrow, correct?" the Duke

asked as he looked at a calendar." His cousin and friend nodded.

"Then we shall have it the last day of March, it is a Friday. I will ask Mrs. Nichols to make sure we have more than enough white soup ready. I do have standards to maintain you know," the Duke affected a look of fake hauteur.

Thus, it was decided; the invitations would start going out the week following the assembly.

~~~~~~~~/~~~~~~~~

Elizabeth loved to walk, but that did not mean she was not an accomplished rider. On this particular afternoon, she was riding her old mare Nellie along the fence that bordered Netherfield when she spied some riders across the fence. She was about to turn Nellie, thinking it might be the arrogant Duke but did not when she spied a young girl of fifteen or sixteen riding with some escorts. Elizabeth knew the Duke had a sister, so she waited to see if she would be approached or if the sister was anything like her objectionable brother.

From the description her brother had given on more than one occasion, Lady Georgiana was fairly certain the solitary rider across the fence from her was the enigmatic cousin she had never met, Miss Elizabeth Bennet. She was also aware that both William and Richard agreed the family connection would not be revealed until there were better relations between the two estates.

Normally very shy, Lady Georgiana approached the fence across which Miss Bennet was watching her, with the green eyes William had quite often mentioned these last few days. "A-as there is no one to perform the office, would you agree that we introduce ourselves?" she asked tentatively.

It did not take Elizabeth long to see that this was a shy young lady, neither proud nor haughty, as she had judged the brother to be. The girl had straight blonde hair, had the beginnings of womanly curves, and the same cerulean eyes Elizabeth had noted when she crossed paths with her brother. "I assume that you are the Duke's sister, and no, I do not object if we introduce ourselves. With you being the higher-ranking person, and now that you have intimated wanting such, I will begin. I am Miss Elizabeth Bennet of Longbourn," Elizabeth offered.

"I am Georgiana Darcy of Pemberley and—well one estate is enough, as you correctly surmised my brother is the Duke," Lady Georgiana forced herself to look the other young lady in the eye rather than look down as her inclination was to do.

"It is a pleasure to make your acquaintance, Lady Georgiana. You know, I believe I met your brother many years ago, in a much happier time," the smile slipped, but Elizabeth schooled her features, "at a cousin's estate."

"Do you mean at Holder Heights when you met the *markess*!" the girl smiled.

"Yes, but how could you know that? You must have been a babe! I do not remember meeting you as a babe," Elizabeth searched her memories and found none that included the girl opposite her. When Elizabeth looked up, she paid attention to the girl's four escorts for the first time. "I am sorry, Lady Georgiana. I am holding you and your party up."

"As I am the one who initiated the conversation, you have nothing to apologise for, Miss Bennet," replied Lady Georgiana. "I was deeply sorry to hear about your sister, brother, and cousins, and then to lose your father. William and I lost both of our parents," she saw the questioning look at the name. "William is my brother, the ogre that stole your apples and bumped into you in Meryton."

Miss Younge was extremely impressed by her charge; she could not remember another instance of her ladyship being so quickly at ease as she was with the young lady across the fence. Better still, the young lady, Miss Bennet, was treating her charge like any other young lady. There was no fawning, and she certainly was not seeking information about the Duke and his preferences.

"It is possible I jumped to some conclusions without allowing him time to respond," Elizabeth owned. "Is it just the two of you in your party?"

Lady Georgiana made a snap decision based on the question. "There are two others, a cousin of mine and a friend of the family. In fact, I believe you know my cousin, his name is Richard, Colonel Richard *Fitzwilliam*."

"Richard is my cousin! His brother Andrew is married to my Cousin Marie, the only one of my cousins not to travel to Jamaica…" Elizabeth stopped speaking as the realisation hit her.

"I know Marie well; she happens to be my cousin too," the younger lady smiled widely.

Elizabeth's mouth formed a perfect 'O' as she processed the information. "That makes us cousins! Goodness, I threw an apple at my cousin, Andrew and Marie's cousin! How long have you all known?"

"With Richard's help, but a day or two. As we are cousins, will you call me Georgiana, or Gigi as all my friends and family do? We are the latter already, and I hope that we become the former sooner rather than later," Georgiana requested.

"In that case, please call me Lizzy. Oh my, I must apologise to your brother, the Duke," Elizabeth realised.

"Do you not mean *Cousin William*?" Georgiana teased. "He is, in reality, an honourable and good person, in fact he is the best brother a girl could ask for." Georgiana did not miss the look of sorrow that crossed her cousin's countenance when she mentioned William being a good brother.

"Absolutely not! He is *Your Grace* to me! I will not blame him if he thinks me a silly young girl the way I have acted and made assumptions about him. I let my prejudices get in the way of my good sense," Elizabeth bemoaned her faulty snap judgements.

"Lizzy, I promise you, William holds nothing against you, and you did not hear this from me, but, if anything, it amuses him," Georgiana assured her cousin. "Now, Lizzy, please say you will join me for tea this afternoon. You will see Richard there, meet Major Wickham, and see my brother is but a flesh and blood man like any other," Georgiana asked, hopefully.

"After the way I have treated your brother, I must accept and take the opportunity to apologise and hope he forgives my bad behaviour. Like Daniel, I will enter the lion's den. What time?" Elizabeth asked, using much hyperbole.

"You are being overly dramatic, newly discovered cousin. How does three sound?"

The young ladies bade farewell to one another and set their mounts to their respective houses.

CHAPTER 12

L ady Catherine was pleased she did not seem to need to send her man Dryden to Meryton to deal with her wayward clergyman, for his first report was gratifying. He had purchased clothing to look the part of a man about town and was with his family at their estate, learning about the habits of the residents of Netherfield.

In Lady Catherine's twisted mind, her long-held desire for Anne to be a duchess was about to be realised. It would allow her to keep control of Rosings Park and have access to the vast Darcy wealth. She was so sure of success that she sent reiteration of the instructions to her pastor to seduce and despoil the girl more than once, thinking to increase the pressure on her wayward nephew a hundredfold.

~~~~~~~/~~~~~~~

The subject of Lady Catherine's reverie was attempting to determine the best way to contact the Duke. After his latest instruction, he knew he could not delay long. He could not simply approach the man; given the Duke's enormous bodyguards, he would not be able to get close to him.

Bingley had no illusions about his mother and youngest sister. They would be useless, as they would only look to turn the situation to their advantage. He was not sure about Louisa until he saw her one morning walking with the younger Bennet daughter and another young lady, all arm-in-arm and very friendly. Not only that, but Louisa was no longer corpulent. She was by no means thin, but she looked well.

He believed Louisa would be his best avenue. He was well aware Elizabeth Bennet was far more intelligent than any of the Bingleys, former or present, and as Louisa seemed close to that lady, he surmised his sister would pass the information on to their stepsister.

He decided he would have to keep a close vigil and find a time when he could approach her out of the company of Elizabeth Bennet, who, he was sure, abhorred the sight of him after his attempt to grab her sister Jane.

~~~~~~~/~~~~~~~

Elizabeth asked Louisa to take a turn in the park with her when she returned from her ride. When they reached the bench under the ancient oak tree, far enough from the house so no one could overhear their conversation, Elizabeth sat down, still trying to assimilate the meeting with Lady Georgiana, *Cousin* Gigi.

"Lizzy, you wanted to talk, yet you sit and do not say a word. What troubles you so?" Louisa asked as she took her friend's hand. The physical contact seemed to spur Elizabeth to focus.

"Lulu, I have to tell you something, but before I do, you have to swear until I tell you otherwise you will not tell another soul!" Elizabeth implored her friend.

"I swear on my life, Lizzy, I will not breath a word to a single being other than you," Louisa promised.

"The story starts when my Mama passed away. What you do not know is that besides Jane and me, we have a brother Tommy, who was two at the time..." Elizabeth told Louisa all. Her father's reasoning for Tommy living with their cousins, who the cousins were and their ranks, everything.

She explained her father's decision not to reveal the truth after Louisa's mother compromised him. She also related that her cousin Marie had married the Matlock heir. She related how Jane and Tommy travelled with her cousins to Jamaica, which was why her father had been wracked by guilt after the ship had disappeared.

"You lost all of your family except for one cousin who is married to a viscount?" Louisa asked in amazement when Elizabeth paused in her recitation to catch her breath. "Why did you not go live with them, and how did you get the neighbours to never mention your brother?"

"The neighbours were keen to help us once they heard what your mother did to entrap my father. My late mother was a much-loved member of the community, which made them all view your mother as a usurper," Elizabeth replied. "I did not go live with my cousins as I will not abandon Longbourn to your mother. As you know, I run the estate; it is a duty I relish. If Tommy and Jane do not return to me in another four years, then Longbourn is mine. I am the mysterious heir," Elizabeth revealed. If Louisa had been surprised before, she was gobsmacked now.

"What of the entail?" Louisa asked.

"There is an entail, but my Papa allowed your mother to erroneously believe the estate would devolve to a male heir. The entail actually prohibits the estate being broken up or sold to one who is not a Bennet by blood, the same restriction which applies to inheriting the estate, but there is no restriction by gender."

"I assume my mother, Caroline, and I will no longer be welcome when you inherit?" Louisa stated softly. "After I aided mother in the compromise, I would understand your action."

"Lulu, you were a child then, and you are now a sister of the heart. You will have a home at Longbourn for as long as you need it. Your mother and Caroline will be gone the day I inherit. I still pray Jane and Tommy are alive and that he will be the next master of the estate!" Elizabeth stated wistfully. "There is more, my friend; there are connections I only discovered this very morning on my ride."

"This morning while you were riding?" Louisa parroted in confusion.

"I met Gigi, Lady Georgiana, while I was riding. She told me her first cousin is Andrew Fitzwilliam, Viscount Hilldale, my cousin Lady Marie's husband," Elizabeth explained.

Louisa cogitated for a few seconds, then it hit her. "You are related to the Duke!"

"So it seems. We are cousins, and I am to visit them this afternoon. Miss Jones will accompany me in the carriage. If your mother and Caroline question me about where I am going, I will tell them it is business related," Elizabeth stated.

"Does that mean you will see Mr. Hurst, the Duke's private secretary?" Louisa asked, as she blushed becomingly.

"I am not sure, but once I explain you are a sister of my heart, I am sure you will be invited to join me next time I visit, if I am invited back after being rude to the Duke twice already," Elizabeth reported, with embarrassment.

"Twice? I only know of once," Louisa looked at her friend questioningly, though not quite able to check her smile at the idea as the last one did involve almost being knocked over by him.

By the time Elizabeth had narrated the happenings in the apple orchard, Louisa was nearly crying from laughing so hard. "I am mortified at my behaviour, Louisa! You do not have to laugh quite so much as that!" Elizabeth smacked her friend's arm, playfully.

"That is the fearless Lizzy I know and love. I am sure he will forgive you; he is your cousin after all." Louisa dried her eyes.

The two walked arm in arm back towards the manor house, and Elizabeth joined in the laughter at herself; it had been a long time since she had laughed so freely.

~~~~~~~~/~~~~~~~~

"Brother, you are not angry at me for revealing our connection to Lizzy, are you?" Lady Georgiana confirmed nervously. "I know you wanted to give her time, but the moment seemed right."

"No Gigi, I am not upset with you at all. You were accurate in reading the situation, so I am quite proud of you. You did very well!" Lord William praised his sister, who beamed with pleasure as she received his approbation; he did not want to see her smile slip, so he did not comment on her use of their cousin's familiar name.

"Our ward is maturing nicely," Richard opined, after the lady in question excused herself to practice a piece on the pianoforte.

"She is, but the comfort level with which she described our cousin, which Miss Younge also reported to me, I have never seen before. Somehow, Miss Bennet was able to coax Gigi out of her shell faster and more fully than any new or long-time acquaintance has before. It seems our cousin has more than just a good arm with which to launch apples," Lord William grinned at the remembrance.

The Duke realised that, had he and his sister been able to attend Andrew's wedding, none of the confusion would have taken place as the Darcys and the Bennets would have met. Not just the time when the intriguing lady with the green eyes was a mite of four. The Duke acknowledged she showed great strength of spirit for one who had experienced so much loss in her relatively short life. He and Gigi had lost their parents, but this young lady had lost much of her family while being left to manage the family's estate.

When she hit him with the apple, he had been more amused than aggrieved. He *was* the one unknowingly trespassing, and taking her fruit without permission, after all. When he had bumped into her in Meryton, he had been deep in thought. For all his wealth and rank, he still had difficulty conversing with those he did not know well. His only regret was his inability to articulate anything before she had turned and stormed off.

Hurst knocked, and when bade to enter, placed some documents needing the Duke's signature before him. He carefully read each document before affixing his signature and seal.

~~~~~~~/~~~~~~~

Louisa Bingley walked into Meryton the afternoon Elizabeth was to visit Netherfield; she was to meet Charlotte Lucas at the tearoom. "Louisa!" she heard a familiar voice call; one she had not heard in some years. At first, she thought it might be her imagination, but then she heard her brother's voice again.

Louisa entered the alleyway where her brother was hidden from view. "Charles, why are you in Meryton? You know you are not allowed to set foot on Longbourn's lands!" Louisa exclaimed. She had no time for her brother; all she remembered was the selfish and vile propensities her brother had when he lived at Longbourn.

"I will not trespass on Bennet land, I promise you. I need to speak to you in private. I promise you on my life, Louisa, I am not here to cause trouble; I am trying to stop it," Bingley insisted.

Just then Louisa noticed Charlotte arrive at the tearoom across the street. "I must away Charles; my friend awaits me. I will be in Meryton alone three days hence. Find me then, and I will judge if you are sincere in your desire to help." Louisa turned and crossed the street before her brother could respond.

~~~~~~~/~~~~~~~

"Welcome, Cousin Elizabeth." Lady Georgiana waited at the top of the stone steps leading to Netherfield's front door. Miss Younge stood just behind her, while Miss Jones followed Elizabeth.

"I thank you for the warm welcome, Cousin Georgiana; it is good to see you again," Elizabeth curtsied to her younger cousin.

"Let us go meet the men," Georgiana invited.

"Is your brother content with my being here?" Elizabeth asked.

"He is," a deep, baritone voice answered from behind Georgiana. "I do not hold you responsible for my trespassing on your land or being a clumsy oaf who became tongue-tied when he bumped into you," the Duke stated, evenly.

"Do not forget to add *borrowing* apples as well, Cousin," Richard added.

"Cousin Richard!" Elizabeth exclaimed. "I have not seen you for so long."

"Could we move to the drawing room?" Georgiana said as she smiled. "I do not believe it is proper to have tea served in the entryway!"

The four entered the drawing room where Mr. Hurst and the Major were awaiting them. "Gigi, will you introduce our cousin to us?" the Duke requested.

Lady Georgiana introduced Elizabeth to the men. "You must allow me to apologise your Grace..." Elizabeth started when he interjected.

"William or Cousin William if you please. May I call you Cousin Elizabeth?" the Duke asked.

"I am Elizabeth or Lizzy," Elizabeth allowed. "In that case, *William*, please allow me to apologise for my behaviour toward you on the two occasions we have been in one another's company."

"It is my belief that I am the one who owes you an apology. I was trespassing and, as Richard reminded us, eating your apples without permission. In Meryton, I wanted to beg your pardon for my inattentiveness, but you seemed to be in a hurry," William said with a grin.

"There is no excuse for the way I reacted. I made assumptions about your intent, so it is my error and not yours," Elizabeth insisted.

"Come, let us not argue over who owns the greater fault and agree that we both erred and move forward. Please accept my condolences on the loss of your family members and then your father," William offered.

"I thank you for the condolences for my father, but until I know for sure they are no longer living, I must believe Jane, Tommy, and our cousins yet live," Elizabeth averred.

"It is understandable you feel that way. I believe Marie also does not accept her parents, brothers, and sisters are no more. She and Andrew manage Holder Heights and the rest of the Holder interests with an eye to the Earl returning to assume the helm once again," Richard stated.

"Richard, Major Wickham, I see you are both wounded. I trust you will both make full and complete recoveries?" Elizabeth had not noticed at first the fact that Richard leaned on a walking stick and had a serious limp. She noted that the Major's arm was in a sling as soon as they were introduced.

"We are well on our way to hopefully being completely hale and healthy, Miss Bennet," Major Wickham informed her.

"Major, please call me Elizabeth, or at the very least Miss Elizabeth. Jane is still Miss Bennet until I find out otherwise,"

Elizabeth insisted.

"Cousin, I understand you manage the estate and have to put up with an unwanted stepmother and her two awful daughters," William intimated.

"One awful daughter. Over the years Miss Louisa Bingley and I have become as close as real sisters could be. Once she matured and saw her mother and sister for who they are, we became extremely close..." Elizabeth told them how things were at Longbourn and how, if the stepmother and her shrew of a daughter did nothing to evict themselves beforehand, they would be expelled if she inherited the estate in four years.

"The day I made your acquaintance in Meryton, I noted Miss Bingley did not seem at all like what I had heard about the three women," Mr. Hurst observed.

"If you were to meet Lulu, that is Louisa, Mr. Hurst, you would see she is a genteel and a most pleasant sort," Elizabeth informed her hosts.

Georgiana looked to her brother, who gave a nod. "When we return your call, we will be pleased to meet Miss Bingley," Georgiana offered.

"I would like nothing better than to have all of you visit me at Longbourn, but the other two residents would fawn and fall all over you. My younger stepsister already claims to be the next Duchess of Derbyshire, Countess of Lambton," Elizabeth related with chagrin.

Elizabeth had thought her cousin, the Duke, to be of a staid and of a taciturn disposition—until he roared with laughter at her intimation. He wiped his eyes as he brought himself under regulation. "The one who tried to apologise for your rudeness fancies that I would look at her in any way other that disdain? She is not close to tolerable enough to tempt me, and we shall not talk about her being handsome, as she is not. I know it is indecorous for me to speak of a *lady* so, but I have never seen such behaviour as that in public before. I am not sure whose behaviour was worse, that of the mother or the daughter!" William's re-energized laugh shook his shoulders. "I know they are from trade, but do they know nothing of protocol?"

"I explained it to them when they wanted to visit here the day after you took up residence—they must have forgotten," Elizabeth's tongue-in-cheek reply was offered in all seriousness, and she smiled at the laughter of all who were listening.

"Will you be attending the assembly this evening, Elizabeth?" William asked.

"I will, along with Louisa and the other two. Please accept my apologies ahead of time for the way those two will behave," Elizabeth replied.

"In that case, may I have the second set with you?" William requested. "I never dance the first as it would set tongues wagging."

"Yes, William, I will dance the second with you, and I understand your aversion to dancing the first," Elizabeth allowed.

"You mean his aversion to dancing at all!" Major Wickham ribbed his friend. "May I have the third, Miss Elizabeth? I am able to dance with one arm creditably." Elizabeth granted the Major's request.

"I would request the first set Cousin, but dancing with one good leg is somewhat harder than with one good arm," Richard quipped.

"May I have your fourth set, Miss Elizabeth?" Mr. Hurst requested. Elizabeth responded in the affirmative.

"Lizzy, do you play the pianoforte?" Georgiana asked.

"I do Gigi; I enjoy music," Elizabeth nodded happily as she looked directly into her younger cousin's eyes and was gratified to see they were on herself rather than toward the floor. Georgiana invited Elizabeth to join her in the music room in the time Elizabeth had left before she had to depart to prepare for the assembly.

"Lizzy has grown since the last time I saw her before we were deployed to the peninsula," Richard opined.

"She is much more than merely tolerable," the Duke said to no one in particular as he sat contemplating the finest eyes he had ever seen.

After Elizabeth had played a duet with her cousin, she and Miss Jones departed Netherfield Park to return to Longbourn.

CHAPTER 13

"Cinder-Liza, you hardly have time to prepare for the assembly, mayhap you should stay home. You *were* rude to my dear Duke, after all, so I am sure he will not want to see you tonight," Caroline sneered.

"Remind me again, Caro, who it was the Duke cut, me or you?" Elizabeth asked innocently.

"Why you," Caroline took a step towards Elizabeth, but stopped when a look of challenge was directed at her.

"What did I say that upset you, Caro? I merely repeated the truth, did I not?" Elizabeth asked with a placid smile, as she could not help but be pleased and could only school herself that far.

"Caroline, ignore her; she is nobody compared to you. When the Duke sees you, he will not want to dance with anyone but you for the remainder of the night," Martha Bennet hissed. "Remember, we have a plan," the mother whispered to the daughter.

Martha Bennet had found one man that was susceptible to her *charms*—the new Bennet coachman. He was a man who had never worked for the Bennets before, and who had been hired when his predecessor retired a month earlier. Martha had seen her chance to have an ally among the servants, and she had taken it.

A sennight after he began his new duties, Martha asked if he was happy with his salary. Luckily for her, being new he had not yet made friends among the rest of the servants. He told her he was happy with his three pounds a month and his full board and lodging.

She had tutted, and when he asked her what was wrong, as

she hoped he would, she began to pour poison in his ear about her stepdaughter. She told him how she, the mistress, had advocated for the same as the previous man, more than double what the coachman was earning, and how the Miss High and Mighty Elizabeth had said he was too much of a fool to know she was paying him less than was fair.

Martha played on his male ego to make him hate her stepdaughter. Her trump card was her body, as she seduced him and told him if he helped her control the uppity Miss Elizabeth, she would make sure he was paid twenty pounds per month.

Caroline Bingley rejoiced at her mother's plan to get their revenge on Cinder-Liza for all the humiliation and degradation they had suffered under the Bennets. The three conspirators scouted Longbourn and found an abandoned hunting cabin near its border with Netherfield. Tonight, after the assembly, the uppity witch would finally pay.

Having never been accused of being a mental giant, Martha planned to offer Louisa the chance of returning to the family fold when they departed the assembly, or she would meet the same fate as Cinder-Liza.

~~~~~~~/~~~~~~~

The residents of Longbourn rode to the assembly together and arrived on time. It was one occasion for which Caroline Bingley did not want to be late. Once there, they split into two groups. As Elizabeth entered the assembly room, she thought the new coachman was decidedly surly. He had been for some time now, and she could not fix the reason for it. She made a mental note to talk to him on the morrow.

Elizabeth and Louisa were standing with the Lucas family and talking happily to Charlotte as a hush fell over the assembly when the Netherfield Party arrived. Given there were more young ladies than men in the area, the arrival of four men was most welcome, especially since one of them was a peer of the realm.

Mr. Hurst led the party over to Sir William Lucas and his family and made introductions at the Duke's request. As had been agreed at tea, no sign of prior acquaintance was shown between Elizabeth and the party from Netherfield. While the other three were making small talk with the Lucases and Miss Bennet, Mr. Hurst approached Miss Bingley.

"It is good to see you again, Miss Bingley," Hurst bowed to her curtsy.

"And you, sir," Louisa returned.

"If I may be so bold, I request the opening set, if you are not otherwise engaged for it," Hurst requested.

"It will be my pleasure to dance the first with you," Louisa responded, and Hurst did not miss the heightened colour of her cheeks.

"May I request the final set as well, Miss Bingley?" Hurst hoped she was not engaged for that set either.

"It is yours, sir," Louisa's blush deepened with pleasure. The man—*a man*—wanted to dance two sets with her—a man she was starting to admire greatly.

Across the room, Mrs. Bennet and Caroline Bingley were seething with anger. As usual, no one would stand and talk to them, but it was worse than that! The Duke and his party were talking to the Lucas party, which included Cinder-Liza! Inexplicably, the Duke had bowed over the chit's hand. If they were not worried about another cut, they would have attempted to insinuate themselves into the group.

"Why is that chit talking to my Duke?" Caroline hissed to her mother.

"It is no matter, Caroline, for after she is ruined by the coachman tonight, she will do anything we desire to keep her secret!" Martha Bannet cackled in anticipation.

They watched as Sir William accompanied the Duke's party to introduce them to the prominent families of the area. They watched with envy as the dancers for the first set lined up. Even Louisa had a partner, and as had happened at every other dance, neither Martha nor Caroline was asked to dance.

Elizabeth danced the first set with the Lucas heir, Frederick. The Duke and Wickham continued their rounds of the room while Richard found a spot to sit and rest his leg. The fact the Duke passed by them without so much as a glance in their direction added to the anger that the two outcasts were feeling.

When the first set ended, Martha and Caroline saw the Duke approach Cinder-Liza and lead her to the dance floor, the two almost had an apoplexy. "Why is *my duke* dancing with that nobody? Did you not say she was nothing to me in looks, Mama?" Caroline demanded petulantly.

Mrs. Long and Mrs. Goulding had been passing by the two when the ugly daughter made the comment about her looks compared to Miss Elizabeth's, and both giggled behind their hands, using all their self-control to hold back the raucous laughter bubbling under the surface. Martha suspected she and her daughter were the subject of the women's mirth, but she was not sure, and knew not the reason.

They watched in horror as the Duke seemed to be enjoying his dance *and* his partner! How could this be, after she had been so rude to the man? The list of the offences to be laid at Cinder-Liza's door was mounting. When the set was over, both Elizabeth and Louisa were returned to the Lucas family, as Louisa had danced the set with the handsome Major.

The set after she danced with Mr. Hurst, Elizabeth sat out her planned sets that she would not dance. It was something that she and others did at each assembly to allow as many ladies as possible a turn to dance. She would sit out two before the final set as well.

"You know Lizzy, if looks could kill, you would be dead. Have you seen the looks those two have been spearing you with?" Richard asked his cousin, as he leaned toward her.

"It is nothing I am not used to, Richard. They do not scare me as they know what will happen should they harm me at all. I cannot wait until Tommy, Jane, or I are able to get rid of those two!" Elizabeth stated, with steel in her voice.

"Be careful with them, Lizzy; you know, sometimes, angry people are unwise people," Richard warned.

"I am aware of that, Richard." The two continued to talk

until Elizabeth was collected by her next partner.

"Did you see that wanton hussy flirting with the crippled colonel after her disgusting display with my duke?" Caroline asked her mother softly—as softly as she was capable of.

"Soon all our problems will be over, Caroline. Have patience my dear daughter," Martha soothed.

~~~~~~~/~~~~~~~

While his family was at the assembly, Charles Bingley was sitting in his room at the Golden Bull Inn at Steveton thinking about his life choices and reaffirming his epiphany that he, and he alone, was responsible for the direction of his life.

In a few short days he would meet with Louisa, and hopefully she would help him contact someone close to the Duke to convey a message to him. It was not only the right thing to do, but Bingley feared that Lady Catherine was so obsessed with her aim of marrying her daughter to the Duke that next she would send Dryden, and it would not be to compromise Lady Georgiana.

When he thought about Jane Bennet, Miss Bennet, he was sad she was lost for two reasons. Firstly, it was plain human compassion—something new for Charles Bingley. Second, he was sad as he would never be able to beg her forgiveness. That night he made a pledge to himself. Once he had helped all of those he could here, he would become a clergyman worthy of that profession.

~~~~~~~/~~~~~~~

When Elizabeth was sitting out the second set, her cousin, the Duke, sat down next to her, after gaining her permission to do so. "It is admirable of you and the other ladies of the area to voluntarily sit out dances so others may have their turn," the Duke stated.

"It is good you know the reason why we choose to. It is not that we are not tolerable enough to tempt anyone, nor have we been slighted by other men," Elizabeth teased.

"You know I was *only* referring to your stepsister," he inclined his head towards Caroline Bingley. "You, I find, are one of the handsomest women of my acquaintance!" The Duke made the declaration before his head overruled his heart. He had never met a woman of Elizabeth Bennet's equal.

She did not simper or fawn over him, and she most certainly did not agree with everything he uttered. In fact, it was quite the opposite. Between Netherfield and here at the assembly, she had shown a willingness to debate and defend her point of view, his rank be damned. He reasoned all he had done was declare she was pretty, and she was—not made a proposal of marriage! Although, his head whispered to him that she would be a perfect mate to share his future.

These whisperings were not wholly unwelcome, but it was far too early in their acquaintance for any of these steps that his heart might be pushing him towards. As he sat talking to her, he admitted to himself he was starting to develop a tender regard for Miss Elizabeth Bennet. If he were completely honest, he would see his feelings had begun the day the fiery woman had launched her apple at him.

If not for her mother's restraining hand holding one of Caroline's spider-leg like arms, she would have charged across the dance floor to pull the chit away from her duke, as she watched him laugh and smile with Cinder-Liza.

"If it is not taken, will you grant your much older cousin the pleasure of the last set?" Again, the Duke's heart spoke before his head could, for he could countenance her dancing a second time with none other than himself.

"Well, Cousin *Methuselah*, if I had an open set, I would grant it with pleasure, but I have no others open tonight," Elizabeth teased him into a less stern expression, surprised at the sensation of loss at not being able to dance a second set with him.

He had called *her* handsome, but there was no denying *he* was by far the most handsome man of her acquaintance. She could not imagine her cousin would be interested in her beyond cousinly affection, but she found that if he ever were, she would not object in the least.

~~~~~~~/~~~~~~~

At the end of the night, Martha pulled Louisa aside as they were waiting for the carriage. "We are going to make sure that Cinder-Liza gets her due for all the problems she has caused us. You are either with us or against us. If against, you will get the same just deserts as she!"

Louisa made a snap decision; she would have to play along and find out what her mother and sister had planned and then seek help. "Mother, I have *always* been with you. I got close to Cinder-Liza so she would buy things for me. Did you not tell me once you attract more bees with honey than vinegar?" Louisa knew her mother had never said such a thing, but she also knew that her mother would want to claim credit for her daughter's deviousness.

"I knew how it would be, Louisa; you could not be so clever for no reason. Keep her distracted in the carriage so she does not see where we are going," Martha instructed.

"Yes Mama, I will start now," Louisa stated. She stood next to Elizabeth as the carriage approached and only had time to say: "My mother and Caroline have planned something, and I may have to act like I am on their side. Please forgive me." Elizabeth nodded.

In the carriage, Louisa was the *dutiful* daughter talking to Elizabeth and distracting her. Elizbeth knew well they were not headed for the house. She understood why the coachman had the attitude he did; her stepmother had somehow co-opted him to her side. She felt disgust, as she knew the only thing the woman had to give was her body.

The carriage stopped. "Get out!" Caroline ordered.

"Where are we?" Elizabeth acted surprised they were not home. "I will not get out, take me home now!" Caroline slapped, her missing the hand in the dark with which Elizabeth punched her with all she had, catching the shrew's mouth, and loosening some teeth.

Martha Bennet saw red and struck Elizabeth from the side, snapping her head back so it hit the wooden brace of the carriage wall. Elizabeth slumped unconscious. The coachman opened the door and was shocked to see one lady within bleeding from her mouth and another unconscious. He had not signed up for murder.

"She lives, you halfwit!" Martha spat at him; all pretence of friendliness gone. "Carry her into the lodge. Now!" When the man hesitated Martha threatened him. "You will do what we agreed, or all of this will be laid at your door, and you will swing! Who will believe a servant over a gentlelady?"

The hapless coachman, who realised he had been played for a fool, did as he was ordered. As soon as she was placed on the dirty floor, Caroline Bingley began to kick Elizabeth's prone and unconscious body. Martha joined in. "Mama, she will be useless to you dead! If she is gone, we will be kicked out as the heir will be notified! What did you want this man to do?" Louisa asked.

"He is to ruin her so we may hold it over her head," Martha shared her disgusting plan.

"Mama you and Caroline must be seen at Longbourn. Tell Mrs. Hill that I am with her at Lucas Lodge, they will believe you. If they ask why poor Caroline is bleeding, tell them she fell when getting into the carriage at the assembly. Then, send your patsy back and I will make sure he does the deed. I have pretended to be her friend for so long, it is time for me to see her suffer." Louisa did not know how she was able to deliver the speech with her friend in pain on the floor.

"Yes Louisa; very smart. It will be as you say," Martha pointed at the coachman, "You will return us to the house and then return to do what you need to do!" With that, Martha and her injured daughter walked out to the carriage.

Louisa whispered to the coachman, "You will return but you will not lay a finger on my friend. I am going for help. Wait here with her. Before you leave the lodge, bring me blankets. If my mother asks why, tell her I am cold. When the time comes, I will be your witness you did nothing except follow my mother's orders so you will not swing—but they may!" The coachman nodded and soon returned with two thick carriage blankets and was gone.

Elizabeth started to moan. "Oh Lizzy, I am so sorry they hurt you. I am going for help! What direction is Netherfield?" It was painful, but Elizabeth pointed with her right hand as she felt searing pain from her left arms and leg. After making sure her friend was well covered, Louisa headed for the fence between the estates and then ran for her life in the direction the sister of her heart had indicated.

~~~~~~~/~~~~~~~

When the carriage arrived at Longbourn, Mrs. Hill was worried that her dear girl or her friend were not within. Also, they were later than expected. Seeing the housekeeper's questioning look, Martha decided to use her clever daughter's suggestion.

"Elizabeth and Louisa were invited to Lucas Lodge, and my poor Caroline fell as she was entering the carriage. There is blood within that needs to be cleaned," Martha told Mrs. Hill as she sailed into the house helping Caroline in with her.

The story seemed plausible, but when Mrs. Hill looked at the coachman, he looked everywhere except at her. The housekeeper had a footman wipe the interior of the carriage, and then the coachman moved the conveyance, not to the stables, but back to the hunting lodge.

~~~~~~~/~~~~~~~

The ship that the Bennets were on was almost three weeks out of Nassau when the Captain announced that they were now out of the area where there were storms like the one that caused them to be shipwrecked and stranded on their island.

With that information, all the Bennets felt the tension that had descended when they had first set sail lift. Given their experience, it had been a worry for all of them—no one more so than the new Viscountess.

"I was so worried, Jamey! The thought of something happening to stop us seeing my Papa and Lizzy again, not to mention Marie and Andrew! We may be aunts and uncles and your parents might be grandparents, and none of us would know it. As much as I want to see our home at Glenmeade, I cannot wait for the moment I see Papa and Lizzy again," Jane stated as she lay in her husband's arms that night.

"We were all concerned until the Captain's announcement my love, myself included. The only islands I want to see ever again are the ones which contain our homes! Your feelings of wanting to see your dear sister and father again are completely just and natural. Can you imagine how happy they will be when they receive our letters? We should be a sennight to a fortnight behind the post." Jamey kissed his wife, and not long after, family and England were temporarily forgotten.

CHAPTER 14

Just when Louisa thought she was running in the wrong direction, she saw the lights of the house up ahead. She banged on the door with all her remaining energy, until the butler, who was about to retire, opened the door with the Duke's two huge bodyguards on either side of him, pistols in hand.

Hurst, who had gone to see what the commotion was all about, was astounded to see the out-of-breath lady in the doorway. "Miss Bingley, what on earth is the matter?" It was then that he saw blood on her dress where she had tried to wipe Elizabeth's head.

"My mother—and sister—attacked Elizabeth," Louisa managed to blurt out between breaths.

"Where is she?" Hurst asked.

"An abandoned hunting lodge, near the border with Netherfield Park," Louisa got out as her breathing began to settle. She told them that Longbourn's coachman should be watching over her by now.

"I know where it is," Nichols stated. Just then the Duke, Colonel, and Major, having dressed again, arrived at the door too.

"What is this?" the Duke asked. Hurst related what he knew, succinctly. Within minutes, with Nichols leading the way, the men were off. Neither Dragoon officer let a little thing like an injury keep them from joining the large group of men that rode out, for their family was in danger.

The coachman arrived at the old hunting lodge at about the same time as the Duke and his riders. Lord William left the others to interrogate the man while he burst into the lodge. He found his love—he admitted to himself that very night that he had fallen in love with Elizabeth Bennet—lying on the floor, thankfully covered with blankets.

He would allow no other man to touch her but picked her petite form up from off the floor. He allowed Biggs to hold her while he climbed up onto Zeus. Once he was seated, she was handed up to him. He sat her in front of him and with one hand held her close to his chest.

"Is there a doctor hereabouts?" the Duke asked.

"Yes, your Grace, Mr. Jones is both a physician and an apothecary. His sister is Miss Elizabeth's companion," Nichols informed his master.

"Have a man summon him with all speed," the Duke ordered. Nichols sent a footman on his way to do the master's bidding. The Duke and his two bodyguards took off for Netherfield, with Nichols trailing them.

It did not take long for Richard to get all the story from the coachman, including Mrs. Bennet's lies, her seduction of him, and her threats. Miss Bingley had told some of the story, and what the man told matched what she had said.

Richard instructed him to wait an hour and then to return the manor house. He was to tell the disgusting woman that the deed had been done, and, in the morning, come to Netherfield to collect Miss Bingley. The man agreed without question, knowing well what could happen if he did not cooperate. Soon, the rest of the men were on their way back to Netherfield.

~~~~~~~/~~~~~~~

The Duke almost rode Zeus up the front stairs, but he stopped him at the base. She had to live; he was not willing to lose her, as now he had found the only woman he would ever love. He handed her down to Biggs and then retrieved her as soon as his feet were on the ground.

Miss Bingley, Lady Georgiana, and the housekeeper were waiting for him in the entrance hall. The former two could not hold their tears back when they saw him holding the limp body in his arms. "She lives," he assured them.

"I have a chamber ready next to Lady Georgiana's, your

Grace," Mrs. Nichols informed her master. The Duke carried her to the bedchamber and placed her gently onto the bed.

"Your Grace, we must undress her and prepare her for Mr. Jones," Mrs. Nichols informed her master.

"Yes, of course," the Duke said, a little embarrassed as he had not thought of moving since placing her on the bed.

"Oh my goodness!" Lady Georgiana exclaimed once they had Elizabeth undressed. She had large red welts on her legs and torso, and there were a few impressions of a lady's dancing slipper, if one could use the term "lady" for one who perpetrated such evil.

Not long after, there was a knock on the door. It was Mr. Jones, who entered and asked Louisa and the housekeeper to remain as he examined Elizabeth. Georgiana joined her brother and the rest of the men waiting anxiously in the hall.

Less than an hour later, which seemed like an eternity to the Duke, Mr. Jones emerged. "What are you able to tell us, Mr. Jones?" the Duke asked nervously, hoping the news was not what he feared more than anything.

"She is unconscious but breathing normally. Her left forearm is broken; her left leg is fractured between the knee and ankle. It was not a complete break, fortunately. It looks like one of those—those females," Mr. Jones could not bring himself to call them ladies, "stomped on her leg, and another on her arm. Thankfully, I do not detect any broken ribs, but that is not to say Miss Elizabeth's injuries are not serious. They are, but unless she develops an uncontrollable fever, I believe she will be well—in time."

"Should I summon my doctor and a surgeon from Town?" the Duke asked.

"It surely will not hurt, and a surgeon will be able to make sure her bones are set as they should be," Mr. Jones replied.

"Hurst," the Duke turned to his private secretary, "Have Mr. Bartholomew brought from London with all haste, and make sure he brings the absolute best surgeon with him."

"Yes, your Grace," Hurst headed to the study to write the

notes. As it was a full moon, a courier would be dispatched that very night.

"We need to summon the magistrate," the Duke stated.

"If I may, your Grace," Louisa interjected, as she stepped out of her friend's suite. "Elizabeth is conscious and requesting your presence. I believe she wants to address the subject you are talking of now."

The last word was barely out of Miss Bingley's mouth before the Duke was at Elizabeth's bedside. "Please do not exert yourself; you need to rest," William took her uninjured right hand and squeezed it.

Elizabeth winced with pain, almost sending the Duke charging toward Longbourn to claim justice on her behalf by his own hand. "I want them left alone until I can confront them. I want to see their faces when they see me and I have them arrested," Elizabeth rasped.

"I do not know if you know this, but I am a distant cousin of the royals, meaning you are as well. What they committed was treason; they will go to the Tower for this," he explained.

Louisa gasped, but then schooled her features. "They must pay the price they are due for what they have done! I have my family, and that is you, Lizzy!"

"From this moment forward you are a Bennet, Lulu. We will be able to acknowledge that openly once they are dealt with. I will not allow them to taint your name." She turned her head slowly to her cousin. "William, I have told Lulu, Miss Bingley, what I want done. I know I will be sleeping most of the time, but please make sure my sister receives all the help she needs," Elizabeth beseeched.

"Anything for you, Elizabeth, *anything!*" the Duke exclaimed, and he meant it.

"Time for me to administer the laudanum, Miss Elizabeth, for you need to sleep so your body is able to heal," Mr. Jones told her as he held a dose of the thick brown liquid to her lips which she drank. Once she was sleeping, a maid stayed while the rest vacated her bedchamber.

"What does my cousin want?" the Duke asked when all were seated in the family sitting room.

"Mrs. Bennet and her daughter do not know Lizzy's writing. I am to write a letter saying she has decided to make a three-month-long summer visit like she used to." No one missed how Miss Bingley refused to call them mother and sister. "I will tell Mrs. Bennet Lizzy passed from her injuries and the coachman and I disposed of her body in the morning. She will see the letter as a way of explaining why Lizzy, or as they call her Cinder-Liza, is away from home."

"Cinder-Liza?" Richard asked angrily. How he wished he and Wickham were allowed to go visit the two women and interrogate them, as he had done during his tenure in the army.

Louisa explained how the name came about. It did nothing to curtail the desire of the men to ride to Longbourn and string the two perpetrators up in the nearest tree of sufficient height. "I completely understand from the thunderous looks on your faces you would like nothing more than to punish those two right now." All four nodded. "Elizabeth wants things done her way, and, knowing her, I believe we should honour her wishes."

The men reluctantly agreed after the Duke relayed the request she had made before sinking into a laudanum-induced sleep. "It will be as my cousin desires," the Duke stated.

After wishing the men goodnight. Louisa accepted Mr. Hurst's arm as he escorted her to her bedchamber, across the shared sitting room from her sister.

~~~~~~~/~~~~~~~

"By now Cinder-Liza should be ruined!' Caroline Bingley crowed.

"I am excited as well, Caroline;" her mother retorted, "however, we must be circumspect about what we say in this house, or anywhere in public. Let us wait for Louisa to return."

Neither was aware Louisa was currently meeting with the Hills, telling them their mistress' plan, and enlisting their help. When she finished meeting with the Hills, she walked until she met the carriage in the lane. Once inside, the coachman drove them to Longbourn's front door.

Knowing Mrs. Bennet and her daughter would be in their bedchambers, she plastered a smile on her face and entered her mother's chambers when she heard her sister's grating voice from within. She made a show of looking up and down the hall to make sure there were no servants in the vicinity, as had been arranged with the Hills. Louisa closed the door and with her finger to her lips, indicated that the other two should be quiet.

"Cinder-Liza died from her injuries last night," Louisa told them with a smile.

"What are we to do? We will be hung!" We should have regulated our righteous anger," Martha worried.

"I am glad she is dead; I hope she is with her uppity sister in hell!" Caroline allowed her vitriol free rein.

"I am not unhappy she is dead, but how will we get away with this?" Martha asked.

"You remember you told me I was not so clever for no reason?" Louisa looked at Martha who nodded emphatically.

"I thought you said eating was all she was good at, Mama," Caroline added nastily.

"Silence, Caroline!" Martha gave her youngest a rare rebuke. "Tell us, Louisa!"

"I wrote a letter, as I am able to imitate her handwriting, telling Mrs. Hill she left on one of her long trips, like she used to take each summer?" Martha nodded. "In three or four months, I will *receive* another letter from her, and she will decide to live there for a long time and appoint me to run the estate in her stead," Louisa spun her yarn.

"You are so clever, Louisa! In three months, we will get what is due us!" Martha exclaimed.

"Mayhap before then," Louisa replied, ambiguously. "In the meantime, we all need to act as if everything is as it has always been. We do not want to raise the solicitor's or her uncle's suspicion. You cannot try to sell anything or do anything you would not, were Cinder-Liza here with us. Please tell me you understand."

"I do not see why it should be so," Caroline whined. Louisa was happy to note that, besides a split lip, Caroline was also missing two teeth from the front of her mouth.

"Your sister is right, Caroline. We need to be just a little more patient; if we are not, we will be in gaol or worse, swing, before we even enjoy the fruits of our labour," Martha stated.

"If you put it that way, Mama, then I suppose it must be," Caroline pouted, quite like the child she was.

Before I leave, I must pack a trunk full of her clothing and possessions and her book *Utopia*," Louisa informed Mrs. Bennet.

"For what do you need that?" Caroline asked, already planning to rifle through her stepsister's things.

"Because, Caroline, it must be like every other time she travelled. Her letter asks for her trunk to be forwarded to her. The coachman will take me and the trunk to some remote location and we will bury it."

"You have thought of everything, my clever girl," Martha praised. Louisa's skin crawled, but she managed not showing her true feelings.

With that, Louisa stood and went up to her sister's chamber, making sure she folded all her clothing just so. Her prized book was placed on top. Two footmen carried the trunk to the waiting carriage. Once Miss Bingley was seated, the coachman departed—just not for the location the would-be murderers believed it was.

~~~~~~~/~~~~~~~

With the winds at their back, the packet ship from Nassau carrying the all-important letters from the Bennets announcing their survival, as well as one from Lord St. John confirming their identity, met a ship from England at about the halfway mark, at a predetermined location. The crews made the exchanges, and after taking fresh stores on board, each ship started the return voyage from whence they came.

~~~~~~~/~~~~~~~

"I feel like I need to bathe after being in the company of those two!" Louisa exclaimed, relating the cavalier attitude of

Mrs. Bennet and her daughter at the news they had murdered Elizabeth.

Mr. Philips was present, and, as far as they knew, the Gardiners and their three young children were on the way from London. While Miss Bingley was collecting Elizabeth's clothing and possessions at Longbourn, Mr. Bartholomew and the surgeon, Mr. Jackson Harrison, had arrived. The two were assessing her state with Mr. Jones while the group were talking in the sitting room.

Louisa had not mentioned her brother's request to meet her to anyone; however, she felt it was important, so she was determined to keep her appointment with him on the morrow. She could not put her finger on it, and now was not the time for her to contemplate it, but there was something different about the way he had talked to her. There was a softness she had never seen from him before.

"Are you sure Lizzy does not want me to have those worthless women arrested, and Longbourn purged of their presence?" Jacob Philips asked. He knew what his late friend had written, but he also knew if Elizabeth wanted to wait, she had good reason to.

"I am sure, Mr. Philips. She was specific about the fact she wishes to be there when they see they have not killed her— only themselves. It may sound callous of me to talk in such a way of the woman who bore me; however, she stopped being my mother years ago, and kept encouraging my sister's false sense of worth. Nobody forced them to do what they did to Lizzy. Further, what they planned to do was so far beyond the pale that if I had not broken with them before, there would have been no choice for me," Louisa stated with emotion.

"As I was with my cousin when she made her wishes known, I am able to verify Miss Bennet's version of what her sister said completely." The Duke looked at Louisa meaningfully. It was the first time anyone called her by the last name that her sister had bestowed on her, and it sounded good.

The Duke explained it had not been a slip of the tongue,

but what his cousin wanted, but everyone present understood that, in public, Louisa would go by Miss Bingley, at least until the criminals were arrested.

Mr. Nichols cleared his throat. "Your Grace, your cousin's housekeeper and butler are here to enquire after her; they are with my wife in the kitchens."

"Please show them to this sitting room, Nichols," the Duke allowed.

A few minutes later, Mr. and Mrs. Hill entered the room nervously. "We apologise for disturbing you, your Grace. We just need to know how our girl is doing. She is the only one of three left; we could not endure losing her too," Mrs. Hill said with much emotion.

"You will not lose her, madam," Doctor Bartholomew assured them as he and Mr. Harrison entered the sitting room, with Mr. Jones trailing them.

"Do you have an update on my cousin, doctors?" Richard asked, hopefully.

Before the doctor could answer Nichols announced a new pair of visitors, "Lord Andrew and Lady Marie Fitzwilliam, Viscount and Viscountess Hilldale."

"Andy! Marie!" Richard pushed himself out of his chair, hobbled over to his brother and sister and hugged them both. "Where are my nephew and niece?"

"Jamey and Amy are in the nursery with their nursemaids. They are a little tired after our mad dash from Holder Heights," Marie informed her brother. "How is my cousin?" Marie saw Mr. and Mrs. Hill and immediately hugged her cousin's beloved housekeeper.

"The doctors were about to give us a report when you interrupted us," the Duke said with a grin. Given his doctor's opening remark, he was feeling more optimistic about Elizabeth.

Before the report could be given, Edward and Maddie Gardiner were announced. Six-year-old Lilly was holding her mother's hand. "Eddie and May have joined your two in the nursery Marie," Madeline Gardiner informed her cousin by marriage.

"Perhaps the doctors will finally give us their report," Jacob Philips returned the attention to, just now, the most important person in the room.

"As I was saying before the new arrivals, Miss Elizabeth will survive. As bad as the injuries to her left arm and leg are, thankfully, they sustained most of the blows. She was extremely lucky that her chest received but a few weak blows. The wound to her head was superficial, and although she did lose consciousness, she shows no symptoms of concussion. Neither Mr. Harrison nor I would have done differently. Mr. Jones did a stellar job," Mr. Bartholomew reported, and there was a collective sigh of relief throughout the room.

"I examined both the arm and the leg. Luckily, the arm was a clean break and as Mr. Jones surmised, the lower leg bone was not a complete break. From everything my examination revealed, there is no need to make any changes to the splints that our colleague applied," Mr. Harrison added his assessment.

"I agree with Miss Elizabeth's request; we do not want her on laudanum in the long term. As of tomorrow, she will be placed on sleeping drafts to help her rest, ones with no opiates in them," Mr. Jones concluded.

"Would you and Mr. Harrison remain for a sennight, just to make sure that there are no complications?" the Duke asked his personal physician.

The two men conferred briefly. "I am able to remain, but Mr. Harrison needs to be back in London in two days, your Grace," Mr. Bartholomew replied.

"Thank you, doctors," the Duke thanked and dismissed them at the same time.

Both the arriving Fitzwilliams and Gardiners had the same question: "What happened?"

Between everyone present who knew pieces of the story, all was related. Once all was known, Andrew Fitzwilliam and Edward Gardiner had to be restrained from riding to Longbourn and doing what the other four men desired to do the day after the attack. With some reasoning by those same four men, they were able to calm down the new arrivals.

"Mr. and Mrs. Hill, where do those two think you are?" Madeline Gardiner asked.

"It is our half day, Mrs. Gardiner. Those two care naught for servants, so they would not have thought to ask, in any event," Mrs. Hill replied.

"Miss Elizabeth is awake," a maid reported, timidly. It was decided that two at a time would visit the sickroom for as long as she was able to bear it. First were her Uncle Edward and Cousin Marie.

When Elizabeth saw Marie, tears for their lost families ran freely from both. Gardiner kissed his niece's forehead and withdrew, allowing the cousins time alone. "Lizzy, it is just us," Marie said between sobs. "I am so glad the doctors say you will recover. I could not lose you as well; you are the last Bennet."

"When did you and Andrew arrive, and did you bring my little cousins?" Elizabeth asked.

"In the last two hours, and yes, Jamey and Amy are here. We are not going anywhere until you are back on your feet, and you rid Longbourn of its current criminal infestation!" Marie stated, firmly.

"As much as I appreciate the sentiment, you and Andrew have your own lives, Marie. I cannot ask you to put them on hold..." Elizabeth stopped when her cousin raised her hand.

"Elizabeth Rose Bennet! We are *not* leaving! Remember, I have as much of the Bennet stubbornness in me as you, so accept it graciously, *little* cousin of mine," Marie stated with a challenging glint in her eye. Elizabeth raised her good hand in surrender.

"I see that you have discovered how my wife does not appreciate being gainsaid," Andrew said as he entered the bedchamber.

"She is like she always was, all of the years I have known her," Elizabeth stated with an arched eyebrow.

"You two know I am in the bedchamber as well, do you

not?" Marie interjected, with mock effrontery.

After a few minutes, Marie and Andrew noticed their cousin's eyelids drooping. They wished her a good sleep and returned to the sitting room to inform their friends and family that the patient was asleep again.

When they heard the name Bingley mentioned by someone, they both looked at Louisa with suspicion until they were enlightened about her. Not long after, Marie and Andrew had requested their adopted cousin Louisa to call them by their familiar names.

CHAPTER 15

As planned, Louisa met with Charles Bingley the day they had agreed to speak. It was not long before she discerned her brother was indeed sincere and genuinely wanted to help. She was surprised when she learned he was offering his assistance, with no intention of gaining something in return.

Louisa had the foresight to have Mr. Hurst and Miss Jones wait for her in the tearoom. She showed her brother in, and after he repeated his tale a second time, he found himself in a carriage with the three and on their way to Netherfield Park.

Still not trusting her brother to the extent of revealing that Elizabeth was in the house, they were shown to a public drawing room rather than the family sitting room near Elizabeth's bedchamber. When the Duke entered the drawing room with both of his Fitzwilliam cousins and Major Wickham, Bingley did not misunderstand the hostility the men displayed towards him. That began to change as he told his story.

When he was done recounting his tale a third time, the livid duke spoke first. "That woman thinks she will be able to blackmail me into marriage by having you compromise my sister, her own niece? And she instructed you to despoil my sister?"

"Correct, Your Grace. She cares for nothing but her own selfish desires. She is obsessed with getting her claws on your wealth," Bingley said. "I know I have done things in the past that would make you doubt my word, but I do have her last letter with me, Your Grace." Bingley handed the missive to Hurst.

The Duke quickly read it and passed it to the Viscount, who shook his head after he read it, and passed it to his younger brother. "She is a loon!" Richard exclaimed. "Who is this Dryden she threatens you with?"

"He is the one that does her dirty work for her, Colonel. They know your cousins are always guarded, so how they thought I would ever be able to achieve what I was sent to do, even had I the inclination to attempt it, is beyond me," Bingley averred.

"This is what we will do…" the Duke enunciated his plan. "You will assist with this, Mr. Bingley?"

"Yes, Your Grace, I am willing to do anything you require."

"It is time to invite my parents to your estate, William," Andrew stated. No one disagreed with him.

~~~~~~~/~~~~~~~

Elizabeth no longer needed sleeping draughts a week after her injuries. First Mr. Harrison, and then Mr. Bartholomew, had returned to Town as they were no longer needed. Elizabeth suffered no complications other than a low fever, which lasted but a single day.

Mr. Jones returned to his abode and had been replaced by Miss Jones. She had received a letter calling her *home* to care for an ailing *friend*. Neither Mrs. Bennet nor her daughter regretted the departure of the companion, as she was a reminder of Cinder-Liza in their home. She had done them a favour, for they were not permitted to dismiss any servants, though they had desperately wanted her gone.

Neither of the criminal women noticed or cared when Mr. and Mrs. Hill began to spend a good portion of time away from Longbourn. They did not care as long as their needs were met. Even though Louisa slept most nights in a house with two attempted murderesses, she was away from Longbourn most days and not a few nights, *at Lucas Lodge*, or so Mrs. Bennet and her spawn believed.

Much to the disappointment of the local populace, the masque ball to be held at Netherfield Park had been cancelled for an unspecified reason. Martha and Caroline were most put out, for they were certain they would have received an invitation and the Duke would have made them his personal guests.

There were few outside of the close-knit circle who knew the true reason; the Lucas, Long, and Goulding families were the only others aware of the true reason for the cancellation.

~~~~~~~/~~~~~~~

A little over a week after the attack, Elizabeth woke from a restful sleep to find her Cousin William reading to her from her beloved *Utopia*. After so many years of reading and then re-reading the book, Elizabeth could recite most of it verbatim, but hearing his deep, baritone voice caressing the words she loved so dearly made her feel warm all over. His voice gave her a sense of comfort, but more than that, she felt safe in his presence in a way she had not since before her beloved father had died.

Miss Jones was sitting in a corner fastidiously working on her sampler. As Elizabeth looked at her incredibly handsome cousin, she did not see a duke, but a man. A man who was compassionate, who would do anything to protect his loved ones, who was intelligent, and who she had fallen in love with!

She could not be certain of his feelings, but unless her perspicacity had deserted her, all the signs pointed to the fact he too felt their deeper connection which meant they were formed for each other. "You know, William," Elizabeth stated boldly, "people may get the wrong idea about your spending so much time with me." She arched her eyebrow. "Please pass me the glass of water."

Before Miss Jones was able to set her embroidery aside, her cousin performed the office himself. "And what idea would that be, Elizabeth?" William asked, his voice heavy with emotion.

"That there is something beyond cousinly affection between us," Elizabeth dipped her head, blushing at having been too forward.

"Miss Jones, it seems I need to have a private conversation with my cousin," William said in his best Duke of Derbyshire voice.

"I will be in the hall, Miss Elizabeth, and I shall leave the door *open!*" She was not cowed by the Duke, but she had no doubt that her charge wished to hear what he had to say.

Elizabeth was looking down at the half-full glass of water

she held in her uninjured hand. She watched as William reached for the glass in her hand. He wrapped his hand around the glass, brushing hers while they were both touching the glass; she felt the sensation of his touch and the warmth of his hand, causing warmth to flood throughout her body. He then lifted the glass and Elizabeth's eyes followed it up until she met William's eyes as he placed the glass on the bedside table.

She broke eye contact and lowered her head as she blushed profusely. Her head was still down when she felt his fingers below her chin gently lifting her head. The frisson she felt at his touch was something she had never experienced before, and while she was not sure what she wanted, she knew she wanted more of whatever it was he had to offer.

"Let people talk, Elizabeth; it is no more than the truth. It is my hope your feelings will one day match my own and you will agree to be my life partner," William stated, unequivocally. "However, if you do not feel as I do, I will be silent on this subject forever."

"How could you be interested in me, the daughter of a man who was but a lowly country squire?" she asked, despite hoping this was real. If it were not, she was sure she would suffer from the greatest heartbreak.

"Do you think me so proud of my position that I would ignore my heart, Elizabeth?" She hated that he looked wounded by her words.

"I hoped not, William, because I find I am falling in love with you, or may be in love with you already," she replied, shyly.

"Then we have that in common. You must allow me to tell you how ardently I love and admire you, Elizabeth. I think it began the day you accosted me for being on Longbourn land; it seems it was Cupid's arrow disguised as an apple!" William related.

"I thought you would abhor my behaviour, especially after my performance in Meryton that led to your being importuned by those two women!" Elizabeth looked chagrined.

"I was tongue-tied because I was so affected by you, Elizabeth. I see if you accept me, I will have to be aware of that quick temper of yours," he half joked.

"Where do we go from here?" Elizabeth asked quietly.

"As your Uncle Bennet is missing, your Uncle Gardiner is your guardian, is he not?" Elizabeth nodded, most appreciative William had said missing and not dead. "In that case, Elizabeth, I request a formal courtship with an eye to the natural conclusion of making you an offer of matrimony."

"Yes, William, I would like nothing more than to be courted by you, but have we not been courting already?" Elizabeth arched her eyebrow. How he loved it when she did that, especially when he saw his love reflected in her shining green eyes.

William rose from his chair and bestowed a lingering kiss on the wrist of her right hand over her pulse, and at that moment it seemed both of their hearts beat in unison. He left to find Mr. Gardiner, and Elizabeth was joined by Miss Jones, who returned to her sampler without a word.

It was not long before William returned with escorts. "You will be a very happy woman, Lizzy," her uncle noted, thereby indicating his consent—not that he would have denied anything for which the Duke deigned to ask.

"Lizzy, you will be my sister!" Georgiana almost squealed and covered her mouth at the unladylike sound she produced.

"*If* William proposes, and *if* I decide to accept, then yes, Gigi, we will be sisters," Elizabeth teased the young lady.

The four were soon replaced by Louisa and Mr. Hurst. "I am so happy for you, Lizzy! Great minds must think alike, as Mr. Hurst—Harold—requested a courtship today, and I have, of course, granted his request," Louisa gushed.

"Oh Lulu, I am so pleased for you. I hope you treat her as the jewel she is, Mr. Hurst," Elizabeth wished the couple joy, as she had longed for such for both her sisters of the heart.

"Her happiness will be my life's work, Miss Elizabeth. We do not plan on a lengthy courtship," Hurst related, as Louisa nodded her agreement.

They were replaced by Marie and Andrew and the Earl and

Countess of Matlock. All four expressed their unreserved pleasure and support for the newly acknowledged, if already long-courting couple. "Catherine will have an apoplexy when she hears of this," Lord Reggie opined.

"That, dear husband, is why she will not hear of it until William has sprung his trap. Personally, I think it is high time she is taught a lesson," Lady Elaine stated, with certainty.

"She is my sister so I wish I could disagree with you, Elaine, but I find I am unable." the Earl stated sadly. The four remained for a few more minutes before taking their leave.

The final group were the Colonel, Major, and Miss Younge. Now, perhaps because she was in love herself, Elizabeth did not miss the tender looks that passed between Miss Younge and Major Wickham. "George and I have extended leave as the doctors have ruled it is still some months, if ever, before we two old warhorses will be able to return to full duty. At least we will be here to witness when you confront those women and see my aunt receive her just desserts," Richard grinned, rubbing his hands together as he relished the idea of justice being served, even if it were too cold for his preferences.

Elizabeth was patient, but she was aware it would not be long before she eradicated the scourge residing in her home once and for all.

~~~~~~~/~~~~~~~

May 1, 1809

Elizabeth had regained much of her strength in the month since the attack, and her relationship with William had grown. The Earl and Countess of Matlock were still in residence, as were Andrew and Marie, for Marie kept to her resolve that she would not leave her cousin until she was completely healthy and had dealt with the cancer at Longbourn.

Elizabeth had been allowed to leave her bedchamber, at first only to go to the family sitting room. As her strength grew and the pain receded, she was allowed anywhere in the house. For her, the best day had been two weeks ago, when she was allowed outside to hobble with crutches in the garden while William walked at her side.

Louisa had fallen deeply in love with Harold Hurst, although her primary motivation in visiting Netherfield was to be in her sister's company. Mr. Hurst had kept his word and proposed a fortnight after Louisa had granted him a courtship.

It seemed love was in the air, as Hurst and his betrothed were to have a double wedding on the morrow. The other couple was George Wickham and Karen Younge, who would marry the same day. As had Hurst and Louisa, the two had realised they were in love as soon as they started spending so much time together. When the couple approached the Duke, he wished them well, and although he did not ask her to do so Miss Younge had been firm in her decision to remain in post until a replacement companion could be found.

With Lady Matlock's help, Mrs. Helena Annesley was found and hired. Georgiana would always miss her former companion, but she grew to love her new companion as well. Mrs. Annesley was older than her former companion but was as kind and considerate to her charge as Mrs. Younge. It helped that Miss Younge pledged to help her replacement learn all about her charge's likes and dislikes.

Colonel Fitzwilliam and Major Wickham returned from their last foray to London. After being re-evaluated by a panel of military doctors, they had been informed that they would never regain combat status. The Colonel and Major Wickham were considering resigning from the army, as neither of them could imagine themselves with a desk job in the war office. They were combat soldiers at heart.

~~~~~~~/~~~~~~~

Life at Longbourn was boring for Mrs. Bennet and Caroline. Neither had the patience to wait for Louisa to write the second letter to Mr. Philips which would grant them access to Longbourn's coffers, although there was no choice. The two were salivating over the prospect of being able to spend the funds long denied them. They badgered Louisa about the second letter continually, no matter how many times she explained that Mr. Philips would be suspicious if a second letter arrived so far from the expected date of Miss Elizabeth's return.

They did not care that Louisa spent no time with them during the day and only slept a few nights each week at the estate. Louisa would be useful in helping them attain the funds they craved, but beyond that they cared not for her. They were much displeased she would not agree to accede to their wishes earlier than planned. After ten days or so, they decided if waiting meant they would get their hands on Longbourn's funds, they would have to wait.

More than a month had passed since they rid the world of Cinder-Liza. The two were now confident they would suffer no consequences for their actions as Louisa had covered up the truth so well for them. While they were bored and had few, if any, funds at their disposal, they were as happy as they were pleased at not having to suffer the barbs Cinder-Liza used to deliver. Neither considered breaking the monotony by going into Meryton due to the way they were received by all those country bumpkins who were so beneath them.

Now all they had to do was find a way to gain the Duke's notice.

~~~~~~~/~~~~~~~

Elizabeth was proficient on the pianoforte but had no chance to practice until her arm healed. On the first day she was without splints or a sling, her cousin Gigi invited her to join her lesson with *Signore* da Funti. The cousins were halfway through the lesson when the Duke asked the *Signore* if he could steal Miss Elizabeth away.

The couple walked outside into the rose garden on the side of the house. Elizabeth used a crutch on her left, even though the splint had been removed and she was pain free, while her right arm was supported by the Duke. Miss Jones trailed them at a distance, and the Duke's huge bodyguards took up stations at either end of the path.

Once he helped Elizabeth sit on the bench under the gazebo

in the middle of the rose garden, the Duke dropped to one knee and took Elizabeth's delicate hands in his own. "Elizabeth Rose Bennet, you hold my heart. Since the day I requested a formal courtship, my regard, my affection, nay, my love for you has only grown in strength. You, my love, see the man, and not my title or wealth. You are beautiful, the most beautiful woman of my acquaintance, but that is only one of your attributes. Your compassion, charity, empathy, and character, all make you my ideal partner.

"There is none save you I would want, or agree to have, as my duchess. I know you will always challenge me and keep me on my toes, and you will not allow me to hide in the corners of a ballroom, as I have been known to do. With you I want to be sociable so all can note I have won the crown jewel of the kingdom as my wife. My life without you would be without love, so I beseech you to accept my hand in marriage," William poured his heart out to the lady he loved above all others.

"Even when I erroneously believed you would not look at me as a helpmeet, I already had strong feelings for you, William, and they grew into love. My love began as small as an acorn and has grown mighty and strong as a huge oak. It has been some time since I have known you are the *only* man I could ever agree to marry, William, so yes, a million times yes! I will marry none, save you!" Elizabeth replied, making her Duke the happiest of men.

William rose from his knees and sat down next to her. Forgetting they were not alone William brushed his betrothed's lips with his own. The touch of his lips on hers sent her heart racing. He was about to do what they both desired and deepen the kiss when Miss Jones tactfully cleared her throat.

Both blushed as they moved a little apart. "I hope you do not require a long betrothal, Elizabeth," her betrothed searched her eyes for her reaction to his request and relaxed at the pleasure he discovered within at his beseeching.

"I do not, William, a few weeks will be enough. I first need to clear my estate of all vermin, and then we will marry," Elizabeth stated, matter of factually.

"And we have Lady Catherine's arrival to anticipate on the morrow," William stated, with resignation.

In his weekly updates, Bingley had led the lady to believe he had met Lady Georgiana and had begun to win her trust. Each subsequent missive had reported more progress, which all those at Netherfield believed would cause the lady to lick her lips in anticipation. The last one sent reported success; he had seduced her as instructed. Her nephew would meet her on the second day of May to hear her terms for silence. The Earl opined that, if they listened very carefully, they might be able to hear his sister's joy from where they sat when she received the last letter.

"Then why do we not say three weeks, William?" Elizabeth suggested. "By then both our problems will be solved, finally."

"Three weeks it will be. I asked your Uncle Gardiner's consent and blessing before they departed for London, so we are officially engaged," William related.

"Sure of my answer, were you?" Elizabeth teased.

"I did have hope, my love, but I would say I was prepared, not overconfident," William grinned.

As they mounted the steps to the house, they heard a horse at full gallop and turned to see Mr. Philips barrelling toward them. He pulled on the reins as the horse halted, sending pieces of gravel flying. He jumped off his horse and withdrew a sheaf of letters from his pouch.

As Philips reached the couple he blurted out: "They are all alive, Lizzy! Jane, Tommy, the Holder Bennets, they are all *alive!*" It was the last thing Elizabeth heard before her world went black.

CHAPTER 16

As Elizabeth came to, she saw the anxious faces looking down at her, none more worried looking than her—she remembered—her betrothed. William had proposed and she had accepted. Then why was she lying here? She remembered Mr. Philips making a frantic dash up the drive and then he said…

"Mr. Philips, did you say they are alive?" she asked, hoping she had not dreamt that part.

"It is true, Lizzy; they are all alive and will be here about a fortnight," Marie informed her cousin, tears of happiness flowing unchecked down her cheeks. "We all wish you and William well, but, as I am sure you agree, this news is what we have wished for beyond all else!"

Elizabeth took the letter her betrothed proffered as she sat up on the settee. She slowly broke the seal and let her hand run over the script she was starting to think she would never see again: Jane's!

March 4, 1809
Nassau, Bahamas.

My dearest Lizzy,
How long have I desired to write that! Two days after we departed Jamaica to return home…

Jane wrote of the shipwreck, how they survived, and their life on 'New England,' the name they gave their island. She told of their longing to be rescued, and how, until their rescuer was sighted, they had seen a handful of pirate vessels and a Royal Navy ship chasing one of the pirate ships. Then Jane continued:

Jamey and I were falling in love in Jamaica, and I believe even before then, but after we had been on the island for more than a year, we decided we could wait no longer so we became betrothed. After we were rescued, we married the very next day on board HMS Charger, a frigate, by a clergyman from the Church of England. I pray you and Papa understand we could not wait any longer after being betrothed for more than eighteen months!

"Poor Janey!" Elizabeth exclaimed, "how sad she will be when she learns Papa is no more." The Duke squeezed her hand in support. She continued reading:

You will not believe how tall Tommy is, Lizzy, he looks like a man; he is boy no longer! I am sure he will dwarf Papa! Phillip has grown so much as well, although he is not as tall as his new brother. Tommy looks like a younger version of our dearest Papa. Tommy and our aunt and uncle have also written to you and Papa.

I cannot wait to see you two. For so long I have dreamt about seeing and hugging you and Papa, Lizzy. From the time you receive this missive, you will not have long to wait, my dear sister, until I see you both, and I cannot wait!

We will depart two or three days after this letter. I must cut my writing short as the packet boat is readying for sea. I will tell you about the rest in person when I see both of you.

Please kiss Papa for me as I asked him to do the same to you from me,

Jane

"Marie, you are my sister! I have four more brothers! William, when we marry, you will be Richard and Andrew's brother! Tommy is coming home to claim his inheritance; I will go distracted," Elizabeth babbled. Then maudlin thoughts invaded her happiness. She remembered she was going to have to tell Jane and Tommy about their father dying.

When she looked up at William, she saw she was not alone, and his compassion proved he understood the direction her thoughts had taken. She would never be alone again. Elizabeth and Marie sat in one another's arms for some time crying tears of joy, although for Elizabeth they were mixed with tears of sorrow as she was reminded of the loss of her father. As happy as she was that Jane and Tommy were alive and on their way home, Elizabeth was struck that had this same news arrived before that fateful day her father rode his stallion while foxed, he might still be alive.

As if he were somehow responsible for her father's death when the stallion was, in fact, innocent, she had refused to ride Orion. Once the woman and her evil stepsister were evicted from Longbourn, and Mr. Jones cleared her to ride again, she would ride him.

Elizabeth realised if she focused on the would-haves, the could-haves, or should-haves of the past, she would court insanity. She remembered her father's voice: *'Only think about the past as that remembrance which gives you pleasure.'* Jane and Tommy were alive, as were all her cousins; that was the most profound and important fact. She would be able to give Jane over three years' worth of letters she had written, thinking they would never be read by her dearest sister.

"Lizzy," Richard said, grinning from ear to ear. "I have had a brilliant idea!"

"You think all your ideas are brilliant," Major Wickham intoned dryly, causing a round of laughter and a playful glower that said 'just you wait' from his friend.

"What are you thinking, Richard?" William asked.

"We should hold the masque ball! I would suggest toward the end of the month, when the *travellers* are here. Invite those two witches to the ball and then all, including your betrothal, will be announced. I suggest Thursday the five and twentieth, as you two plan to marry two days after," Richard proposed.

"Receiving an invitation to your ball will send Mrs. Bennet and Caroline into raptures," Louisa agreed. "They will never expect that they will not be leaving the ball as free women. After what they did and tried to do to my sister, they deserve nothing less!" It irked Louisa that she had to act a part around them, but she did it to maintain the illusion that all was well.

"As long as our family will be here. If not, I am sorry, William, but our wedding will wait until they arrive. I do, however, like the idea of the masque ball. They will claim they have no money for dresses. I suppose that is their problem, is it not? Mayhap the mother can sell some of her useless baubles," Elizabeth stated. As much as she wanted to marry her William, she would wait for Jane, Tommy, and the rest of the Bennets to be present as witnesses. Elizabeth had an idea. "If you agree, William, and if Jane agrees, the celebration after the ceremony will be for both couples. I am sure they did not have much of a wedding breakfast on board a Royal Navy warship.

"But of course. On a grimmer note, when Lady Catherine arrives tomorrow you will need to keep out of sight Elizabeth," William informed his betrothed. "We do not want to take any chances she or Bingley will see you." Elizabeth did not object; she had never met the lady and had no interest in doing so now.

~~~~~~~/~~~~~~~

Even though it was an ungodly hour to rise, Lady Catherine did so with glee on the appointed day. She had acquired a special license from Town. Once her daughter and nephew were betrothed, she would not allow her nephew to drag his heels.

She felt almost giddy. At long last she would humble a Darcy. More importantly, her daughter would be a duchess, and Lady Catherine would use the Darcy coffers as her personal reticule. She was already imagining all the things she would be able to buy that she was currently refused due to the restrictions her late husband had put on estate funds.

When she did not launch into society as well as she had expected she would, and after her failed compromise of the late duke, only a marquess at the time, her parents arranged a match for her with the much older Lewis de Bourgh. Her parents had lectured her on the immorality of trying to gain what she felt she was due by forcing the man's hand, but now she would triumph, getting what she wanted, regardless of the time it had taken her to do so.

Anne de Bourgh's only interest now was to remove herself

from under her mother's thumb. She was about to turn five and twenty, and she was sure her mother was not aware that she knew the terms of her father's true will—not the fabrication Lady Catherine had presented to Anne as his will.

As she was close to the birthday that would make her mistress of Rosings Park, her desire to marry her cousin, regardless of his rank, was nil. It had been a few years now since Anne realised the betrothal her mother went on and on about existed only in her mother's mind.

As the carriage rumbled on, Anne smiled to herself. Her mother's mood was giddy, but she was amused that her mother believed the duke, well-guarded at all times, had allowed their bumbling, Peeping Tom of a parson anywhere near one of the things most precious to him in the world, his sister. She imagined her mother was in for a very rude awakening.

~~~~~~~/~~~~~~~

Bingley was seated in a private parlour at the Red Rooster Inn in Meryton. His patroness had questions she wanted answered before she made her way to Netherfield Park to force the Duke to do her bidding.

Lady Catherine swept into the parlour with Dryden an hour before they were expected at the Duke's local estate, just after half past the hour of ten. "You have done very well, Mr. Bingley; I am impressed. I did not think you had it in you to seduce my niece," Lady Catherine pronounced.

"What will you do, your Ladyship, if your nephew refuses to acquiesce to your demand that he marries Miss de Bourgh?" Bingley asked for the benefit of the Duke, Earl, Viscount, Colonel, and the magistrate who were all listening just behind the servants' door as they stood huddled together in the servants' passageway.

"My nephew is soft, and he will do as I demand. He would not want his sister's ruination known abroad. This is my due, and I *will* have his compliance. If not, I will allow Dryden to convince him. I will have him take my insipid niece, and if my recalcitrant nephew still refuses me, I will have him end her life as he did that of my useless husband. If only I had him change his will first! I digress; it will not come to that, as my nephew will do anything in his power to protect his little sister, which is why I gave you the task I did and allowed you to experience her highborn flesh." Lady Catherine had no understanding she had just admitted to solicitation of murder, and more, before multiple witnesses.

"It seems you have considered all possibilities, Lady Catherine. We have ten minutes before we should depart for the estate; it is but two miles distant," Bingley informed the preening woman. She assumed he admired her well-thought-out plan to gain that which she had long coveted.

~~~~~~~/~~~~~~~

Just before half past eleven, Lady Catherine swept into the drawing room at Netherfield Park. What she did not know was that, as soon as she had entered the house, Dryden had been arrested for the murder of Sir Lewis de Bourgh and other crimes. While she was gloating over her perceived victory, Dryden was singing like a canary in a vain attempt to save his neck.

"Lady Catherine, what brings you to my estate when you have been told more than once not to set foot on Darcy land?" the Duke asked calmly.

"Why, you impudent pup! You will show me the respect I deserve unless you want one and all to know of your sister's cavorting, unwed, with my parson," she pointed at Bingley.

"I see. So you are here to extort me. What leverage do you think you have, and what *exactly* are you asking for?" the Duke asked evenly.

"I know it all! Your sister is naught but a common trollop, lying with the son of a tradesman!" Lady Catherine insisted.

"Mother, how can you say such a vile thing about your own niece?" Anne de Bourgh spoke up.

"Be quiet, Anne! What I do, I do for you. One of us will finally be Duchess of Derbyshire!" Lady Catherine glowered at her daughter.

"Where is your proof, Lady Catherine?" the Duke asked.

"As you correctly pointed out, this man is the son of a trades-man. Who would believe him, or you, with alleged second-hand knowledge of a phantom compromise, over my word?"

"You would deny the truth and let some man raise her bas-tard if she is with child?" Lady Catherine was positive she would carry the day. "I have a special license here! It has your name and Anne's. If you marry today, no one will ever hear of my niece's shame!"

"Hurst," the Duke nodded towards the termagant and the licence she was waving about like a lace cloth.

Before she could stop him, the Duke's private secretary re-lieved her of the special license and tossed it into the fire. Lady Catherine sat, her mouth opening and closing like a fish out of water. "Everyone will hear of your sister's ruin; you will be slighted by all; no one will receive you again!" Lady Catherine yelled.

"I disagree with you, *Lady Catherine!*" Lady Georgiana, who had slipped in behind the woman, stated clearly. "Why are you lying about me?"

"You hussy, how can you say that when your lover is in this very room!" Lady Catherine spat.

"And who is my supposed lover?" Lady Georgiana asked.

"Do not act all innocent with me; I know it all!" She pointed at Bingley. "He is there, now deny it if you dare!"

"*This* is your niece? I have never met her before." Bingley stated, with a straight face.

"You wrote to me and told me..." Lady Catherine started to say.

"That I had had success. I did not say what the success was, did I?" Bingley challenged the lady.

"But...how...why?" Lady Catherine could not grasp how things had not gone as she had determined they would.

"All of this, Cathy, so you could cheat your daughter out of her inheritance," Lord Matlock stated from behind her. Lady Catherine stood and turned slowly, and her face fell when she saw her brother, sister-in-law, their two sons, and the Viscountess looking at her with disgust.

"Reggie, why are you here?" Lady Catherine asked lamely.

"To have you arrested for your crimes, Catherine. We were behind you today when you admitted to having Lewis murdered, and your man Dryden is in the process of enumerating every illegal action you ordered him to take. You did not even have the sense to tell him verbally, as you did with Bingley; you wrote your instructions down. Our parents, if they were alive, would disown you, just as we are about to do," the Earl stated, sadly.

"By the by, *Mother*, I have a true copy of my father's will, and even were you not about to be arrested, by next week you would have no longer been mistress of Rosings! Your Grace, allow me to apologise. I went along with my mother's plans to marry you in the past, as I was selfish and wanted to escape her and her dictatorial ways," Anne looked down in shame.

"You cannot do this to me! Do you know who I am?" Lady Catherine attempted to bluster.

"You are a woman with an overblown sense of her own worth and position in life. You are not a peer; you have a courtesy title which has no significance. It is time for you to learn just how insignificant you are," the Duke stated firmly. "Not that is any of your business, but I am already betrothed. My lady was wise to decline meeting one so cruel and insipid."

The magistrate nodded, and two constables took charge of Lady Catherine. "Reggie do not let them do this! Think of the family," Lady Catherine pleaded.

The Earl raised his hand, and the two men stopped and turned their prisoner around to face those in the drawing room. "Now you mention family. What cared you for family when you treated you own daughter as a captive? When you ordered the murder of your husband and others? When you tried to compromise our late brother Robert, twice mind you, and now you send a clergyman to compromise your niece! You care naught for anyone but yourself, and whatever happens to you now was decided by your own hand. May God have mercy on your soul,

Catherine."

With that, the magistrate and his men left with their prisoner, who seemed to be in a stupor, attempting to understand how everything had gone so very wrong. "It is sad, but there was no choice, Reggie," Lady Elaine soothed her troubled husband.

"I know, Elaine, but she is, or, at least, she was, my sister," Lord Matlock sighed.

"Anne, I hope you know you are welcome to stay for as long as you would like. And please, no more of that 'your grace' nonsense. It is William now, just as it was when we were younger," William offered.

"Thank you, William. Are you truly betrothed, or was that for my mother's benefit?" Anne asked. She smiled at her cousin in response to his, neither of them guarded after so many years of suffering the denial of cousinly affection.

"I promise, she is very real, Cousin," Andrew said with a grin. "He only asked her yesterday, and she accepted him—even with all of his warts and wrinkles."

"In that case, I wish you and the lady who will take you on happy, William. Will I meet this paragon soon?" Anne enquired.

"You will, Anne," was the only answer the Duke offered.

"Mr. Bingley, you have done me and my family a great service. We have canvassed your past, and you have owned up to your errors and pledged to keep walking an honourable path. You are sure I cannot reward you?" the Duke asked.

"It was my pleasure to be of service, Your Grace. No, what I did, I did because it was the right thing to do, not for any pecuniary advantage. While I thank you for the thought, I must decline. I will return to my parish and become the parson that my parishioners need and deserve." Bingley looked to Anne. "I look forward to working with you as my patroness, Miss de Bourgh."

Anne inclined her head; Bingley bowed to all and took his leave. Per the master's instruction, once the confrontation in the drawing room was over and Lady Catherine and Bingley had departed, Nichols informed Miss Elizabeth and Miss Louisa it was safe to join the family in the drawing room.

"This," William said as he extended his hand to Elizabeth, "is my betrothed, Miss Elizabeth Bennet of Longbourn, who happens to be cousin to Marie, so she is your cousin too, Anne. Elizabeth, our cousin, Miss Anne de Bourgh of Rosings Park. The other young lady is Elizabeth's sister Miss Louisa Bennet, formally Bingley. She also happens to be the sister of your clergyman."

"It sounds as if there is a good story there, William," Anne surmised. For the next hour Anne was regaled with the history of both Bennet families, the good and the bad, and the fact that those feared lost were expected to arrive in England within the next fortnight.

~~~~~~~/~~~~~~~

Ten days later, a Dennington Lines ship, which left Nassau more than two months previously, docked on the Thames. When the Bennets set foot on English soil, their odyssey, which began almost four years previously, came to an end.

A man from Holder House had been watching the berth ever since the Earl's letter was received. Other than all the children being much grown, the coachman recognised the family instantly. Before the Bennets knew it, they were being shepherded into two Holder coaches. There were only two trunks between all of them and Parrot was a remarkable point of interest for all who saw him.

By the time the two coaches pulled up at Holder House, word of how the Holder Bennets had returned was spreading through London society, with the speed of a warm knife cutting through butter.

Later that afternoon, a Holder carriage pulled up at number 23 Gracechurch Street. When the Gardiner's housekeeper opened the door, she almost fainted when she saw the missing Miss Jane Bennet standing in front of her, with a handsome man on her arm. Next to them was a young man who seemed oddly familiar.

The shocked housekeeper led Jane, Jamey, and Tommy

into the drawing room where they found their Aunt and Uncle Gardiner. "Jane! Tommy!" Uncle Gardiner exclaimed, "and, I assume this is my new nephew," Gardiner looked toward Jamey.

"Dearest Jane, we wish you well on your marriage. My goodness, Tommy, you look like…a younger version of your father! When do you all depart for Hertfordshire?" Madeline Gardiner asked.

"On the morrow, Aunt; we cannot wait to see Papa and Lizzy," Tommy replied, his voice now that of a man.

"Sit; there is much we must relate…" Aunt and Uncle Gardiner proceeded to tell them all that had occurred. They shed many tears for the father neither would ever see again. At least they were assured that Lizzy was healed, and they were ready to confront the criminals still in residence at Longbourn. They took some pleasure in the assurance that they would be present when the Bingleys were called to account. Before they left, the Gardiners sent an express to Netherfield, as the one the Holder Bennets had sent announcing their arrival in England had been directed to Jacob Philips's offices.

CHAPTER 17

To say the reunion at Netherfield the next day was emotional would have paid a great disservice to the word. No one knew who to hug first. Tommy hugged Elizabeth, lifting her off the ground as he swung her around. "Tommy, you do know my leg was recently injured, do you not?" Elizabeth smiled at the exuberance of her little brother.

No, she could no longer call him her *little* brother. He was as tall as her betrothed, inches taller than their late father had been. With a sheepish look, Tommy put his sister down most gently. Elizabeth was then engulfed in Jane's arms as the two cried tears of both joy and sorrow simultaneously. "If only Papa could be here to witness this," Jane sniffed as she held onto her younger sister for dear life, as if, were she to let Elizabeth out of her arms, she would awaken and find it was all a cruel dream. She pinched herself just to be sure it was not a dream.

"Jane, why on earth did you do that?" Elizabeth asked through her tears.

"I was afraid this was a dream, so I had to make sure," Jane averred with a watery smile.

Marie was enfolded in her parents' arms, something she had been fearful to admit, she believed would never happen again. Cassie, Allie, and Phillip joined the group as Marie was surrounded by her parents and three of her four siblings.

Jamey was with his wife and the recipient of one of his new sister's big hugs, which had earned the nickname *Lizzy-Bear*. "I am so happy to have you all home!" Elizabeth exclaimed. "You two remember my betrothed, William?" Elizabeth asked as she drew the man to her side. William had been standing back, allowing the family their time until his betrothed pulled him into the fray.

"Yes, we all know William," Jamey retorted as he shook the man's hand.

"The last time I saw you, Your Grace, I was but seven or eight," Jane stated.

"I remember, and please, my name is William; we are soon to be brother and sister after all," William lifted his soon-to-be sister's hand and bowed over it.

Elizabeth motioned Louisa over. "Jane, you remember our *sister*, Louisa?" Elizabeth asked with arched eyebrow. Luckily, Louisa's unstinting support of her sister had been part of what the Gardiner's had told her the previous day.

Louisa was not sure what her reception from Jane Bennet would have been, had she not already known of the close friendship she and Elizabeth had formed. All her worries were for naught when Jane enfolded her in a hug. "Thank you for all you have done to help *our* sister," Jane said quietly in Louisa's ear, and Louisa could not help but beam with joy. "This handsome devil here," she indicated Jamey, "is my husband, Jamey Bennet. Jamey, our sister Louisa." Jamey bowed to Louisa.

"Well met, Louisa. Another sister is most welcome, one can never have too many." Jamey grinned at her.

"This shy young lady is the Darcy you did not meet. Jane and Tommy, our Georgiana. You may remember she is called Gigi by all who know and like her, and one cannot know her without liking or loving her! She will soon be our sister too." Elizabeth soundly complemented the younger girl, who blushed furiously at her words. While well-pleased by the compliment, she was also embarrassed.

Georgiana blushed even more when she greeted the extremely handsome Tommy, but when she met Phillip Bennet her heart skipped a beat. There was something inexplicable about the young man that attracted her to him. She dismissed her feelings as being caught up in the moment, pushing them to the recesses of her mind.

Lizzy was hugged by her aunt, uncle, and cousins, whom she had not seen these long years. "Uncle, Aunt, Cassie, Allie, and Phillip, I would like you to meet my sister, Louisa." Louisa curtsied to the Earl and his family. Any worry she had about acceptance from Elizabeth's cousins was washed away as each of the five she had not yet met welcomed her to the family warmly.

The Earl of Holder turned to William. "Is there not a question you wish to ask me, your Grace? I *am* Lizzy's legal guardian, after all," he sported with the Duke.

"In that case, may I..." William started and was cut off by a grinning Earl.

"Yes William, you have my consent and blessing. I could not think of a better or more honourable man to whom I can entrust my late cousin's daughter. Welcome to the family." The two men shook hands vigorously.

Richard Fitzwilliam could not believe the beauty he saw before him, Lady Cassandra Bennet. The last time he had seen her she was a young girl barely out of the school room. Being on the peninsula, he had missed seeing her when Andrew and Marie married, and now she was a poised and intelligent woman standing before him. He would have to take the time to know her all over again, and his heart constricted with the hope that she would want to know him as well.

"Now that we have all calmed down somewhat," Elizabeth stated, as she sat on a settee with William to her left and Jane and Jamey to her right, "I have a suggestion. William and I will marry on the seven and twentieth of this month, and we would like to know if the wedding breakfast may be used to celebrate both weddings, ours as well as Jane's and Jamey's." She looked toward her sister and brother-in-law. "I am not sure what kind of wedding breakfast you had on one of his Majesty's war ships."

"There was a lot of grog involved," Phillip piped up.

"Our brother has the right of it," Jane smiled. "Unless Mother Amy or my husband object, I would like to accept Lizzy's and William's thoughtful offer."

"There is no objection I would allow," Lady Amelia's smile

was genuine as she again and again scanned all her family here in the room, known and new.

"Nor I, Wife," Jamey stated.

"Then it will be so, but I would think we need to have the breakfast here, as Netherfield has far more room. It will be a larger event than Longbourn can accommodate," Elizabeth opined. Elizabeth then pointed to a small trunk next to the settee. "When you have time, Jane, there are a *quite a few* letters I wrote to you while you were away *enjoying* life on your island. Sometimes I wrote more than once a week; it made me feel as though I could still talk to you. They are all in the trunk for you to read at your leisure."

Marie summoned a footman and said something quietly to him. The man nodded and withdrew. Some ten minutes later, two nursemaids entered. The arriving Bennets all went quiet when they saw a little boy holding his nursemaid's hand until he spied his mama and ran into Marie's welcoming arms. The second nursemaid was holding a babe, a little girl if all the pink was to be believed.

"Mama and Papa, I would like to introduce your grandchildren. This is Jamey Thomas, not yet three, and Amy Cassie, who is being held by her nursemaid; she is eight months old." She looked at her son as he stood holding onto her for dear life, wide-eyed with all the new people before him. "Jamey, you remember I told you about your other grandparents besides Grandpapa Reggie and Grandmama Elaine?" The little boy nodded tentatively. Marie turned him towards her parents. "This is Grandmama Amy and Grandpapa James."

"My new grandmama has the same name as Amy?" little Jamey asked, and his mother nodded. "An' my new grandpapa has my name?"

"You are named after him and your Uncle Jamey, but in essentials you are correct, my son. Be a good boy and go see your grandmama and grandpapa." Marie gave her son a gentle nudge in the direction of her parents.

Lady Amy's eyes flooded with tears of joy. Here were two

miracles she had never thought to meet. Here in this moment, when she was seeing her family again, which she had also once believed impossible she felt an inner peace. As it was with young children, it did not take little Jamey long to warm to his newly met grandparents as well as the slew of new aunts and uncles.

Little Amy looked at each successive adult who held her with good cheer, and the biggest blue eyes, ones that were a common hallmark of a Fitzwilliam. Half an hour later, little Amy began to fuss, so Marie excused herself with a nursemaid in tow to go feed her daughter. A little while later, little Jamey's nursemaid returned him to the nursery for a nap, as he was fading fast.

Once Marie returned, the arriving family was apprised of the plans for the masque, and the revelations that the two despicable women would be subjected to.

"The masque will serve as a betrothal ball for you and William, will it not?" Lord James asked. Both nodded. "Also, it will be a reintroduction, or for many an introduction of your family, namely us?"

"That is correct, Uncle James. What are you asking?" Elizabeth questioned.

"Just this, Lizzy. Why have this unpleasantness spoil what would otherwise be a joyous celebration? Why wait? Let us go see them on the morrow and have them arrested and be done with it. As William stated, by attacking you they have committed treason. There is no need for a dramatic scene at your ball. Believe me, it will be but minutes before all in the neighbourhood are aware of their perfidy and crimes." Lord James said nothing further, allowing his suggestion to percolate.

"I think my friend's suggestion has merit," Lord Matlock agreed.

Elizabeth looked at her betrothed who gave her a nod, then she looked to Louisa who also nodded. "It seems we agree; we will rid Longbourn of the vermin on the morrow. We need to contact Mr. Philips and have Sir William ready with some of his constables."

"I will contact Mr. Philips," Mr. Hurst volunteered.

"And I will send a note to Charlotte to ask her father to wait on you this afternoon. In fact, should we not invite the Philips, Lucas, Long, and Goulding families to see for themselves that Jane and Tommy are alive and well, rather than at the masque along with everyone else?" Louisa suggested.

"Lulu, you are brilliant! I should have thought of it myself; I can only plead my brain was addled by the excitement. Oh! Do not forget the Hills! William, please have them sent for now." Elizabeth knew the Hills would be overjoyed when they saw Jane and Tommy hale and healthy.

While the notes were being written, Jane turned to her sister. "Lizzy, you say our stepbrother has turned his life around; is it genuine?"

"It is, Jane. He helped dealing with Lady Catherine without any expectation of reward. When William offered him a substantial reward, he refused. He came to his epiphany years after Lulu, but it is real," Elizabeth shared with Jane.

"If that be the case, if I ever see him and he asks me, I will forgive him," Jane allowed.

"Jane, before we received your letter, I planned to ask Lulu to stand up with me, but you are here now, so if you agree, I will ask you stand up with me as well," Elizabeth shared her quandary.

"Louisa has been a saving grace; it was she who offered you friendship when you needed it most; it is right she should stand up with you. If you desire it, I will be more than content as a bridesmaid," Jane replied with complete sincerity. The sisters hugged again. They had many years of hugs to make up for.

~~~~~~~/~~~~~~~

A little more than an hour later, the Hills were shown into the drawing room at Netherfield Park. One of the Duke's coaches had waited for them in the lane next to Longbourn to convey the couple.

When Mrs. Hill saw Jane, and then Tommy, she stood with her hand over her mouth as tears streamed down her cheeks.

It became real for her when Jane enfolded the long-time house-keeper in a welcoming hug. Mr. Hill looked pleased and non-plussed at the same time.

Not much later, the three families from the neighbourhood arrived. When Charlotte saw Jane, she shrieked and then pan-demonium broke out with much crying, laughing, and hugging as the three families welcomed the long-believed-dead Bennets back home. Those who did not know the Holder Bennets were introduced, and the younger children were led outside by the Ladies Georgiana and Allie, who were assisted by Phillip and Tommy.

Once there were only the adults remaining, the tale of the attack on Elizabeth was related, and the plan for the morrow. Sir William, normally jovial and affable, looked as if he were ready to commit murder himself. "I wish I had known right away." He looked at Charlotte in an accusatory fashion; she would not look her father in the eye.

"Sir William," the Duke called Sir William's attention away from his daughter, "Elizabeth and I swore Miss Lucas to silence. My betrothed and I support her completely." The surprise on the faces of the neighbourhood residents caused William to remem-ber they were unaware of his betrothal. "Elizabeth wanted to be the one to deal with the despicable women. I could not deny her that. Would any of you?"

The men and women all nodded; they would not deny Elizabeth the closure she was seeking. "Sir William, I ask that you and some constables be present on the morrow. They *will* be leaving Tommy's estate under arrest, and they *will* be trans-ported to the Tower to answer for committing treason," Eliza-beth stated with steel in her voice.

'Papa, how I wish you were here to see this! Not only to see Jane, Tommy, and all our family alive, but cleansing Longbourn of them on the morrow! I miss you, Papa, but it is a little easier now with all of my family standing with me,' Elizabeth looked to the heavens as, in a moment of solace, she offered her message to her father.

~~~~~~~/~~~~~~~

Monday, the two and twentieth day of May, was no different than any other day before it for Martha Bennet and her darling daughter, though it was one of the few days Louisa had remained at home. Caroline was whining about the lack of entertainment and the fact no invitation to the upcoming masque had been received from Netherfield Park.

"Mayhap our invitation will be delivered today," Louisa suggested.

"How well that sounds. I am sure some servant dropped our invitation and has just found it," Martha deluded herself. The three ladies sat up when they heard a knock on the front door.

"Mama!" Caroline Bingley jumped up and down with excitement. "I recognise the crest on the first carriage; it is the Duke's!"

"Sit, Caroline; you must appear ladylike when the Duke comes to solicit your hand for two or three sets," Martha fussed to straighten her daughter's skirts. Louisa shook her head at the delusion they both lived in.

"Mr. Harold Hurst, private secretary to the Duke of Derbyshire, Earl of Lambton," Hill announced.

Mr. Hurst entered the drawing room bowing as the ladies curtsied, and he shot his betrothed a quick smile. "His Grace requests an audience with the Bennet and Bingley ladies," Hurst intoned.

"His Grace, and any he cares to bring, are welcome at any time," Martha preened.

Mr. Hurst turned and nodded to the door. The Duke, Lady Georgiana, the Earl and Countess of Holder, Viscount Glenmeade, Tommy Bennet, and Sir William entered the drawing room. Caroline shifted over, hoping the Duke would take the hint and sit next to her, but he sat as far from her as possible.

"Would you introduce your friends, Your Grace?" Martha asked, demonstrating for all her lack of knowledge of protocol.

"You know, Jane, given the number of times I informed those two about protocol, you would have thought they had learnt something," Elizabeth said as she and Jane sauntered into the drawing room arm in arm.

Mrs. Bennet and her terrible daughter were in absolute shock and horror as Elizabeth and Jane entered the room. Both had contorted faces as they shook their heads not believing their own eyes. On reopening their eyes, to their chagrin, the two sisters were very much alive and standing looking at them with pure disdain.

"*WE KILLED YOU!*" Caroline Bingley screeched.

"Do I look dead to you, Jane, William, Gigi, family?" Elizabeth asked mockingly, as she looked from one to the other.

"Y-you are dead!" Martha spluttered as she looked at Jane, her eyes as huge as saucers.

"Lizzy, did you hear what that woman said? I, too, am supposedly dead." Jane scoffed at the gaping woman.

"As I refuse to call you a Bennet, Mrs. Bingley, and Miss Caro, do you know the charge for attempting the murder of a relation of the Queen and royal family?" Elizabeth asked, evenly.

"You, a relation to the Queen? You are naught but Cinder-Liza, the one who often gets cinders and soot on her face from reading in front of the fire!" Caroline tried to stand, in an attempt to get to Elizabeth, but an enormous hand pulled her back into her chair, and none too gently. Biggs and Johns had taken up positions, one behind each lady.

"Did I omit to mention to you, my *dear* stepsister, my connection to the Duke? You see, my cousin, *Lady* Marie Fitzwilliam, née Bennet, is married to Viscount Hilldale, who just so happens to be the Duke's cousin, so that makes me cousin to his Grace, and, by extension, his cousins, the royals."

"What of Louisa; she helped us that night," Martha was clutching for any straw she could think of.

"You mean my sister, Louisa *Bennet*, who saved my life that night? She played along so she would be left with me and got help as soon as she could. You may wonder who these other people are." Elizabeth watched as the two women who were now whiter than a sheet looked at those unknown to them. "We may not have mentioned that my late father's cousin is the Earl of Holder, Lord James Bennet, and his wife the Countess, Lady Amelia Bennet. Their son and heir, Viscount Glenmeade, happens to be Jane's husband. Sir William you know, and the young lady and my future sister is Lady Georgiana Darcy."

"You are betrothed to my Duke!" Caroline screeched, vainly struggling against the hand holding her in her seat.

"Are you really that delusional, Miss Bingley?" the Duke drawled. "The one time you tried to talk to me, I cut you. If you were the last lady alive, I would not offer for you. You disgusted me a long time before you attacked my betrothed. It is but her desire to see you thrown out of her home in person that stayed my hand from having you hung the day after your despicable attack on her person. You have lived in for far too long, but that all ends today!"

"And this tall, strapping fellow is the one you have asked after so many times." Martha and Caroline looked at Tommy, not knowing who he was, but not failing to note he looked eerily like the late master of Longbourn. "My *brother*, Thomas Bennet Junior, the heir of Longbourn!"

Martha was stupefied as blow after blow kept punching the air out of her lungs. All her bad decisions seemed to be coalescing around her this day. "I may have advocated for transportation had you showed even an iota of remorse for what you did to my betrothed, but the only thing I see is regret that you have been caught!" the Duke told the two with disdain.

"Louisa, how could you do this to us?" Martha screeched.

"As you believe, and have said many times, I am only here for the food. I have done *nothing* to you, madam. It is by your actions and those of your disgusting daughter that have led to your well-deserved consequences. Not that it is any of your business, but I will be Mrs. Harold Hurst before the masque!" Try as she might, Louisa could not summon any sympathy for the two. She knew, had she asked it, Elizabeth would have had them transported; however, the last remaining bonds between her and the woman who bore her were irrevocably torn asunder the night they had attacked and kicked her sister on the filthy floor of the hunting lodge.

"We are done here, Sir William. Please have your men remove this rubbish from our house," Elizabeth stated dispassionately.

Four constables entered the drawing room at Sir William's nod. A pair lifted one of either Martha or her daughter by the arms and carried them out as they screeched invectives at anyone they could see. The last words they heard from Caroline Bingley was something about Cinder-Liza, but then, thankfully, there was quiet in the house.

Mr. Philips waited in the hallways until the two criminals were arrested. "Now that Lord Holder is returned, he becomes Miss Elizabeth's guardian until she marries, and Tommy becomes his ward until he reaches his majority. Additionally, the Earl will manage Longbourn for Tommy until that time," Philips explained after a question from the Earl.

"I do not know if we will find anyone to manage Longbourn as effectively as Lizzy has since my cousin passed, but I believe we will look for a steward," Lord James stated.

"There are one or two under-stewards at Pemberley who would more than fit your requirements, Holder," William offered.

"If memory serves, Andrew told me we have a good candidate who is under-steward at Holder Heights. I think Tommy and I should interview all three and then make a decision," Lord James stated.

"Papa would have loved to be here this day, when the interlopers were dragged out of Longbourn," Tommy said, as he looked to the heavens.

"I am sure Mama and Papa are looking down on us with love and pride," Elizabeth told her brother.

"Lizzy is correct, Tommy; Mama and Papa had a love for the ages. I too am sure they are together again looking over us. If, since the start, Mama and then Papa were not watching over us, do you think we would have survived the shipwreck and the years languishing on *New England*?" Jane asked.

"I suppose not," Tommy replied, thoughtfully.

Before they departed a much more peaceful Longbourn, Jane, Elizabeth, and Tommy spoke to the Hills and requested they have the house cleansed of any remnants of the Bingley presence, and ready it for a small wedding breakfast on the morrow, and so they would be able to sleep at Longbourn the night before Elizabeth's wedding. The Hills gave their word that the house would be ready by that time.

Everyone returned to Netherfield Park to inform those who had remained behind of the outcome of the arrest and removal of the vermin. After the exit of the two evil woman, Elizabeth was never called Cinder-Liza again.

CHAPTER 18

When Charles Bingley heard of his mother and sister Caroline in the Tower awaiting execution, he would have liked to have expressed surprise, but he could not. It was sad his relatives had come to this end, as it would have been with any human being; however, after reading Louisa's letter he could only agree that his mother and Caroline had done despicable things and had earned their prescribed punishment.

He had never imagined them capable of attempted murder, but he supposed years of coveting that which they would never have, materially or socially, and the frustration of never being able to attain it, had poured out in the disgusting attack on his stepsister.

Bingley was pleasantly surprised that he was invited to Louisa's wedding, and, furthermore, that he would be the one giving her away to her new husband. He read the reports in *The Times of London,* which had been repeated in every broadsheet in the Kingdom, of the recovery of Jane Bennet, now a viscountess, and her family connections. He had believed there was no chance he would be invited to a wedding where she, her sister, or her brother would be present.

From what Louisa told him, the family had been impressed by his desire to change his life, and the Viscountess was willing to hear him if he felt he had anything to say to her. Bingley knew, no matter how many years in the past he had committed his offence against Jane Bennet, he would have to apologise fully and without trying to excuse his behaviour in the past.

When he met with Louisa in Meryton, he had made his apologies to her for his behaviour and offences against her when they were growing up. In her magnanimity, she had forgiven him. He had met his future brother-in-law when he helped the Duke, and Hurst had impressed him as an excellent sort of man.

When Bingley arrived in Meryton the night before the wedding, he noticed his reception from the locals was decidedly warmer than it had ever been before. Word must have been disseminated about his change of heart and the way he had assisted the Duke against his obsessed aunt.

Where before he had been shunned, he was welcomed. He was given one of the best rooms at the inn in Meryton and told it had been already paid for by his future brother. He looked forward to meeting Louisa at Longbourn Church on the morrow, the first time he would be allowed to set foot on Bennet lands since his ill-advised attempt to attack the then Miss Bennet. If he needed a reminder of his folly, all he need do was look at the scar of her teeth on his hand, still clearly visible.

~~~~~~~/~~~~~~~

Since Miss Anne de Bourgh had been resident in Hertfordshire, she had become much closer to her aunt, uncle, and cousins. There was no more formality between Anne and any of the group of friends and family residing at Netherfield Park. She had become especially close to Karen Younge and George Wickham.

The three were sitting outdoors one afternoon, the day before the double wedding that would unite Miss Younge with the Major and Louisa with Mr. Hurst. "Are you resolved to return to the Dragoons, Major?" Anne asked, as the three sipped lemonades in the shade of the gazebo.

"I wanted to, but I fear the injury to my arm will leave it permanently too weak to wield a sabre," Wickham lamented.

"It does not please me you were injured, George, but I cannot repine the fact you will no longer be put in harm's way. I would hate to lose you on a battlefield after finding you. It may be selfish to articulate such feelings, but I do not want to lose you," Karen Younge stated, softly.

"Well I know it, Karen. Mayhap it is not too late for me to

seek a career in the law," Wickham surmised.

"There may be yet another option. You learnt a lot from your father when you grew up at Pemberley, did you not, George?" Anne asked.

"I suppose I did," Wickham replied.

"I am aware I will never be able to bear a child, an heir due to my health. I am the last of the de Bourghs, and I find I have an estate to run. My mother cosseted and closeted me, never allowing me to be educated or allowing me to know about my inheritance. At five and twenty years old I am in possession of a large estate and have no idea how to manage it," Anne explained.

"Are you offering me the position of steward? I thought William said the current gentleman in the position is more than competent," Wickham asked.

"No, I am not asking you to be my employee; I am asking you to come live at Rosings Park as the future *master*!" Anne delivered her bombshell.

"Excuse me. Did I hear you correctly?" Wickham asked in a state of shock. "Surely one of your cousins, especially Richard, is far more worthy than I? I am not without the ability to support a wife; I invested my legacy from the late Duke, and it has grown nicely."

"Your question makes you even more worthy, George. I am not making this offer because I think you unable to support your wife. William has more estates than he knows what to do with; if he had ten sons, he would have an estate for each of them. Andrew has Hilldale, and will, one day have Snowhaven and the Matlock estates. Richard has Brookfield as one of Aunt Elaine's brothers passed away without a direct heir and left it to Richard, whose legacy from Uncle Robert has also grown nicely. Like Rosings Park, Richard's estate has a profit of about seven thousand pounds per annum," Anne related. "So you see, I chose you because my other choices all had their own estates," Anne teased.

"We do not know what to say," Karen Younge said, recovering her power of speech.

"There is no need. You have both become my good friends

with no expectation of any sort of reward. I know the state of my health – I will not live to old age. You will be giving me far more than I you," Anne told the couple. "Can you imagine the look on my *dear* mother's face if she hears the next master of Rosings Park will be the son of Pemberley's former steward?" Then Anne smiled as a thought struck her. "She should be happy; there will be a connection between Pemberley and Rosings at last!"

Once Anne announced her intention to the assembled family, there was not a single voice of dissent among them. Many toasts were drunk to the couples who would marry on the morrow.

~~~~~~~/~~~~~~~

During the wedding breakfast after the double wedding, held at Longbourn, Charles Bingley approached the Viscountess Glenmeade gingerly. "Lady Bennet, please allow me to apologise for my inexcusable behaviour to you all those years ago," he pleaded after she had greeted him politely, her husband waiting at her elbow in case he was needed.

"Mr. Bingley, I have it from most reliable sources that you have made genuine and permanent changes to your life. I forgive you whole-heartedly. It helps that Louisa is my sister now. I do not know if I am ready to call you brother—yet. Who knows what the future will hold? I wish you the best of everything in your life. Have a good day, Mr. Bingley." Bingley understood he was being dismissed by the Viscountess, but he had gained her forgiveness.

~~~~~~~/~~~~~~~

"It seems that, in a way, you will be following in your father's footsteps, George," the Duke clapped his friend on the back.

"You are right in a manner of speaking. However, I do not think either of our fathers envisaged me being an estate owner one day!" Wickham smiled. How his life had changed because he decided to take responsibility for his actions when the late Duke took him to task all those years ago! He would never have imagined he, the son of a steward, and his wife—how well that sounded, would one day be master and mistress of a large, thriving estate.

A few days earlier, he and the former Colonel were in London, where both resigned from the army and sold their commissions. As they were barred from returning to combat, it had made the decision palatable. General Atherton was loath to part with two of his best officers but understood their decisions to move on as gentlemen.

~~~~~~~/~~~~~~~

Harold and Louisa Hurst made the rounds of well-wishers at the wedding breakfast. Louisa had never looked prettier; she had not noticed it in herself, but all the walking she had begun once she and Elizabeth became friends had paid off! She had been shocked when her friend had taken her to the modiste, who told her she needed to be measured again because she was so much smaller in the waist.

She had obtained all the things her former mother had craved by doing the exact opposite of what the condemned Mrs. Bingley had advocated for. Louisa felt the same sorrow she would have felt for the loss of any human life, but nothing more than that. Based on the application by the Duke of Derbyshire, which was supported by the Earls of Holder and Matlock, the ecclesiastical court had granted a posthumous annulment to Thomas Bennet so that when the woman met her maker, it would be as Mrs. Bingley; there would be no link to the Bennet name.

But this was not the day to think of such things, Louisa reminded herself as she looked at her husband standing next to her. She, who thought she would never marry due to her size and looks, was loved, respected, and appreciated. She returned those same sentiments to her husband.

As much as Hurst enjoyed working for the Duke he had always dreamed of owning his own estate. A medium-sized estate near Longbourn, Purvis Lodge, had come on the market after the widow Purvis passed. Her heir lived in Ireland, on a remarkably successful horse breeding estate, and had no need for the property or desire to manage one so far from his own. It was a perfect situation for Hurst, an answer to his dream. He had saved and invested most of the money he earned, so he had more than two-thirds of the price being asked for Purvis Lodge readily available. The Duke, circumventing any attempt for Hurst to refuse his gift, paid the remainder of the price and purchased additional land adjoining the estate as a wedding gift. The Hursts changed the name of the estate to Hurst Haven as soon as the deed was presented to them.

"Lulu, you are glowing," Elizabeth said, as she took one of her friend's hands in her own.

"How could I not be, Lizzy? I just married the love of my life!" Louisa gushed. "On a more serious bent, are you sure you want me and not Jane or one of your other cousins, or Gigi to stand with you?"

"It has to be you, Lulu! You were my light at the darkest time in my life. If it were not for you, I may have accepted I deserved no more than to be called Cinder-Liza, and then who knows what would have been had they broken my spirit? No, Lulu, you are the one to stand with me, and believe me when I say, Jane agrees fully. Please do not question it again!" Elizabeth assured her sister and friend.

"I suppose you do owe me," Louisa teased with a smile, "Harold and I are delaying our wedding trip to attend your ball and wedding, after all!"

"That you are, sister of mine, that you are," Elizabeth agreed, gratefully.

As both newlywed couples would attend the masque and the subsequent wedding, the Wickhams would spend their first few nights as man and wife in Netherfield Park's dower house, while the Hursts would spend their first nights at Hurst Haven.

Once both couples had spent an acceptable amount of time at the wedding breakfast, they departed for their respective destinations, and were not seen again until the night of the masque.

~~~~~~~/~~~~~~~

The three children of Thomas and Fanny Bennet looked

around the manor house with pleasure. All the items Elizabeth had been forced to remove in order to protect them were restored to their rightful places. Most pleasing of all was seeing the book room restored to its former state. The three swore they could feel their father's presence there. Orion became Tommy's horse, as Elizabeth would have the choice of available horses at Pemberley once they journeyed home after the wedding.

~~~~~~~/~~~~~~~

For the masque, Elizabeth took her mother's dress to the dressmaker in Meryton and requested she make wings and a mask to match the gorgeous gown. The creative seamstress used the same light blue gossamer as the dress's overlay with blue stones sewn in. The wings would be secured by a loop to either side and threaded through almost-invisible slits added to the back of the dress near the sleeves; the fabric would loop under Elizabeth's arms and over her shoulders. The mask itself was fashioned to match the dress.

The local economy was booming, thanks to the flurry of activity at Longbourn and Netherfield. The newly returned Bennets had acquired but a few clothes in Nassau, so they had much to buy. The local tailor and dressmaker hired temporarily help to cope with their orders, though a lot more purchases would be made in London, where the family would be for the month of June before heading to Holder Heights and Glenmeade.

As the ladies sat in the tearoom in Meryton, they were approached repeatedly by residents wishing to see their Jane again and to commiserate with Elizabeth Bennet, as the perfidy of the Bingley women was now widely known. Louisa, who was made known as a Bennet sister prior to her wedding, was not tarred with the same brush as Mrs. Bingley and her daughter.

"To be sitting with all of you here in Meryton is a dream come true. I would not, could not, allow myself to believe you were never coming back," Elizabeth told the rest of the Bennet women.

"We never gave up hope of seeing you again, Lizzy," Aunt Amy replied. "If only we had been saved before your father allowed despair to consume him."

"As much as I love my late Papa, he was self-indulgent at the end. We all make choices; mine was to believe in hope, but he chose a different path. I wish he were here to see us all together, especially Tommy assuming his rightful place as the heir of Longbourn. I have to believe he and Mama are with us in here," Elizabeth placed her hand over her heart, "and always will be."

"Lizzy, is it true that the first time you saw William, you pelted him with an apple?" Allie asked.

"She did," Georgiana giggled. "William says that was the day he started to fall in love with her."

"Only my Lizzy," Jane shook her head as she smiled and patted her sister on her hand.

"Have you started to read my letters, Jane?" Elizabeth asked, quietly.

"I started with the first one and am working my way forward chronologically. There are well over a hundred, so it will take me some time, but I will read them all. They are a good window into your lives while we were stranded on *New England*," Jane explained her intent and belief.

"It was part of my affirmation you were all alive," Elizabeth owned. "I do miss Lulu as she has been with me daily for years, but I have a feeling she is not missing any of us!"

"Cassie," Allie turned to her next oldest sister, "you seem to be spending a lot of time talking to Richard."

"You know I have an interest in the war," Cassie hedged as she blushed furiously. "Allie, stop teasing me!" Cassie swatted playfully at her younger sister.

The ladies finished their tea and cakes and boarded coaches to return to Netherfield Park. Since they were betrothed, William and Elizabeth should not have been residing in the same house, but it was decided that, with the number of chaperones and the imminent wedding there was no point in making changes.

~~~~~~~/~~~~~~~

The night of the masque, Netherfield was ablaze with the

light of thousands of candles, while the drive was lit with torches. "Lulu! Harold! It is so good to see you two. How go things at Hurst Haven? Or have you been too busy to notice?" Elizabeth arched her eyebrow.

"Lizzy, you are incorrigible! We have been enjoying our new home, thank you very much," Louisa replied with a huge smile. "My goodness, Lizzy! How well you look in your mother's dress. Are you wearing the glass slippers?"

Elizabeth lifted her hem slightly to show her sister the slippers on her dainty feet. "Louisa has the right of it—you look like a fairy princess with those wings, Lizzy," Jane told her from her other side.

"I must admit, I am excited to dance with William tonight. It will be the first time we have danced since we were betrothed. I had the pleasure only once, at the assembly he attended right after we discovered the connection between us," Elizabeth stated, dreamily.

"Do not forget, my Elizabeth, you have promised me the first, supper, and final sets," the deep baritone voice she loved said from behind her.

"Forget about the pleasure of dancing with you, William? I would sooner call my former stepmother a wit!" Elizabeth turned and smiled as she saw her betrothed's waistcoat matched the colour of her dress.

William had always thought his betrothed a beauty, but the vision he saw before him this night exceeded all his expectations. He counted himself as the luckiest of men to have been accepted by the phenomenal woman who stood before him, with her impertinent and challenging look of expectation.

~~~~~~~/~~~~~~~

It was not the time to speak of it, but Mrs. de Bourgh, formerly known as Lady Catherine, and her henchman had paid the ultimate price at the end of a rope, two days ago. The day before the executioner at the Tower had earned his money by beheading the two Bingley women. The Duke had been told, right up until they had knelt at the block, the delusional women held to the belief *their* duke would come and save them. It had been the last thing they had thought of in this world.

~~~~~~~/~~~~~~~

The receiving line formed. It consisted of the Earl and Countess of Holder, Viscount and Viscountess Glenmeade, Elizabeth Bennet, and His Grace Lord William Darcy at the head of the line, for it had been decided the ball would celebrate the betrothal as well as the recovery of the Bennets.

Once all the guests had arrived and the receiving line disbanded, William and Elizabeth took their place at the top of the line forming for the first set. They were followed by Jane and Jamie, the Holders, the Matlocks, Marie and Andrew, Cassie and Richard, Georgiana and Phillip, and Allie and Tommy. Georgiana was allowed to dance with family only. Given how many men who counted as family were present, Georgiana would dance practically every set.

Bingley, who had been at his sister's wedding and the subsequent breakfast, had been invited to the masque; surprising everyone, he danced the first set with Charlotte Lucas. It seemed that out of general notice, Charles Bingley and Charlotte Lucas had spent time together while he was helping the Duke and since his return for his sister's wedding.

Phillip had requested and was granted the supper set with Georgiana, but both of her guardians agreed as she was not out yet, she would not dance more than two with any one person. The decision to grant two had been cogitated on by both before agreeing.

Richard Fitzwilliam had been much pleased to have been granted the three major sets by Lady Cassandra Bennet. He planned to seek an audience with her after his cousin's wedding to request a formal courtship. His heart was well on its way to being lost to the middle Holder-Bennet daughter, and unless he was mistaken, it was the same for the lady as well.

Allie was almost three years older than Tommy, but they had become extremely close while on *New England*. They had always been close as cousins, but the last few months, unbeknownst to any of the rest of the family, their feelings had changed from familial to romantic. They had discussed the fact Tommy would begin Cambridge in September, and there could be no declaration until he reached his majority and completed his studies. They both agreed anything worth having, was worth waiting for.

Karen and George Wickham, who could not have looked happier, danced as many sets together as propriety would allow. Their love seemed to deepen with each day they spent together. After the wedding, William had given them use of Seaview Cottage near Brighton for their honeymoon, as William was taking Elizabeth to Ireland and the two estates owned by the Darcys on the Emerald Isle.

As they danced the first set, Elizabeth looked up at her handsome betrothed. "Come now, William, we cannot go a half hour complete and not talk, what will people say?" Elizabeth asked mischievously.

"I am at your disposal my love; name a subject and I will pontificate on it," William returned, with a dimple-revealing smile.

"I will never repine accepting my uncle's suggestion to remove the vermin before the ball. It is so much more pleasant this way," Elizabeth opined.

"You will hear no argument from me on that, Elizabeth," William replied.

The rest of the dance passed in companionable silence. Before they knew it, they had danced the supper set. Once everyone was seated with their food, the Earl of Holder stood and made the official announcement of the marriage of his son Jamie to the former Miss Jane Bennet. He then announced, for the few who were not aware of the fact, his ward Elizabeth Bennet had accepted the proposal of the Duke of Derbyshire, Earl of Lambton some weeks ago, and they would marry two days hence. After the cheers died down, everyone returned to their meal, and the rest of the ball passed as would be expected.

Both couples accepted many wishes for their future felicity

from their long-time neighbours.

CHAPTER 19

T he night before the wedding, Elizabeth was in her bedchamber at Longbourn once more. It was the first time back in her room since the late Martha Bingley had moved her to the one above, next to Louisa. She felt the presence of her mother and father in the walls of the house, as if their love had infused itself into its very structure.

Unlike most who had one person to talk to them the night before her wedding, Elizabeth had four: Aunt Amy, Jane, Aunt Maddie, and Marie. First, the aunts sat with her on her bed and assured her as she was entering into a love match, marital relations would be a pleasure, not a chore, as some characterised them. They gave her the practical facts about how it might hurt somewhat when her maidenly barrier was breached the first time she joined with her husband. They warned her there might be some blood, but it was quite natural and nothing to be concerned over, and it would only be that first time.

Elizabeth was assured mutual pleasure was to be desired rather than to be eschewed. Both aunts advised her not to be shy in telling William what she found pleasurable, and to ask the same of him. When Elizabeth asked about marital relations when she was with child, she was informed her body would tell her when it was no longer able to accommodate her husband. Also, they made sure she understood it was nothing but a myth some propagated about marital relations somehow harming the babe in the mother's belly, and once a woman was with child, she should refuse her husband entry to her bedchamber.

When Elizabeth told her aunts she felt like a wanton at times as her desire for William grew and it would have been easy to give into her passion, while assuring them she had not, her aunts made sure she understood relations between married, consenting adults were never wrong in private. By the time the aunts completed their talk, the apprehension Elizabeth felt had vanished.

Once the aunts kissed Elizabeth's cheeks, they were replaced by Marie and Jane, who reinforced what the aunts had said. "What of it not being acceptable to share a bed?" Elizabeth blushed. "Is it not frowned upon by polite society?"

"Lizzy, since when have you allowed the mores of others to dictate to you? Jamey and I have not spent a night apart since our wedding night, and, other than during my confinement, we do not *ever* intend to!" Jane told her sister emphatically.

"It is the same with Andrew and me, especially on the long and cold winter nights. Sleeping with your husband in the bed is worth more than all the warming pans in the Kingdom! Marie looked Elizabeth and Jane and said, "When you enter your final confinement, the midwife will try to chase William and Jamey out of the birthing chamber. Do not allow it if you and your husbands wish to remain together for the birth! Andrew was by my side for the birth of both of our children—and I would have it no other way. His support was worth more than his weight in gold!"

"It seems those of us in this family do not follow the dictates of the *Ton*, for I know you feed your babe yourself, Marie, though I know you have a wet nurse. Does she ever work?" Elizabeth asked.

"Uncle Thomas, may he rest in peace, was accurate in his assessment of the members of polite society. They make arbitrary rules, yet the behaviour of so many supposed paragons of society is disgusting. They are excused because of their wealth and rank. So, I do nurse my child, and I suggest both of you follow your own paths; decide what works for *your* family. Excuse me for saying this, but the *Ton* be damned!" Marie stated. "The wetnurse feeds little Amy at night or if I am unavailable, that way I am able to sleep a full night unhindered."

"Mother Amy told me she felt a bonding with you and your siblings when she fed you as babes," Jane stated.

"My mother is correct; I felt the same way with my son and now my daughter, and I will continue to do so with any future children we are blessed with," Marie agreed.

"William and I have discussed it, and we agree with you on both issues, sleeping arrangements and my feeding our future children, if I am able to. Once we are married, I never want to be parted from him." Elizabeth blushed a little as she prepared to ask a question. "The aunts told me never to be shy to tell William what pleases me and ask him the same for himself, is it how you learned what yours prefer?"

"Absolutely, yes," Marie replied, and Jane nodded her head vigorously.

"In that case, I believe all of my questions have been answered. I thank you both." Marie gave her sisters-in-law a hug each and then departed for Netherfield Park, while Jane and Jamey were to spend the night at Longbourn with Tommy, the Gardiners, and Elizabeth.

The sisters talked about anything and everything until well after midnight, claiming many missed hugs during their conversation until Elizabeth fell asleep at close to one in the morning.

~~~~~~~~/~~~~~~~~

While Elizabeth was talking to the ladies at Longbourn, the Duke was sitting with his relatives, and those soon to be so, in the billiards room. They had played some games, but now was the time to relax. At almost eighteen, Phillip was with the men, and had a snifter of brandy in his hand as they did. Richard, Andrew, and the Earls were more restrained in their ribbing of the groom, due to the young man's presence.

"Do you regret you are as inexperienced as your bride, William?" Uncle Reggie asked quietly, as they sat in a corner away from the others.

"I do not, Uncle Reggie. The attitude that a lady is to be as pure as the driven snow, while we men are lauded for our prowess and conquests is one of the many hypocrisies I soundly reject. Anyone who looks at my Elizabeth and still calls women the weaker sex is, in my opinion, fit only for Bedlam. If I expect her to be pure on our wedding night, should she not rightfully be able to expect the same of me?" William stated, and he meant it.

"There is truth in your words, Nephew. I suppose you will learn together," the Earl opined.

"I may be a duke, but I am still a farmer, and she grew up on a farm as well, so I believe we will both bring a knowledge of the mechanics with us. Luckily, we are both voracious readers who like to study subjects of interest," William grinned.

"She is your perfect match, you know," the Earl noted, as he looked off into the distance. "Both my sister Anne and brother Robert would have loved her, William. It is sad that between you two there are no parents left to see you marry on the morrow. You know Elaine and I think of you and Gigi more as son and daughter than nephew and niece, do you not?" Lord Matlock put his hand on his nephew's shoulder, his voice gruff with emotion.

"We both love you as surrogate parents, and we always will," William returned.

"Enough chit-chat you two; I would like to beat William at billiards for once," Richard said.

"At least you have the excuse of your limp now when William beats you," Andrew clapped his younger brother on the back. The men retired two hours later, although the Duke did not fall asleep for an hour or so after he retired, unable to check his grin while thinking it was his last night to sleep alone.

~~~~~~~/~~~~~~~

While the men were entertaining themselves, and once Lady Amy returned from Longbourn, the two Countesses, Cassie, Allie, Georgiana, and Anne were upstairs in the family sitting room entertaining Parrot, as he was with Phillip this week. He had become a favourite with all of them—his sometimes-colourful language aside. Parrot was also a favourite of the children of the neighbourhood, so everyone had been working hard to teach him other words and phrases so he would not be as apt to squawk out what the crewmen who were stranded with the family taught him.

"Amy," Lady Elaine called her friend's attention to herself, "it was most generous of James to pay the back wages of all three crewmen who were castaway with you, even that Sparrow fellow who perished. From what I heard; he paid each family many times what the men's actual wages would have been."

"It was the least he could do. With their skills, all three were integral to our survival. With their men presumed dead, the wives and children had a hard time of it. All three families will be housed in cottages at Holder Heights, and there will be employment for any who require it. The two men already have positions, as does Mrs. Sparrow, who is a seamstress."

"You cannot believe how my niece has blossomed since Elizabeth has been in her life," Lady Elaine changed the subject, looking at Gigi, who was sitting across the room from her with the younger ladies.

"Lizzy has always been able to draw others into conversation, regardless of how shy they might be. She is still so unassuming; it is not becoming a duchess she is excited about, rather, it is becoming William's wife. I am glad both Jane and Elizabeth will be close to one another, and to Holder Heights. Tommy will be with us when he is on break from Cambridge so they will be able to be in company with one another often," Lady Amy stated.

"With Snowhaven close to all the family estates, and Hilldale but five miles from your estate, Jane and Jamey are the most distant, but they are but four hours away by carriage. We are not much farther, but you and James are less than an hour from those sweet grandchildren of ours. As you missed the first years of little Jamey's life and your namesake's birth, it is only right for you to reside much closer to them," Lady Elaine said, as she squeezed her friend and fellow grandmother's hand.

Georgiana and Cassie were trading questions about Phillip and Richard, respectively. Georgiana was aware she had several years to wait, and that was *if* Phillip remained interested in her, but, for Cassie, time was not a concern. Even though Allie was older, she and Gigi had become remarkably close, both gratified that, after the wedding on the morrow, they would be considered sisters-in-law.

The younger two girls put Parrot in his night-time abode, a big cage, which they covered, and then they followed the rest to bed.

~~~~~~~/~~~~~~~

The morning of her wedding, Elizabeth was awake before dawn broke in the east. She walked out to the stables with two apples, one for Nellie and one for Orion; both chomped theirs gratefully.

"I am sorry I neglected you, boy. What happened to Papa was not your fault, so there was no reason for me not to ride you." The stallion nuzzled her, almost as if he understood her words, after he enjoyed his apple. "Tommy will take good care of you, I promise." Elizabeth rubbed his neck and then walked around the back of the house to the park.

She sat herself on the bench under the big oak tree, the same one all five of them would sit on, their young Tommy on mother's lap, Elizabeth on father's and Jane seated between them. "How I miss you, Mama and Papa," Elizabeth raised her eyes to the heavens as the sun peeked over the horizon, casting haloes behind the clouds. "I wish you could have met my William. He is the best of men, and we will have a love like you had, one for the ages.

"As much as I wanted you to walk me up the aisle, Papa, Tommy will stand in your stead today. He looks just like your portrait painted when you were at Cambridge." Elizabeth paused as a little breeze wafted around her, as if her parents were letting her know they were there with her, and suddenly she felt completely at peace. "I will always love you, Mama and Papa," Elizabeth told the heavens as she stood and made her way back to the house, where Jane and Aunt Maddie were waiting for her.

~~~~~~~/~~~~~~~

Lord William Darcy, Duke of Derbyshire, Earl of Lambton, also woke with the dawn. Like Elizabeth, he too was without his parents, their mothers having passed within twelve months of each other. His father had been gone longer than Thomas Bennet, but it did not make his longing for his parents any less on this most special of days.

The Duke was relieved that few members of the *Ton* had been invited. An invitation had been sent, as a matter of protocol, to the royals, who had wished the couple joy, but declined the invitation. The Queen had requested for him and his Duchess to inform her lady in waiting when they were in Town so she could invite them to tea. Elizabeth would have to be presented. Jane had been, but given what happened, frivolous things like presentations were not a priority for the remainder of the Bennet family.

From the description sketched of Elizabeth's father—first by Elizabeth and then by her siblings and the Holder Bennets—the Duke was sure he would have enjoyed Mr. Bennet's company greatly. He lamented the fact he had never met the man who had fathered three honourable children and was a fellow bibliophile to boot.

When he looked ahead, he envisioned a joy-filled life with Elizabeth at his side. Life would never be boring with her. He was sure they would argue—after all, they were both strong-willed people—but he also knew the strength of their love would overcome any problems which might present themselves in the future.

After his soak in a steaming bath, Carstens shaved him and assisted his master to dress. Following some advice from his uncle and uncle-to-be, William had a tray before his bath to make sure he had something to eat and drink as he knew his Elizabeth had, or would have, at Longbourn before her bath. He was thankful the reaction to the vision he had of her naked in her bath subsided before he stepped out of the bath into the towel his valet held up for him.

By the time William joined the group downstairs, the Holder Bennets had already departed to Longbourn. Richard was to stand with him, while Andrew and Wickham would be groomsmen.

~~~~~~~/~~~~~~~

"Lizzy, you are a vision," Cassie told her cousin once she had joined them in the entrance hall at Longbourn. Her dress was simple, a cream-colored flowing gown with an empire waist, puffed sleeves and long cream gloves to match. There was a train, but it was a short one.

"That is an understatement, Cassie!" a glowing Louisa Hurst stated as she looked at her sister. "My goodness, Lizzy, your William will want to carry you off from the vestry and skip the wedding breakfast when he sees you."

"Our sister does look gorgeous, does she not," Jane beamed. It was the one time she would not collect a hug—well, at least not before the ceremony.

"My Lulu, you are looking happy. I take it married life, or at least some aspects of it, are treating you well?" Elizabeth arched her eyebrow at her best friend and sister.

"Lizzy! Just wait until I see you after *you* have been married a few days!" Louisa threatened playfully.

"As we will be on our way to Ireland, I will be safe," Elizabeth retorted, smugly.

"I think it is time, Lizzy," Tommy informed her, and his sister started, not yet used to his deep bass voice.

Everyone departed to make the short walk to the church, leaving Elizabeth with Tommy, Louisa, Jane, and Marie. With the Hills looking on, and not a few tears escaping the long-time housekeeper's eyes, the bride and her attendants were escorted by Tommy to Longbourn's church a few minutes after the rest.

~~~~~~~/~~~~~~~

William, Richard, Andrew, and Wickham all noted the entrance of the Holder Bennets. Richard's eyes tracked Cassie as she walked up the aisle with her family and took her place in the Bennet pews.

It was Andrew's turn to stare next as his wife walked up the aisle looking even more beautiful to him than the day they had married. Jane followed her, and her husband's eyes followed her intently as she glided up the aisle.

There was a slight pause, and Hurst was bursting with pride as his wife followed the bridesmaids and stood opposite the former Colonel near the altar. There was a hush as the vestibule doors were closed and the vicar signalled his congregation to stand; then the doors opened again.

William was transfixed as his beloved Elizabeth approached him, on her brother's arm. She could have been wearing even a sackcloth, and she would not have looked any less beautiful to him. He noted that she reached toward Charlotte Lucas, who was sitting next to none other than Charles Bingley, and Charlotte held her hand out for her sister of the heart, Eliza, to squeeze, as the bride and Tommy proceeded forward.

The groom was so entranced, it took more than a gentle nudge from his cousin to propel him forward so he could claim his soulmate from her brother. Tommy lifted the sheer gossamer veil, kissed his sister's cheek, and, after gently lowering it, he placed her hand on William's arm. Both bride and groom felt the tension leave their bodies as they relaxed at the physical contact.

It seemed like an eternity as they approached the waiting vicar, but in reality, it was a matter of less than a minute. He gave the signal for the congregants to be seated, and as they complied, he opened his copy of *The Book of Common Prayer*. "Dearly beloved…"

Before they knew it, they had recited their vows and had both given, and received, rings. The vicar intoned the final benediction, and then presented Their Graces, Lord William and Lady Elizabeth Darcy, to the cheering congregation. The newlyweds were escorted to the vestry accompanied by Richard and Louisa, where the last thing they had to do to be legally wed, had been completed—all four of them signed the registry. Louisa and Richard then slipped out to give the bride and groom a private moment.

"Alone at last, my dearest, loveliest Elizabeth," William said, his voice filled with desire as he pulled her to him with purpose. Her arms snaked around his neck, as she was as keen as he to seal their wedding with a kiss.

During the wedding preparations, they had had hardly enough time to steal more than a few chaste kisses, with so many around them at all times, so when he captured her lips hungrily, she was just as needy as he. Elizabeth had read of a toe-curling kiss in a novel somewhere, but these kisses not only curled her toes, but also made her weak at the knees. Luckily, with her husband's arms around her waist, and hers around his neck, she was held in place so she could enjoy the feel of his desire for her, which matched hers for him.

After a few minutes, knowing their families were awaiting them in the church, they reluctantly separated, with the promise of more to come later.

CHAPTER 20

Jane and Jamey waited for Elizabeth and William outside Netherfield's ballroom. Mr. Hill stood ready to open the doors with Mr. Nichols stepping aside so the former Bennet girls and their husbands could be announced by Longbourn's long-serving retainer. At a nod from the Duke, the doors were opened wide, and all turned toward them.

"My Lords, ladies, and gentleman, their Graces Lord William and Lady Elizabeth Darcy, Duke and Duchess of Derbyshire, Earl and Countess of Lambton. James Bennet Junior and Jane Bennet, Viscount and Viscountess Glenmeade." Mr. Hill proudly stepped aside. Mrs. Hill was standing just outside the doors with her husband, and each former resident of Longbourn squeezed her hand as they passed her.

A loud cheer went up from the assembled guests as the two couples entered the ballroom. Although the cheer was mainly to celebrate the two couples, there were not a few Meryton residents who put some extra effort into their cheering so as to celebrate the permanent removal of a certain two hated women. So happy were the people of the area that these women were not in the neighbourhood any longer that no one allowed the names of the two criminals to pass their lips.

Departing in opposite directions, the couples made their rounds of the guests. No matter how many times the neighbours heard the story of their survival, they were always hungry to hear it again, in case there was even a single detail they had missed on prior retellings. Those who asked were indulged by Jane and Jamey without impatience, for it was a story worth retelling.

When the Viscount and Viscountess reached Charlotte, she

was on the arm of Charles Bingley. It had taken some getting used to by both the Bennets and many in the neighbourhood, but as it became evident the changes the pastor had made were both genuine and permanent, the number of those against him had dwindled to a few watching him with a gimlet eye, though it was about making sure Charlotte was happy, not about his past sins.

"If that coy smile is anything to go by, you have some news to share, do you not, Charlotte?" Jane asked, her head cocked to one side in question.

"We were going to wait until the morrow to say anything, but as you have asked, Charles requested a formal courtship and I consented, and my parents gave their blessing," Charlotte smiled widely.

"I am very happy for you, Charlotte," Jane told her, as she leaned in to hug her friend.

Jamey shook Bingley's hand and leaned forward so only Bingley could hear him. "Charlotte is a best friend to my wife and my sister Elizabeth; do I need to point out what will occur should you ever hurt her?" Jamey asked, quietly.

"My purpose in life will be to make sure that Charlotte never repines accepting me, if she does when the time comes," Bingley averred sincerely. Jamey nodded once at Bingley, then the couple continued with their rounds to greet and thank their guests for helping celebrate their marriage. The two couples met their family members, who were seated near where the musicians would normally be for a ball.

"I hope this is a *little* better than your first wedding breakfast, Jane," Elizabeth teased her older sister.

"The best part about it is there is no fish!" Jane exclaimed. She, as well as the rest of the former castaways, had steadfastly stuck to the decision of give fish a break. Some, like Jane, said forever, and certainly it was for at least a long while.

"I take it you will not want to join us when we go fishing at Pemberley, Jane?" Uncle Edward teased his niece.

"Edward!" Madeline admonished.

The newlyweds sat with Jane and Jamey as both couples had some repast and quenched their thirsts. After they felt refreshed, the couples walked in opposite directions, as they had when they started to greet the guests. An hour later, no guests had been missed, and the couples were able to relax with their families.

Elizabeth arched her eyebrow when she and her husband arrived where Charlotte and the rest of the Lucases were seated. After greeting and accepting good wishes from the rest of Charlotte's family, Elizabeth cocked her head toward Charles Bingley.

"I know you have made a change for the positive, Mr. Bingley, but if you ever hurt my friend, a sister of my heart, I will not rest until you are dealt with," Elizabeth told Bingley quietly as they stood a little apart from the rest of the Lucases.

"I will tell you the same thing I told your brother the Viscount, Your Grace. If Charlotte accepts me, it will be my life's work to make her happy," Bingley related, sincerely.

"I hope so. Talk is cheap; we will see by your actions. Charlotte looks happy and she is a good judge of character, so I will give you the benefit of the doubt," Elizabeth allowed. Bingley inclined his head to the new Duchess.

After talking to Sir William and Lady Lucas for a few minutes and extending them an invitation to Pemberley, the newlyweds continued their walk around the second half of the room.

"When will you depart for Holder Heights?" William asked Lord James when he sat down after completing his duties to their guests.

"Three men arrive on the morrow for us to interview them for the position of Longbourn's steward, so I believe we will depart Meryton for London within a sennight. We will be in Town for up to a month and then depart for Staffordshire. I am in anticipation of seeing our estate again," Lord James clapped his son-in-law Andrew on the back, "and I owe this young man an enormous debt of gratitude."

"It was my pleasure to look after your interests for you,

Holder. You would have done the same for me," Andrew averred humbly.

"It is time, William. I am going to change for travel," Elizabeth told her husband as she stood, and Jane and Louisa accompanied her, to assist if needed.

~~~~~~~/~~~~~~~

"It is hard to say goodbye to you after just getting you back, Janey," Elizabeth told her sister as she hugged her tightly in the front of the house while the last of her luggage was loaded.

"We will meet again in about six weeks, Lizzy, and Glenmeade is near the Derbyshire and Leicestershire border, which is little more than four hours from William's—your—estate, I am told. I promise we will try to make sure to see each other at least once a week! This is as much a new adventure for me as for you. We both remember Holder Heights, but we never saw Glenmeade before, so it will be another first. Now go, Lizzy," Jane told her sister, sending her back to her husband after a kiss on the cheek.

As she did with Jane, Elizabeth spent time with Tommy, who took pleasure in calling his sister *Your Grace*. She also spent time with each of the cousins—sisters and brothers now— with whom she had so recently been reunited. After hugging and wishing everyone else goodbye, her Aunt Amy and Uncle James were the last two she hugged and kissed.

Tommy was the last to shake his new brother's hand. "I could give you the 'never hurt her speech' but I know it is not needed, William." Tommy jested. "Lizzy could not have asked for a better husband for herself, and brother for Jane and me. Have an enjoyable wedding trip, and hopefully your voyage to and from Ireland will be uneventful." Tommy clapped his new brother on his shoulder.

"And I believe you, Jane, and the rest of the Bennets will be the best of brothers and sisters. Both Gigi and I are happy our family has expanded so greatly," William returned.

With all goodbyes completed, the new Duchess was led into one of the large and extremely comfortable Derbyshire coaches by her Duke. With a rap on the roof with his cane, the driver gave a flick of the reins, the conveyance gave a little jerk, and it started rolling forward, away from Elizabeth's childhood home.

Before the coach had made the turn from Longbourn's drive to the lane beyond, William moved to the forward-facing bench where his wife was seated and drew her on his lap with alacrity. Each time they kissed, Elizbeth felt her heart skip a beat. Some kisses were passionate and when his tongue sought entry into her mouth, which she granted, with pleasure, she was sure her heart skipped two beats or more.

After some time, William pulled back a little. "Elizabeth, as much as I want you, the carriage is not where I envisioned us experiencing our first time joining. Like you, it will be my first time, and I want us to be able to take our time and have pleasure in our bed."

"You are not experienced? I thought men always..." Elizabeth did not need to say the rest.

"For most men, I dare say it is the norm, but not for me..." William explained his philosophy, and when he was done, the respect Elizabeth already felt for her husband had grown exponentially.

In a world where women were no more than chattel, she had found one of the few who saw them as equals, as partners in every way. As much as she had missed her father not walking her up the aisle to William, Elizabeth was mollified by the fact that had he met William, he would have approved of the man, *not* his wealth and rank, just as those were not factors for her. His wealth would have meant nothing if her late father had not thought his daughter would be protected and loved. Her father would never have entrusted her to one less worthy.

She knew beyond a shadow of doubt her mother would have loved William too. Even though Elizabeth had been young when her beloved mother was lost, she still retained many warm memories of the late Fanny Bennet.

William was having similar thoughts of his parents as he

hugged his wife close. She rested her head on his shoulder, and it was not long before he heard a change in her breathing as she fell asleep. As he watched his beloved wife sleep, he wished his parents could have lived to meet this woman he loved so ardently.

William had not known it was possible to love with the depth of feeling he felt for his sleeping wife. He would never regret the day she launched the apple at him; it would be an amusing story to tell their future children and grandchildren. With pleasant thoughts of his new wife in his head, William, too, succumbed to sleep.

~~~~~~~/~~~~~~~

The plan was to sail from London on the morrow. Though it made the trip to Ireland longer, it saved them three or four days travel to Liverpool and allowed for a night in the comfort of Darcy House. In addition to being comfortable for the night rather than at an inn, Elizabeth would be able to see one of their homes in town. She would be able to see Derbyshire House when they returned to London for the season.

Both were still asleep when a footman opened the carriage door at Darcy House and coughed politely. After the footman woke them, he closed the door and waited until his master rapped on it once, before opening it again. It took the couple a minute to wake and put themselves to rights. The Duke stepped out, then turned and handed his Duchess down.

The Killions, the housekeeper and butler at Darcy House, were waiting for the Duke and Duchess on the top step. "Welcome home, Your Graces," the Butler intoned with a deep bow, as the housekeeper curtsied.

"Our butler and housekeeper, Mr. and Mrs. Killion," William told his wife.

The housekeeper smiled broadly. Even the normally stoic Killion's lips curved up when the Duke swept his bride up in his arms and carried her over the threshold. The servants, who were in three lines, waiting to greet their master and new mistress to their home, smiled at the playful display by their normally proper master.

William put his wife down gently, then turned to the servants, "I introduce you to Her Grace, Lady Elizabeth Darcy. From this day forward, your mistress." He grinned down at her, and there was a rousing cheer from the servants.

"It may take me longer than I would prefer to learn all of your names, but that will be my aim in short order. I thank you for taking the time to welcome me and His Grace home on this happiest of days in our lives. Please, carry on," the new Duchess dismissed the servants.

"As you do not have a lady's maid, your Grace, I have assigned Barker to you. She is fully trained in that role. Please let me know if, and when, you would like to interview permanent candidates if she is not your choice while in residence," Mrs. Killion informed her new mistress.

"I am sure she will fill the role well, Mrs. Killion. I will let you know if I need to make a change," the Duchess replied.

"She is waiting for you in your chambers, your Grace," Mrs. Killion returned.

William gave his wife a tour of the public rooms on the entrance level, which included a large ballroom, three dining parlours, two drawing rooms, a music room, and three parlours. Elizabeth was impressed at the understated elegance of the décor and furniture in the rooms they viewed. It seemed from what she saw that her husband was more interested in comfort than show which pleased her no end.

William led Elizabeth up the grand marble staircase to the first floor—the family floor. To the right, the doors to the mistress and master's studies and the library were pointed out before they turned to the left and William led her to three doors.

"The left door leads to my bedchamber; the middle door is to our private sitting room. This door," he pointed to the right-hand door, "is your bedchamber. It was last decorated over thirty years ago. You are free to redecorate it and any other room, in this or any of our other houses." With that, William led his wife into their sitting room.

"So far there is nothing I would care to change, William. I

will not make changes because I am able to, but only if they are needed," Elizabeth stated.

"Enough about décor," William growled as he captured his wife's lips. It seemed as if their hearts were beating together, as kiss followed kiss, and their hands explored the other's body through their clothes. "How much time do you need, Elizabeth?" William asked, his voice gruff with passion.

"Half an hour," she answered, almost lightheaded from the surge of passion she felt. With one more toe-curling kiss, the couple separated and made for their own chambers. The Duke dismissed his valet as soon as he gained his chambers, removing everything except his breeches and lawn shirt, which he untucked.

When Elizabeth entered her chambers, she was met by her new lady's maid. "You must be Barker?" the Duchess enquired, and the maid curtsied in reply. "I would like to change into the yellow nightgown and matching robe."

The nightgown and robe had been a wedding gift from Aunt Maddy. Once she donned it, with her maid's assistance, Elizabeth looked at her image in the full-length mirror. The nightgown was as sheer as could be, revealing all her womanly assets. Seeing herself thus and knowing William would soon be looking at her caused her pulse to race in excitement. Barker held the robe open for her and Elizabeth slipped her arms into it, tying the bow loosely as she dismissed her maid, telling her she would ring when needed.

Only seconds after her requested half-hour, there was a knock on her bedchamber door. When she called "enter," William walked in. She had always thought him handsome, but she was not prepared for how good he looked dressed only in his shirt and breeches.

Her breath hitched and her heart raced after she scanned her handsome husband from head to foot. His shirt was open halfway down his torso, revealing a thin covering of black hair on his muscular chest.

William could not believe the vision that was his wife. She

was clad in a yellow robe over what seemed, from the little of it he could see, a sheer yellow nightgown. He felt his appendage start to become tumescent as he drank in the beauty before him. Wordlessly, he reached his hand out to her; Elizabeth took it without question, and he led her through the sitting room into his bedchamber.

Elizabeth discovered his rooms were exactly as she had imagined them, very masculine and tastefully decorated. His bed was the most enormous one she had ever beheld. As William stood transfixed, she untied her robe and dropped it, allowing it to pool on the floor behind her.

If William had been aroused before, the vision of her body, from her well-rounded breasts with the pert nipples to the dark triangle of hair between her legs, brought him to the brink of release.

Their eyes speaking volumes, William lifted his lawn shirt over his head and flung it away. Seeing his whole well-muscled torso caused Elizabeth to suck in air as her heart skipped a beat, then started to race.

Their eyes met as he opened his breeches and peeled them off as Elizabeth slid the straps of her nightgown off her shoulders, letting it fall to the floor around her feet. She reached out her hand and their fingers intertwined as he led her to the bed. Given their depth of need, their first joining was over before either would have liked, but it was not long before William was aroused once more. This second time he was able to go more slowly, allowing them to savour the pleasures they were discovering longer. By their third or fourth time joining, William was starting to learn what to do to bring Elizabeth to her release before his.

They both ascribed to the theory that in order to be proficient, one needed to practice prodigiously. It was dark when they rang for baths and requested trays of food in their sitting room, and it was after one in the morning before they finally allowed sleep to claim them, intertwined in one another's arms.

CHAPTER 21

Six weeks after leaving London, the Duke and Duchess of Derbyshire, Earl and Countess of Lambton, arrived in Liverpool, where they were met by one of the large, comfortable Derbyshire travelling coaches.

It was a party of six who departed London the day after the wedding: the Duke, the Duchess, and their personal servants, Biggs, and Johns. In the six weeks since their wedding, the Derbyshire Darcys were no longer inexperienced in lovemaking and each had learnt much of what the other found pleasurable, although they agreed it was one subject which would require many more hours of intense study. Both had read books on the subject prior to their marriage, but the practical application of their knowledge was much more pleasurable than either could have imagined.

As they sat in the coach on the way to Pemberley, Elizabeth could not but marvel at all the places she had seen while in Ireland that she had only read about before. After a few days in Dublin, they had made a ten-day circuit of the surrounding countryside.

They travelled south to County Cork, where they visited the ruins of Blarney Castle and the famous Blarney Stone that was said to gift one with eloquence if they kissed it. Elizabeth joked she did not need it but, suggested her husband might benefit from doing so. He merely laughed.

From there they travelled northwest, towards the town of Limerick in the county of the same name. From Limerick, they turned northeast and headed for the Glenbeg Estate in County Kildare, named for the small glen located on the estate's western side. They had originally planned to visit two estates in Ireland but chose to delay their visit to a second estate, further north, until a subsequent visit.

Elizabeth loved seeing the horses raised at Glenbeg and fell in love with a three-year-old mare. She was light brown with white socks, and a white mark in the shape of a triangle on her forehead. Her husband, who held her felicity as his first priority, gifted the mare to his wife, who named her Aphrodite.

When their visit to Ireland was at an end, Aphrodite came with them. The Duke paid for a stall to be constructed in the hold for the relatively short voyage to Liverpool. She was to be ridden by a Darcy postillion on their journey to Pemberley.

Normally Pemberley to Liverpool was an easy one-day journey, however as the ship had arrived around midday, they broke their trip at a coaching inn reserved for their exclusive use.

~~~~~~~/~~~~~~~

As the coach crested the rise, Elizabeth's breath was taken away. She had never seen a place where nature had done more for with so little counteracted by the awkward tastes of man. Across the valley on rising ground stood the manor house, which gleamed in the morning sun, imbuing the Derbyshire stone of the façade with a golden hue.

"William, your home is beautiful!" Elizabeth exclaimed as she squeezed her husband's hand.

"Do you not mean *our* home, Elizabeth?" William corrected. "I am happy you approve."

"Who could not approve of such an estate? We have been travelling through miles of forest since we passed the gate house. How big is the park, William?" Elizabeth asked, as excited as she used to be when, as a girl, she was waiting to open presents on Christmas day.

"It is ten miles around, my love," William informed his wife.

"I will be able to walk or ride a different path every day and not take the same one twice for the best part of a year," Elizabeth stated in wonder. She had thought Holder Heights large until she saw Pemberley and was just now beginning to understand how enormous her husband's primary estate was.

It took another twenty minutes before the carriage arrived at the inner courtyard, which had the largest portico Elizabeth had seen, guessing that, with the severe weather during winters in the north, it was a necessity. Elizabeth thought she was dreaming when she saw their extended family waiting to welcome them home.

As a surprise to his wife, William had arranged for Gigi, the Fitzwilliams, the Holder Bennets, Tommy (with Parrot on his shoulder), Louisa and Hurst, Jane and Jamie, and the Gardiners to be present when they arrived home. If things went according to plan, Anne and the Wickhams would arrive on the morrow from Kent.

"William, did you do this?" Elizabeth asked before the carriage came to a halt.

"I did, my love. Are you happy to see everyone again?" he asked hopefully.

"Of course I am! I had to put up with only you for company for six weeks, after all," Elizabeth teased him, with her impertinent eyebrow arched.

"Minx," William growled, and would have extracted penance for her teasing had it not been for their proximity to their guests.

Just as it had been when they all reunited at Netherfield, Elizabeth did not know who to hug first. As she was hugging Jane, Elizabeth heard Parrot squawk "Your Grace, Your Grace!"

Jane smiled and, as explanation, simply said, "Tommy."

"Do you like what I taught Parrot, Lizzy?" Tommy asked cheekily. Tommy was tall and well built, the size of a man, but still a boy at heart.

"Very funny, Tommy!" Elizabeth said, with mock afront.

"You never know what a parrot is able to learn with six weeks' intensive repeating," Tommy related, immensely proud of his accomplishment.

"If I hear Parrot repeat that too much, it will be off to the Dower House with you and him!" Elizabeth looked at Georgiana.

"There is a dower house, is there not?" Gigi nodded with a big smile.

"You would not dare!" Tommy retorted.

"Just try me," Elizabeth replied pertly.

"He will reside in the conservatory while he is with us, as long as he does not eat all of the fruit on the trees," William offered. "He will think he is back home."

William motioned two members of Pemberley's staff forward. "Elizabeth, our housekeeper Mrs. Hannah Reynolds and our butler, Mr. Peter Douglas. Mrs. Reynolds, Mr. Douglas, Her Grace, Elizabeth Darcy.

Mrs. Reynolds had known the Duke since he was four, so felt protective of him and his sister; they were almost like the children she never had. She had heard from Mrs. Killion how happy the master was, and she had hoped it was true. Then the shy Lady Georgiana had arrived with the extended family, and to Mrs. Reynold's wonderment she was no longer shy.

Seeing the way the master beamed at his wife and the utter adoration the new mistress directed at him, she was convinced her Master William had found the one woman who was his true partner in life. She had a gut feeling, and her gut feelings were seldom, if ever, wrong.

After all the hugs and kisses were over, the family followed William and Elizabeth into the house.

~~~~~~~/~~~~~~~

After dinner, there was no separation of the sexes, and Gigi, Cassie, and Allie delighted the assembled family with their playing. While William and Elizabeth had been away, Allie and Georgiana worked on duets, both playing and singing, and were impressive when they exhibited the results of their efforts.

Elizabeth was sitting with Jane, Louisa, and Marie on a settee. "Is there any news from Charlotte?" Elizabeth asked.

"Yes, I received a letter about ten days ago. Mr. Bingley asked for her hand, and she accepted him. They will marry from Meryton in three weeks," Jane reported.

"Will you go to the wedding, Jane?" Elizabeth asked.

"Of course I will, that is *if* I am allowed to travel," Jane stated cryptically, continuing before Elizabeth could enquire what she meant. "I have forgiven him, and he has proven many times already his change is genuine."

"It is as Jane says, Lizzy. My brother strives to be a good man every day, where before, he was barely tolerated by his parishioners. From the letters I have received from Anne and Karen, he is much loved now and works every day to improve the lives of his flock," Louisa informed her sister.

"In that case, I am happy for Charlotte. When we are invited, I will ask Fitzwilliam if there is any conflict which would preclude us attending." Elizabeth paused as she remembered Jane's words. "Jane what did you mean, *if you are allowed*? Is there something wrong with you, or is it the good news I suspect it to be? Please tell me, Jane," Elizabeth asked, with arched eyebrow.

"It is nothing that will not resolve itself in about seven months," Jane patted her belly. Elizabeth's mouth formed a perfect 'O', as her suspicions were confirmed. "It is not common knowledge yet, so please do not share it beyond William and Harold. I should feel the quickening in the next month or two."

"That is the best news, Janey!" Elizabeth whispered, ecstatically.

"I am so happy for you, sister," Louisa added.

"You will be such a good mother, Jane," Marie opined.

"How could I not tell my married sisters?" Jane asked with a beatific smile. "Jamey and I discussed the subject and agreed I could share it with you, and I have told Mother Amy as well."

"When do we get to see the *little* gift you brought back from Ireland?" Marie asked.

"I will ride Aphrodite on the morrow, and, if I understood William, there are a surfeit of horses in the stables, several of them trained for side-saddle. Do you have your own horse at Glenmeade, Jane?" Elizabeth asked.

"I do. She is called Calista, but for good reason, I do not ride her currently. One of the grooms will exercise her until after my confinement and I have been churched," Jane replied.

"You look very much contented, cousin," Richard remarked, as he sat in a group with William, Andrew, Hurst, and Jamey.

"We are brothers now, Richard," William pointed out.

"True, but we were cousins first," Richard retorted.

"As to your statement, you are right. I could not be happier," William looked longingly at his wife as she sat with her sisters across the music room from them.

"He just spent six weeks in his wife's exclusive company, and the man is so besotted that he pines for her when she sits across the room," Richard ribbed.

"Just you wait, Richard," Andrew stated. "Do you think any of us have not noticed how you look at Cassie? You have been courting her since just after his wedding," Andrew indicated William with his thumb, "so why have you not made your proposal yet?"

"Not that it is any of your concern," Richard returned, "but I intend to ask her on the morrow. I received your father's blessing today for a private interview," Richard said, looking at Jamey.

"I suppose I will have to suffer two Fitzwilliams as brothers. Well, you are my brother already, Richard," Jamey said with mock exasperation. "Just look after her!"

"I intend to. Before acquiring Brookfield, I never could look for a wife seriously, even with the legacy Uncle Robert left me. Cassie is perfect for me; she will never allow me to step out of line; she will be my commanding general!" Richard stated. "You could have brought *me* a stallion from Glenbeg William; you know how much I admire the horseflesh there." Richard was only half joking.

"If my sister-in-law is short-sighted enough to accept you, Richard, you may select a stallion for yourself and a horse for Cassie as a wedding present. You will only need to pay for shipping them home," William allowed.

An hour or so later, people started to drift off to bed and, as was expected, the host and hostess were the final two to retire.

They finally found sleep almost two hours later, after testing the strength of the bed frame in the master's bedchamber.

~~~~~~~/~~~~~~~

When the riding party returned from their morning ride, they spied two of the de Bourgh carriages pulling into the courtyard. Karen Wickham told her hostess they had broken the previous night less than three hours south, as they had made sure the legs of the journey were short enough so Anne de Bourgh would have ample rest between the times she was required to spend in the coach.

Anne was looking better than any of her family could remember. Only her tiring quickly reminded everyone that her time was limited. Her body was weak, but she was at peace. She was surrounded by people who loved her, and Rosings Park was once again a pleasurable place to live, something it had not been since her father's murder.

After Wickham had washed and changed and while his wife remained with Anne, he met with some of the men in William's study. "How are you getting on at Rosings Park, George?" William asked his friend.

"It is a process, but I am learning. It does not hurt that the steward is both competent and a good teacher. You know you are all invited for Easter? Anne would like to revive the tradition abandoned because no one desired to suffer her late mother's machinations," Wickham said.

"I am sure the invitation is buried in this mountain of correspondence," William pointed to the prodigious pile of post, "I suppose I need to hire a new personal secretary." He looked at Hurst with a grin, "My old one had the temerity to fall in love with my wife's sister and become my brother!"

"Then allow me to assist by sorting through the candidates for the position, Your Gra...William. Sorry, old habits die hard." Hurst looked a little chagrined as he had been reminded, more than once, that, as part of the family, he was to use their familiar names.

"That is a most welcome offer, Harold; I shall take you up

on it," William happily accepted. Then he turned to his child-hood friend. "I am sure there will be no impediment to us joining you." He turned to Holder. "Did you and Tommy select a steward?"

"We did. Tommy decided the under-steward from Holder Heights was the best fit. There was nothing wanting in the two from Pemberley; they too were strong candidates," Holder informed William.

"Before I left Netherfield, the steward there mentioned he wishes to retire by the end of this year. I will speak to both and choose one for Netherfield. That will allow the new man several months with his predecessor before he retires," William told the group.

That evening at dinner, toasts were drunk to Cassie and Richard who had become officially betrothed on receiving her father's consent and blessing. Richard's brothers-in-law made sure they pointed out his longing looks at his betrothed when she was not by his side.

The family enjoyed their time together, as would be expected in such a close-knit group. After a sennight, departures to their own homes began, the final group to depart being the Wickhams and Anne de Bourgh.

~~~~~~~/~~~~~~~

Less than a month later, the family reunited in Hertford-shire for the wedding of Charlotte Lucas to Charles Bingley. Between Longbourn, Netherfield, and Hurst Haven, there was more than enough room to accommodate all the guests.

Charlotte Lucas may not have been the comeliest of women, but on the day of her wedding, she was radiant. There was no denying that Charlotte and her groom were deeply in love, for their union obviously had no financial motive. She brought only five hundred pounds with her, and he was building up his funds once again; he saved and invested with Gardiner and Associates, rather than gambling. Once Edward Gardiner had seen the genuine change his late friend's son made to his life, he had no reservation about accepting him as an investor.

Bingley had struck up a friendship with George Wickham, which boded well for the time when Wickham would become Bingley's patron. The proximity of the parsonage at Hunsford to Rosings Park was a plus for both women, given that Charlotte and Karen were already friends.

Unfortunately, Anne's disease had progressed to the point where she no longer travelled; her family hoped she would still be at Rosings Park when they all came to visit for Easter.

The wedding went off smoothly, and, after a well-executed wedding breakfast at Lucas Lodge, the newlyweds departed for Hunsford.

~~~~~~~/~~~~~~~

After the wedding, Jane, Elizabeth, and Tommy were sitting in what was now Tommy's study. "Are you looking forward to starting at Cambridge, Tommy?" Elizabeth asked.

"I am. It is time, and I will be following in father's footsteps," Tommy stated.

"As both you and Phillip will be at school, who will keep Parrot?" Jane enquired.

"Allie and Gigi have volunteered. He will live at Holder Heights, but before you take offense Lizzy, he did enjoy living in the conservatory at Pemberley," Tommy replied.

"This is where I would sit to feel Papa's presence when I was not reading *Utopia*," Elizabeth patted her pocket. Even as a duchess, she still made sure the copy her father gave her was on her person each day when she was dressed. "I am happy that the new steward is confident in his ability to increase the estate's yield, I only maintained it when I managed the estate," Elizabeth stated in a subdued fashion.

"What twaddle, Lizzy!" Tommy insisted. "Without you, there would be nothing for me to inherit. You know full well the reason the yields are increasing is we have added land, thanks to your husband, and I will continue to purchase any that become available. Do you know the Gouldings are quitting Haye Park? They inherited a much larger estate in Surrey. Uncle James offered to purchase the estate, and they accepted his offer. The house will remain as a dower house, and the land will be annexed to Longbourn as soon as the sale is final, which is in a matter of days."

"I too feel Papa here," Jane shared, "but Mama too. You remember how much time they spent in this study together, do you not, Lizzy? You were too young to remember, Tommy."

"You have the right of it, Jane, I forgot that. It is no wonder you can feel the strength of their love in here," Elizabeth stated, as she looked around the room where she had spent so much time with her father, and countless more hours after his accident.

"That is why *those* two were never able to break you, Lizzy. Their hatred was not close to equalling the love we were brought up with, and which still resides in this house. They never had a chance!" Jane stated with exuberance.

"No matter what they called you, Lizzy, they are no longer here!" Tommy added. "We live, and always will, in a family surrounded by love."

"Talking about love," William stuck his head around the door, "are you ready to return to Netherfield, Elizabeth?" Elizabeth nodded.

The three siblings hugged in the love-filled study and then Elizabeth took her husband's hand and walked with him towards the carriage. "Take me home to Netherfield and love me, William!" She instructed.

Her husband happily complied.

EPILOGUE

"Lord Bennet Robert Darcy, you will be thirteen soon, and gentlemen do not pull their sister's hair," Lady Francine Beth Darcy, called Fanny, at eleven, remonstrated with her older brother. Her governess, Miss Jones, looked on with amusement, ready to separate the two if needed.

"Would you like me to tell Mama and Papa you pulled my hair?" Lady Fanny asked, her arms akimbo with the same fire in her green eyes her mother had. Her father had been delighted when their second born was a girl who, as she grew, became more and more her mother, in both looks and character. "Otherwise, if you prefer, I will beat you up again, and you can run to Mama and Papa, crying like you did the last time!"

Lord Bennet knew there was only so far he could push his sister before it was too far, and then, he would pay a dear price. He had reached that line. "Sorry, Fanny," he managed, before he turned and made himself scarce.

"Come, Lady Fanny, let us return to the nursery and join your younger brother and sisters," Miss Jones directed her charge. Other than the eldest two, who both had their mother's fiery temperament, the next after Fanny was almost ten, Thomas, Viscount Kympton, who was called Tom. With more than one son, the titles had been split among the first two—Ben was the Marquess of Pemberley. After Tom there was Emily Anne, who was six, and the baby, Annabeth, who would soon be three.

After two years of marriage without conceiving, Elizabeth

had begun to be concerned she was barren, or worse, that the attack by the two executed criminals that she had survived had made her unable to bear children. Just when she was ready to give up the dream, she finally became with child, and nine months later, a little more than three years since marrying her William, she presented him with his heir and first son, Ben. After Ben, there was no further thought of being barren and it was the last time Elizabeth had thought about the cowardly attack on her person, or those who perpetrated it.

This year, the family was at Netherfield for Christmastide. Tommy, Allie and their three boys were at Longbourn, now by far the largest estate in the area, and would join them on the morrow. Allie was with child again, hoping very much to be blessed with a girl this time, but she and Tommy would be happy, regardless of the gender, as long as both mother and babe were healthy. They had married two years after Tommy graduated from Cambridge, now ten years past, in a double ceremony with Gigi and Phillip.

Gigi and Phillip had four children so far, two of each gender, ranging from nine to eight months old. When Phillip married Georgiana, the Duke and Earl, each contributed fifty percent and purchased an estate not five miles from Pemberley's southern border, as the owner, an older man who had no heir, wanted to enjoy his remaining years in Bath without worry. He had sold the estate, which brought in more than six thousand clear per annum, for considerably less than market value. He was simply happy to have someone who would look after Broadmoor as it should be. For the Duke's part, he would have paid the full price happily, as it ensured his beloved sister would remain in the neighbourhood.

Jane, Jamey, and their six children were scheduled to arrive later that afternoon, as they had been in London at Glenmeade House. They had two girls before the first son arrived; he was followed by another son, a daughter, and finally, another son.

Although they used Glenmeade House in London, Jane, Jamey, and their children lived at Holder Heights. Some two years before, the Earl of Holder decided to effectively retire and left the running of the estate to Jamey. There was no health reason for the Earl to retire; it was a choice so he could spend as much time with the family as possible. Lord James and Lady Amy split their time between their children's homes and the Darcys' houses. They treated the Darcy children like their own grandchildren, so their time was devoted to spoiling their myriad of grandchildren as much as possible. The Viscount and Viscountess would travel to Netherfield with their parents, and the Matlocks, as there had been a final session of the House of Lords that morning. Lord James would attend a session if, and when, his voice and vote were pivotal.

Lord Reginald Fitzwilliam had passed away a little more than two years previously, and he had been mourned by all the family. He had a weak heart from a disease he contracted a year or so before his death. For William and Gigi, it had been an especially hard blow as he had been a surrogate father to them, so it was like losing a second father.

The new Earl and Countess of Matlock had five children; the oldest was Jamey, now eighteen, who held the Viscount Hilldale title. Amy was almost sixteen, and had been followed by two more sons and a daughter. The boys were thirteen and ten, and the baby of the family was six. Marie and Andrew Fitzwilliam doted on one another and their children, and never held with the *Ton's* theory that children should be seen and not heard, as they, and the entire extended family, believed the opposite.

The Dowager Countess split her time between Snowhaven and Brookfield. Cassie and Richard had married fourteen years previously and had six children. Andrew was heard to joke that Richard had to one-up him. Cassie had only suffered through four confinements thanks to two sets of twins. Her first confinement, a year and a half after their marriage, produced twins, a boy and a girl, followed by two sons, and then identical twin daughters. The older twins were twelve, the two brothers were nine and seven respectively, and the twin girls a little more than three.

Louisa Hurst went five years without becoming *enceinte*. She was convinced it would never be. What Louisa did not know was that, thanks to her punishing schedule of exercise and diet, as well as her intention to never become corpulent again, without knowing it she had affected her monthly courses, as they had ceased.

Hearing his wife's disheartened determination to give up on her dream of having a family, her husband took her to see a doctor, an accoucheur who specialised in diagnosing birthing problems. The doctor advised Louisa to cut back drastically on her exercise, while increasing her intake of food, and two months after she began this regimen, her courses began again.

The first one was, as the accoucheur predicted it would be, very heavy and painful, but by the next month they were normal. Three months later, her courses stopped again, and as she began to despair, she began to feel tired and was ill in the mornings. When the accoucheur confirmed her state, she was both overjoyed and felt tremendous guilt at her habits having caused a delay in becoming with child.

It took Elizabeth to remind her of her father, the late Thomas Bennet's philosophy to pull her out of her despair, and Louisa concentrated on what was to come, rather than what had been. Her first was a girl she named Beth, after her sister of the heart. Beth was followed eighteen months later by Harold Junior. Almost three years after the birth of little Harold, baby Cheryl was born. For Christmastide, the Hursts would sleep at Hurst Haven and spend each day with the family at Netherfield Park.

Charles Bingley, rather than reverting to his bad behaviours prior to his epiphany, had gone from strength to strength and was as good and honourable a man as any. He and Charlotte were both happy and comfortable at the Hunsford parsonage. He had been offered other livings in addition to Hunsford but had turned all of them down. He did not want any distractions to ministering to his Hunsford flock, and he did not believe he deserved money to do nothing and have a curate do all the work in other locations.

The Bingleys were blessed with five children, three girls and two boys, from the ages of thirteen down to four. They were close to the master and mistress of Rosings Park, George and Karen Wickham and their five sons and two daughters, ranging from fourteen to two years—George Junior, down to baby Robert.

Although Anne de Bourgh's health was deteriorating slowly, she was in her element with all of her loving family during Easter of '10. It had been sad for the whole family when she passed away, three months later, bringing the family back to Kent for a much more sombre occasion. Anne lived the last part of her life surrounded by love, so Karen was able to remind everyone that, when she died, she had promised it was with no regrets.

When her last will and testament was read, George and Karen Wickham inherited everything—the estate, Anne's dowry, and the de Bourgh fortune. They vowed they would help others with some of their new fortune and did so.

Their children were taught the same lesson the late Duke taught their father—anything worth having is worth working for, and honesty is not just the best policy, it is the *only* policy. The Wickhams had been adopted as cousins by the family, and so were included in all family events. They would depart for Netherfield in two days, bringing the Bingleys and their children with them.

As was their wont to do, Elizabeth, William and their children visited Longbourn to see Allie, Tommy, and their children a few hours before the first guests were due to arrive. As arranged, Louisa, Hurst, and their offspring were visiting as well.

Leaving their spouses with the children, Elizabeth on Aphrodite, Louisa on her horse, and Tommy on an aging Orion, who would be put out to pasture soon, rode to the spot where the Bennets' father had met his end in the riding accident that fateful day, so many years ago.

Tommy helped his sister and Louisa dismount. Elizabeth

had not told William yet, but she suspected she might be increasing again, so there was no galloping, as her state was unconfirmed. If confirmed, she would take a break from riding until after her confinement, as she had, each previous time she increased.

Louisa looked at Elizabeth with raised questioning eyebrows; she had an uncanny sense and could detect whenever anyone she was near was with child. She would often be correct, even if the subject of her guess did not suspect yet. Elizabeth shrugged her shoulders telling her sister she did not know yet.

"Papa would have been overjoyed at the man you have become, Tommy. You have taken Longbourn to heights he could have only dreamed of. He would have been as we all are, extremely proud of you. Even if you are a little taller than William, you are and always will be my *little* brother," Elizabeth said as they stood next to the spot where their father's life ended.

"Not little, Lizzy, younger," Tommy corrected her, as he always did, when she called him her little brother.

"What a life we are all having, Papa and Mama. It could not have been better if we had fairy godmothers to grant our every wish," Elizabeth told her late parents, with her head lifted to the heavens.

"I would have wished for my mother to have never compromised your father," Louisa added softly.

"It happened as it should have, Lulu. Were it not for that, we would not be sisters, and I would have gone my whole life without meeting my best friend in the world! Never say that, because I do not want to imagine my life without you in it!" The sisters hugged for a long time.

"Lizzy has the right of it, Lulu," Tommy added. "Never forget what you mean to all of us, and always will."

"Is Phillip bringing Parrot with him? Is it not your year next, Tommy?" Elizabeth asked.

"Yes, he is, and my children cannot wait to see the old bird again. All of our children lament when Parrot leaves their home. But for us, he is a symbol of hope; he always gave us something to think about when we were on *New England* rather than to contemplate our never being found," Tommy averred, thoughtfully.

As they always did when they accompanied Elizabeth to this spot, everyone gave Elizabeth some time alone before returning to the house. "Papa, I will always miss you and Mama, but it is easier for me, as I know you are together in heaven. I have the kind of love with William that you and Mama had, a love that will last for eternity. If only, you both could have met him and all your many grandchildren.

"Papa, I want you to know I still read *Utopia* from time to time. Not as much as I used to, and no longer sitting in front of a fire at night. It has been many years since I have smudged soot on my face from having done so. We will see you again one day, Papa and Mama, though I hope it is not for many years. It is again time to return to my husband and children. I love you both," Elizabeth told the heavens, then she kissed her hand and placed it on the spot where her father had been found.

She joined her brother and sister and the three turned back, riding slowly toward the manor house, to their loving families waiting for them.

The End

COMING SOON

<u>The Take Charge Series</u>:

The Take Charge series are all stand-alone books. There will be at least four books in the series and as they are not sequels or not connected one to the other, you may read them in any order you choose.

The series tells a Pride & Prejudice Variation/Vagary tale in which one of the characters we know and love from canon takes charge and assert themselves. We see how the actions of that particular character affects the others and the trajectory of each individual tale, both known from canon and some non-canon characters.

We know Elizabeth Bennet and Fitzwilliam (William) Darcy well and how they are depicted in the original, they will not have a book in their names, but will, as it should be, feature very heavily in each of the stories where someone else takes charge.

Book 1: Charlotte Lucas Takes Charge: (September/October 2021)

None of the books in this series are just about the title character, but how their taking charge affects those around them.

Fanny Bennet dies of an apoplexy two years prior to the start of this story.

As in canon, the Bingleys, Hursts, and Darcy arrive in the area residing in the leased Netherfield Park. Up until the Reverend William Collins arrival, things are not far from canon. Collins is the sycophant we all love to hate and sets his sights on Jane. Bennet tells him in no uncertain terms he will not consent to such a man marrying **ANY** of his daughters.

Charlotte Lucas overhears Collins ranting to himself about how he will evict the Bennets from Longbourn the day Bennet passes. He then tried to woo Charlotte hours later and she too rejects him. He is derisive when she rejects him out of hand, he tells her that no man would ever offer for one on the shelf, without fortune, and as homely as her.

Collins then proposes to Matilda Dudley, Lizzy's friend and Longbourn's widowed parson's daughter. Matilda accepts him much to Elizabeth and Charlotte's surprise.

Collins's words to her spur Charlotte to take charge, the story tells the tale of what she does and how it affects the lives of not a few people. The book examines how Charlotte actions change the trajectories of some of our favourite (to love and hate) characters.

BOOKS BY THIS AUTHOR

A Change Of Fortunes

What if, unlike canon, the Bennets had sons? Could it be, if both father and mother prayed to God and begged for a son that their prayers would be answered? If the prayers were granted how would the parents be different and what kind of life would the family have? What will the consequences of their decisions be?

In many Pride and Prejudice variations the Bennet parents are portrayed as borderline neglectful with Mr. Bennet caring only about making fun of others, reading and drinking his port while shutting himself away in his study. Mrs. Bennet is often shown as flighty, unintelligent and a character to make sport of. The Bennet parent's marriage is often shown as a mistake where there is no love; could there be love there that has been stifled due to circumstances?

In this book, some of those traits are present, but we see what a different set of circumstances and decisions do to the parents and the family as a whole. Most of the characters from canon are here along with some new characters to help broaden the story. The normal villains are present with one added who is not normally a villain per se and I trust that you, my dear reader, will like the way that they are all 'rewarded' in my story.

We find a much stronger and more resolute Bingley. Jane Bennet is serene, but not without a steely resolve. I feel that both need to be portrayed with more strength of character for the purposes of this book. Sit back, relax and enjoy and my hope is that you will be suitably entertained.

The Hypocrite

The Hypocrite is a low angst, sweet and clean tale about the relationship dynamics between Fitzwilliam Darcy and Elizabeth Bennet after his disastrous and insult laden proposal at Hunsford. How does our heroine react to his proposal and the behaviour that she has witnessed from Darcy up to that point in the story?

The traditional villains from Pride and Prejudice that we all love to hate make an appearance in my story BUT they are not the focus. Other than Miss Bingley, whose character provides the small amount of angst in this tale, they play a small role and are dealt with quickly. If dear reader you are looking for an angst filled tale rife with dastardly attempts to disrupt ODC then I am sorry to say, you will not find that in my book.

This story is about the consequences of the decisions made by the characters portrayed within. Along with Darcy and Elizabeth, we examine the trajectory of the supporting character's lives around them. How are they affected by decisions taken by ODC coupled with the decisions that they make themselves? How do the decisions taken by members of the Bingley/Hurst family affect them and their lives?

The Bennets are assumed to be extremely wealthy for the purposes of my tale, the source of that wealth is explained during the telling of this story. The wealth, like so much in this story is a consequence of decisions made Thomas Bennet and Edward Gardiner.

If you like a sweet and clean, low angst story, then dear reader, sit back, pour yourself a glass of your favourite drink and read, because this book is for you.

The Duke's Daughter: Omnibus Edition

All three parts of the series are available individually.

Part 1: Lady Elizbeth Bennet is the Daughter of Lord Thomas and Lady Sarah Bennet, the Duke and Duchess of Hertfordshire. She is quick to judge and anger and very slow to forgive. Fitzwilliam Darcy has learnt to rely on his own judgement above all others. Once he believes that something is a certain way, he does not allow anyone to change his mind. He ignored his mother and the result was the Ramsgate debacle, but he had not learnt his lesson yet.
He mistakes information that her heard from his Aunt about her parson's relatives and with assumptions and his failure to listen to his friends the Bingleys, he makes a huge mistake and faces a very angry Lady Elizabeth Bennet.

Part 2: At the end of Part 1, William Darcy saved Lady Elizabeth Bennet's life, but at what cost? After a short look into the future, part 2 picks up from the point that Part 1 ended. We find out very soon what William's fate is. We also follow the villains as they plot their revenge and try to find new ways to get money that they do not deserve.
Elizabeth finally admitted that she loved William the morning that he was shot, is it too late or will love find a way? As there always are in life, there are highs and lows and this second part of three gives us a window into the ups and downs that affect our couple and their extended family.

Part 3: In part 2, the Duke's Daughter became a Duchess. We follow ODC as they continue their married life as they deal with the vagaries of life. We left the villains preparing to sail from Bundoran to execute their dastardly plan. We find out if they are successful or if they fail.

In this final part of the Duke's Daughter series, we get a good idea what the future holds for the characters that we have followed through the first two books in the series.

The Discarded Daughter - Omnibus Edition

All 4 books in the Discarded Daughter series are combined into a single book. They are available individually, in both Kindle and paperback format.

The story is about the life of Elizabeth Bennet who is kidnapped and discarded at an exceedingly early age. It tells the tale of her life with the family that takes her in and loved her as a true daughter.

We follow not only Elizbeth's life, her trials and tribulations, but that of the family that lost her and all of those around her, immediate and extended family, and the effect that she has on their lives. There is love, villains, hurt, and happiness as we watch Elizabeth grow into an exceptional young woman.

If you are looking for a story that only concentrates on our heroine, then this is not for you.

Surviving Thomas Bennet

Warning: This book contains violence, although not graphically portrayed.

There are Bennet twins born to James Bennet, his heir, James Junior and second born Thomas. They boys start out as the best of friends until Thomas starts to get resentful of his older brother's status as heir.

The younger Bennet turns to gambling, drink, and carousing. In order to protect Longbourn, unbeknownst to Thomas, James

Bennet senior places and entail on the estate so none of his son's creditors are able to make demands against the family estate.

Thomas Bennet was given his legacy of thirty thousand pounds when he reached his majority. He marries Fanny the daughter of a local solicitor in Oxford where Thomas is teaching. He is fired for being drunk at work. He manages to gamble away all of his legacy while going into serious debt to a dangerous man in not too many years.

When James Senior dies, Thomas and Fanny Bennet arrive at Longbourn demanding an imagined inheritance. They find out there is no more for them and leave after abusing one an all roundly swearing revenge.

James Junior, the master of Longbourn, and his wife Priscilla have a son, Jamie, and daughters Jane, Elizabeth, and Mary. Thinking he can sell Longbourn if his brother and son are out of the way, Thomas Bennet murders them and James' wife by causing a carriage accident.

The story reveals how the three surviving daughters are protected by their friends and how they survive the man who murdered their beloved parents and brother. Netherfield belongs to the Darcy's second son, William. There are many of the characters that are both loved and hated from the canon in this story, some similar to canon, a good number of them hugely different, there are also some new characters not from canon.

Unknown Family Connections

This is a book of two volumes, but all in one book. It is a one off, standalone story.

Over 150 years in the past an Evil Duke plotted to separate his first and second sons. He was a man who had two interests:

money and status. Lord Sedgewick Rhys-Davies, the 3rd Duke of Bedford sets off a chain of events that ultimately ends up doing the exact opposite of what his original evil intent was in the far future.

Mr. Thomas Bennet lives with his second wife and family on his estate Longbourn in Hertfordshire. As far as he knows, he is an indirect descendant of the last Earl of Meryton whose line died out with him over 150 years ago. The family has owned Longbourn and Netherfield Park for as long as anyone remembers. There is an entail on Longbourn, but not the one we are used to. As in the canon, this Bennet dislikes London, and the Ton and he and his family keep away from London society. His second wife is the daughter of an Earl but just goes as Mrs. Bennet.

The Bennet's new tenants at Netherfield Park are the Bingleys. One of the major deviations from canon in this tale, Jane Bennet has more than a little backbone while Bingley has little or none. How will Darcy behave, will he make assumptions and act on them? Will Elizabeth allow her prejudices to rule? When Wickham slithers onto the scene will he cause havoc?

The 7th Duke of Bedford is ill, and he will be the end of the line as there are no living relatives to inherit the dukedom and vast Bedford holdings. He removes an old letter from a safe in his study written by the 4th Duke. Witten on the outside of the letter is: 'Open ONLY if there are no more Rhys-Davies heirs.'

The Duke opens the letter and learns of the 3rd Duke's evil and there is in fact an heir, although a direct descendant, he is not a Rhys-Davies.

This is the story of different families and what happens when their lives intersect and are changed for ever. There is quite a bit about Lizzy & Darcy, but there are not always the main focus of the story as the title infers.